DANGEROUS
JOURNEYS™

DANGEROUS JOURNEYS™

The Anubis Murders

by

Gary Gygax

A ROC BOOK

ROC
Published by the Penguin Group
Penguin Books USA Inc., 375 Hudson Street,
New York, New York 10014, U.S.A.
Penguin Books Ltd, 27 Wrights Lane,
London W8 5TZ, England
Penguin Books Australia Ltd, Ringwood,
Victoria, Australia
Penguin Books Canada Ltd, 10 Alcorn Avenue,
Toronto, Ontario, Canada M4V 3B2
Penguin Books (N.Z.) Ltd, 182–190 Wairau Road,
Auckland 10, New Zealand

Penguin Books Ltd, Registered Offices:
Harmondsworth, Middlesex, England

First published by Roc, an imprint of New American Library,
a division of Penguin Books USA Inc.

ISBN 0-451-45214-3

DANGEROUS
JOURNEYS™

1

DEATH IN YS

"Another rotten night!" The complaint was loud and harsh, but the November wind whipping across the ocean and into the city on the high spit of land tore the sound into shreds.

"Only a pair of fools like us would put up with this duty," the second man agreed, drawing his heavy cloak of maroon-and-blue wool closer. The air was cold and damp, the cloth was heavy with salt spray, and the act was more for comfort than effect. "We should have joined one of the free companies."

"And die in the godsforsaken forests in Teutonia? Yer a damn fool, Ollo!" the taller man said.

"I may be a fool," the shorter city watchman allowed with a snarl, "but it was your foolin' round with that doxy of the sergeant's that got us posted to this duty!"

"Now just take that and—"

The second man grabbed his comrade's arm. "Quiet!" His fingers bit into the man's flesh,

even through the outer garments. "I heard somethin' weird . . ." He trailed off, listening. "There,
Alaine. It was a howling sound. Did you hear?"

"It's the wind."

"No, it wasn't like that. It was real eerie,"
Ollo said so softly that his companion could
hardly discern the words above the stormy night.
"Damn! Look there—what's that?!"

Alaine took his companion's arm and turned
him away from the shadows near the high wall
which marked the boundary of their watch.
"Who gives a rat's ass?" he growled, and headed
back toward the narrow streets and alleys of Ys'
waterfront slum district. "Anything goin' near
that place can pass, as far as I'm concerned."

Ollo hesitated for a moment, peering beyond
the grim wall—and a brief shower of purple
sparks danced around the high tower. The watchman averted his eyes quickly, made a sign to
ward off evil, and hurried after his comrade.
The thugs and thieves of the harbor were at least
known entities. Ollo scurried to catch up with
the long-striding Alaine. "What should we report?" he asked breathlessly.

"You can report whatever you like," Alaine
said with a shrug, "but all I seen was a couple
of mongrel dogs sniffin' along the street, and all
I heard was the wind."

"There was a half dozen of them things,
Alaine. Black as soot and big!"

"Black? There wasn't enough light to tell red

from brown, stupid! I saw plain old wild dogs, smallish ones mostly, in fact. Since when's stray curs in Ys somethin' to run and report?" He paused and stared at Ollo. The smaller man started to say something, stopped, and looked resigned. "That's that, chum," Alaine said when he saw his comrade's uncertainty. "We need to stay the hells away from anything out of line now so's we can get reassigned to better duty before winter, right?"

"Sure . . ." Ollo agreed uneasily.

"Come on, then! Let's check up on what's doin' at the Sailor and Sirene. There's always a good excuse for checkin' on a dive like that, and the mulled wine's good there, too." Ollo needed no further urging, and the two patrolmen garbed in the uniform of the Watch of Ys headed up a twisting alleyway and out of sight.

Hot eyes of orange-red followed their progress, but when the pair disappeared around the curve of the narrow passage, the orbs winked out as if someone had shuttered them. Soft pads made no sound on the rounded cobbles, and the clicking of long nails was lost in the shrieking of the wind.

Six dog-like animals trotted along the road, keeping close to the buildings which lined it. The street rose toward a long spit of land, a rocky promontory which thrust out into the cold waters of the ocean. Though all of Ys was built on a peninsula, this portion of the ancient city jutted off spur-like, due west, as if determined to separate forever the wild waves of the Lantlan Ocean from the choppy waters of the Channel of Avillon. The out-thrust ridge was walled by both natural cliffs and human construction. Where it met the land to the east, Ys proper, it was also shielded by thick granite. Squat, square towers and crenelated battlements marked the place where the city ended and the isolated tongue of stone stabbed forth into the ever-gray waters. As the six creatures came to the massive barrier and closed gates, twice their number came forth to meet them.

There was no light save the little illumination from the distant stars. The low clouds parted and the faint rays glimmered on the damp old stones, the dark iron, and the creatures that resembled dogs. But dogs do not have eyes of lambent fire. And these creatures exchanged no whines, yelps or barks. The six black things sat on the stones, and the dozen who emerged from the deep blackness near the wall joined them. The whole pack sat absolutely still and silent for the space of a hundred heartbeats, then rose and slunk off. Some went north toward the wave-dashed rocks of the shore; others stole belly-low toward the southern verge of the high spit of land. There were darker shapes in the black waters of both places, lupine heads which barked wetly and were answered from shore. Six of the soot-hued things sat before the closed gates of the citadel on the promontory, silent and unmoving.

Perhaps those glowing orbs were able to pierce the iron-bound timbers which sealed the fortress from the rest of the ancient Bretton city. Ys boasted thirteen towers along its walls; thirteen and the great landward gate which was a mighty castle itself. The thick old wall dividing city from promontory was as different from its neighbors in construction as were the squat towers beyond it from the ones which guarded the citizens of Ys. The city walls had been assailed by barbarians, pirates, imperial legions, and once even a ravening humanoid tribe, but not even the latter had dared to assault the citadel crouching on the cliffs of the westernmost peninsula. That place was the Academie Sorcerie d'Ys. Even berserkers preferred the prospect of hails of crossbow bolts and boiling oil to what awaited the uninvited in that place. There dark dweomercræfters gathered, necromancy was commonplace, and sorcerous conjuration a staple. If the black things squatting outside the gate to the Academie Sorcerie quailed at what lay beyond the portal, none showed such fear.

The walls surrounding this place of darkest magick were strong in many ways. The strange carvings covering the gray-brown blocks of stone were enchanted. The leering faces, twisted forms, and oddly disquieting sigils hewn into the hard granite were but outward manifestations of the castings laid there to ward off foes. The forces of magicks cast layer upon layer were as thick as the stone, as impervious to attack. Furthermore, the shieldings and guards were woven so as to cover the air above the college of magicians, the rocky earth below, and even extend to the waters which dashed themselves on the cliffs of the westward-jutting spur. Antipathy, aversion, and terror too were bound into the blocks which faced the city. But these castings had no effect upon the dark, dog-like things as they sat nearly touching the rock and stared with unwinking eyes of flame at the twin gates.

There were no sentries on the walls; the sorcerous inhabitants of the citadel-college were confident that no living guards were needed. Perhaps they were correct. The dog-things were outside, and inside all was tranquil. A straight avenue ran almost the entire length of the peninsula. There was first an outer yard. It had gatehouses and two small buildings set in each corner of the east wall facing the inner towers of the yard's west curtain wall. This place, with grass and flowers and shrubs, was as far as any stranger was ever permitted, unless that outsider happened to be a mighty prince or master of magicks. At night, phosphorescent shapes flitted around the gardens. Even insects were fair game to these vampiric wraiths, and nothing living moved in this outer courtyard after the setting of the sun. There was another gatehouse, the second, set in the inner wall, and the avenue ran straight through it, too.

Beyond was a much larger space, where side streets angled off, and old buildings were scattered along the thoroughfares and byways. The whole was not larger than six or seven city blocks, if a rambling place such as Ys might be said to have blocks. The Academie Sorcerie was comprised of structures large and small: shops, schools, dormitories, laboratories, private dwellings of the demonurges, and the huge buildings where the promontory met the sea. Southward was a massive shell keep. To the north, a pair of wide towers were bridged by a long hall.

The college of magick awakened as the ancient city to its east prepared for sleep. Though many dim streets and alleys in Ys spawned night life, most of its inhabitants were abed by midnight. On any given night, the inside of the Academie Sorcerie was alive with traffic. Most was underground, filling the honeycomb of passages and hand-hewn chambers beneath the upper world. The upper buildings were filled too, but with students and scholars, not the workers and servants who made up the majority of the subterranean complex. Lectures and classroom teaching, study in quiet halls or the several libraries, experiments in laboratories, contests of a magickal nature—these activities (and the normal ones of eating, drinking, and socializing) all occurred at night. A hundred conjurers and spellbinders dwelled in the place, and a thousand others served their needs. That population excluded the demonurges and their servants, for those august ones lived apart. The two great fortresses to north and south of the peninsula belonged to the masters of sorcerous magicks, and no lessers entered those sanctums without invitation.

"Who seeks entry?" asked a brass imp's head set into the iron door of the northernmost tower of the twin fortresses.

A cowled figure, short and broad, stood alone before the imp. With a short baton of thick bone, the cloaked man drew a burning rune in the air. As the figure thus conjured burned whitely, he said, "All-master Marcellus."

The imp's brass face contorted as if in pain as the brightness struck its surface. The door fairly flew open, soundlessly, as the high-pitched voice squeaked, "Pass, Great Nethercræfter Marcellus," and then swung shut so quickly as to nearly catch the all-master's trailing garment.

This was the eleventh night of the dark month of November. It was a high festival night at the Academie Sorcerie. That and more. Many of the greatest of the thaumaturge noirs were to come to the college to join in the celebration. The greatest of the great were to conjoin to call up a mighty elemental prince, bind that entity, and compel it to labor on their behalf. Not even the demonurges of the academy could manage the summoning and force obedience without assistance from outside. The diverse and disparate heka-wielders of Brettony and Francia who worked in the Black Arts were more prone to disrupt each other's work than to aid and abet one another. Here, though, was an undertaking which was bound to profit all concerned. None dared to violate the truce of Beltaine, the immunity of the college's sanctuary, and no secret formulae or arcane knowledge would be revealed by participation. Each of the masters involved would benefit by exacting from the summoned entity a service which they could not otherwise extract. The whole was a known magickal operation, but it required tremendous power—the power of combined dweomercræfters of the highest skill and ability.

Hundreds of neophytes and initiates held revels above and below. Most would never progress beyond those stages and eventually would go forth as petty practitioners of cantrips and other small magicks to earn modest livings. Some few would join the apprentices now overseeing the whole of the Beltaine festival at the college. These journeymen sorcerers had earned the right to remain as long as they desired. Of course, most could not progress beyond a moderate level of heka-binding capacity. Demand for their talents, however, was high. Lesser nobles were always seeking those able to command magickal forces for castle and court. Cities demanded their services. Merchants needed magickal work

of all sorts, from goods production and care, to
service in ship or caravan train. There was private practice, too, and the moderately skilled
practitioner, even one who utilized the dark arts,
could expect to become wealthy and respected
in but a few years of setting up shop and plying
the magickal powers gained at the Academie
Sorcerie d'Ys. A handful of doddering and de-
crepit demonurges were around to oversee all of
this, for combined with students and staff, almost two thousand people were there, all in high
spirits.

The most promising apprentices and most of
the demonurges were gathered in the same twin-
towered fortress where so-called All-master Marcellus had recently entered. The masters were
there to assist their exaulted brethren in the
great ceremonial ritual which was to occur that
very night, precisely at the stroke of midnight.
For hours the castings and summoning would
continue—four hours, to be exact. It was demanding, exhausting, and dangerous. But with
such skilled practitioners, masterful support,
and two-score lessers to draw upon for energy,
there could be no question of failure. In truth,
the chosen apprentices were eager for the operation to commence, for if they did well this night,
one or more of them could expect promotion and
access to the great store of magickal knowledge
reserved for perusal by the demonurges.

"This is the last opportunity for refreshments,

Exaulted Masters," murmured a dozen androgy-
nous servants as thy passed through the upper
vault of the tower in which the ceremony was
to take place. "Purest water? Infusions? I have
coffee, erythrox, cocoa, and tea. There are various forms of tobacco and herbal stimulants in
the salon yonder. May I be of assistance?" So the
solicitation proceeded as the various timepieces
showed the twelfth hour fast approaching.

Sand and water showed but a few minutes remaining. So, too, a thick set of marked candles.
A sidereal clock agreed, as did the mechanical
gears of a huge, ticking mechanism which was a
wonder to all but the most jaded of the thauma-
turges present. Massive gears of bronzewood
clacked, a silver pair of fins spun and caused
a breeze to skitter nearby candle flames. Select
apprentices and the younger demonurges stared
at the open working as there came gnashings and
groanings and accompanying movements within
the device. A massive hammer came down to
beat upon an iron tube.

BONGgg . . .

A flurry of last-second efforts to complete arcane inscriptions in the intricate interweaving
of pentacles, haxacles, and thaumaturgic trian-
gles on the chamber floor accompanied the stroke.

BONG . . .

Metallic powders, chalk, and pigments were
placed in exacting detail, so that no figure was

unfinished, no symbol lacking. Each utterance written was letter perfect.

BONG . . .

There was a stir as several hefty conjurers moved to positions on either side of the great timepiece. That was both symbolic and practical, for the noise was deafening.

BONG . . .

The last of the servitors left the high-ceilinged hall, their bare feet making whispering noises as they exited in nervous haste.

BONG . . .

Bolts made loud snicking sounds in the otherwise still chamber. The world below the topmost space in the tall tower was now shut out.

BONG . . .

At the sixth stroke in the count toward midnight, many of the demonurges laid enchantments upon the two doors and four windows which pierced the solid stone walls of the room. Because preparations had been made well beforehand, this took only a few breaths to conclude, and the last of their incantations droned into silence as the hammer fell once again.

BONG . . .

The incenses and herbs in the copper braziers in each corner of the hall were set alight with coals from nearby pots. Smoke began to rise in varicolored spindles.

BONG . . .

The dark, oddly shaped candles were set

alight. These fat wax cylinders were ensorcled to never go out no matter how gusty the wind or how fervent the attempt to quench them, save a single magickal command. Each of the three sets—thirteen in an outer ring, eleven in the inner figures, four placed in the conjuring diagram—was carefully compounded to assure a burning time of more than four hours.

BONG . . .

The supporting heka-wielders assembled, each in his or her assigned place. There were rustlings as robes were straightened, various materia made ready.

BONG . . .

The six master demonurges who would be principals in the summoning now took their places in the magick circles so carefully prepared. The last of them, a broad-shouldered man with long, greasy black hair, a stone-faced fellow with dull eyes the color of his hair, took sole position in the triangular figure, the chief place of ritual working in a sorcerous conjuration.

BONG . . .

The eleventh stroke. Everyone in the big room was mentally counting the strokes. The dull eyes of the chief demonurge of the Academie Sorcerie d'Ys burned suddenly with fervid light. Bertrand Frontonac, Haut Omniurge of the college, drew forth a black fan and cleared his throat. The five others nearby likewise made ready to serve as invocators—instruments and voices harrumphing as would a body of minstrels in preparation for some performance. There was a chorus of indrawn breaths as the huge wooden gears continued to turn and the hammer rose and dropped for the final time.

BONNGGG ...

Even as the first chant was voiced, a deep and monotonous litany, the works of the miraculous timepiece were stopped short as if to freeze the world at midnight, the instant between one day and the next. To the bass accompaniment of the lesser sorcerers, the demonurgists began to voice their separate parts in the ritual. All time and none at all passed, and in the center of a carefully prepared space there began to grow a whirling smoke or mist. As this grew and thickened, the air in the chamber became cold, and a growing wind tore through the room. When the gusts rose to the force of a shrieking gale, the stuff in the quatragram of conjuration grew to a livid purplish color and slowly formed itself into a discernable shape.

Ominurge Frontonac was now fully animated, feet moving to some inaudible rhythm, hands and arms waving in ceremonial passes as he spoke the final words of the ritual summoning of aerial elementals. Eyes alight with pride and anticipation, voice confident and commanding, Bertrand Frontonac concluded: "You are now called, chained, and compelled, Great Sylph,

Paralda, Prince of Air, Lord of All in that Rari-fied Element, appear and obey!"

The five assisting demonurges made similar assertions in unison as the accompaniment rose from a shimmering hum to a frenzied chant cele-brating the summoning and binding ritual. The dark shape in the quatragram solidified, its mon-strous pinions beginning to unfurl, testing the constraints of its space. And just as the assem-blage was settling to stillness, there came a col-lective intake of breath, the stirrings of a startled crowd.

The wings were not feathery pinions after all. The towering entity inside the quatragram was not an elemental prince of air. The drawn figure used for the summoning was breached. The gasps were of horror.

A red-eyed demon was loose among them all.

"NO!" the great sorcerer cried in denial.

"Oh, but yes!" the demon fairly chortled in an incongruous contralto whose sweetness was quite at odds with its tusked mouth and taloned hands. "You are mine according to the grant of the jack-al-headed one of the North, the stealer of the sun," it added almost in a titter. The iron-hard nails shot forth and gripped Omniurge Fron-tonac. Blood spurted, and the doomed sorcerer uttered a wail of agony and despair as the others in the hall remained powerless. The apprentices shrieked and tried to flee. Two of the lesser demonurges joined the panic. The rest stood fast and worked frantically to ward themselves. The fiery-eyed demon cast its gaze momentarily toward the five others nearby and chortled. "Perhaps I'll return for you later." Then it folded the bloody form of Omniurge Frontonac, tucked the corpse under its left arm, and vanished in a clap of iron thunder far louder than the striking of the huge clock.

Only a reek of vilest sort and a few spatters of gore remained to prove that demon and Frontonac had ever been in the oddly silent chamber. The Academie Sorcerie d'Ys had just lost its master. It was an event from which the college and all associated with it might never recover nor live down.

The howling of something like wild dogs was heard distinctly that night in Ys at about the fourth hour after midnight. Oddly, certain fishermen reported similar howlings coming from the sea around the promontory. That, of course, was dismissed.

2

MEN AS GAUNT AS DEATH

Color began to streak the horizon, and the tops of the rolling waves glistened with a tawny hue. "When will you break your fast, great lord?"

Setne Inhetep had obtained the villa on the Mare Librum only a few days before. The staff which went with the spacious grounds and dwelling were not yet accustomed to the strange habits of the Ægyptian. Although Setne did not turn, his reply was polite. "Later, thank you, Carlos. You may return to the villa and await us there. It will be no more than half an hour."

The Iberian shrugged, then gave a slight bow toward the tall foreigner's back. "As you command, lord," he murmured. He was careful to withdraw silently, his sandals making only soft shushing sounds in the sand. Carlos knew that all Ægyptians were rumored to be mages, and the tall, red-complexioned fellow who was the villa's current master openly admitted to being a wizard-priest Carlos had no reason to doubt, what with the man's shaven head, hawk nose, and sea-green eyes which seemed to look through to the very brain! Carlos made a sign to ward off the evil eye, again careful to do so with his hand shielded from the thin stranger. No sense in taking chances, for the Magister Inhetep might have an eye in the back of his head.

In fact, Setne was vaguely aware of what Carlos was thinking and doing.

Perhaps it was a sixth sense, possibly a mere quirk. Certainly whenever anyone concentrated on the ur-kheri-heb—a wizard-priest when translated from Ægyptian to the Iberian or any other tongue—he was able to sense it, unless the individual was one with strong heka hiding his thoughts or Inhetep was distracted. In any event, Setne was not paying attention because Carlos was a simple fellow. He broadcast everything, but it was of no consequence. Besides, the Magister had eyes only for Rachelle. There was one worthy of attention. If only she were so plainly discerned by his powers. . . .

Rachelle raced along the shore, oblivious to all. It was part of a ritual she performed every morning at first light. The regimen consisted of running, calisthenics, various sorts of gymnastics, and swimming, too, whenever possible. This setting was perfect for her. Rachelle shot a glance towards where the Ægyptian stood. He was watching, of course. That she was naked bothered Rachelle not a bit. She waved as she sped past him, and Setne gave a little wave in return. If possible, Rachelle exercised at other times of day as well as at dawn. Often, however, because of their travels, it was not possible. She was glad that there was time now. Setne had promised that they would spend at least another few weeks here in Valentia. The red edge of the sun rose, seeming to force its sphere through the waters of the sea in order to reach the air above. Rachelle stopped and stood panting slightly. This was a spectacle she would not ignore.

Inhetep joined her where the waves lapped the sand. "Are you finished?"

Rachelle flashed the tall man a smile of greeting. He had taught her to love sunrises such as this. "No ... not quite. I will swim a little longer."

"An excellent prospect," Setne agreed. "It will give zest to my appetite, I am sure. Wait a moment and I'll join you."

The huge solar disk now balanced on the horizon, creating a pathway of red-orange brighter than orichalcum. Rachelle laughed, sprang ahead and, seconds later, was out in the low waves. "Old sluggard!" she shouted as she ran farther out. "You'll be plodding about forever, and I need to be active." With that Rachelle dove as if she were a mermaid.

It took only a moment for the Ægyptian to slip out of his one-piece white cotton garment, girdled like a kilt and tunic. Setne simply loosened the girdle, pulled the folds of the blouse open and off his arm, and dropped it onto the sand. Still in his loincloth, he followed the girl, although far less precipitously. He was lean, and well over six feet tall. Setne never revealed his age, and it was nearly impossible to guess. Sometimes he looked but thirty, at other times he appeared to be forty. In fact, he was older. As a rolling surge came in, Inhetep launched himself smoothly into it. He was a strong but obviously unexceptional swimmer. "Beware, girl! Wizards do not take kindly to being japed at!" Inhetep shouted as he splashed out toward Rachelle.

There was no possibility of him catching her. Rachelle was able to literally swim rings around the Ægyptian. She did so, including several even more insulting maneuvers which took her under and over him, as if a dolphin were sporting with some lesser denizen of the sea. "Come on then, bald priest of Thoth. If you're such a marvelous magician, let's see you sprout fins and catch me!"

Knowing all along that it was a hopeless matter—unless he did somehow transform himself into fish or aquatic mammal—Setne swam in a straight path, away from the beach, ignoring the girl's tauntings and antics. After a few minutes, Rachelle grew bolder and tried to dunk Setne's head into the clear greenish water. "Ahah!" Inhetep managed to cry in triumph as he caught the girl's hand with a movement as quick as a striking cobra. "Now you shall know what true justice is!"

"No!" Rachelle blurted. How many times had she been caught thus? Would she never learn? She was young, lithe, quick, and strong—very strong and very athletic. Rachelle did a somersault, twisted, tore with her free hand at the Ægyptian's hold, and found Setne's grasp as unbreakable as a giant and hungry octopus. She heard him answer, "Yes!" and then she was deep beneath the water. Inhetep descended with her. Rachelle knew she could hold her breath for minutes, and her mentor could at best manage a few dozen seconds. She would win.

Setne went along too willingly to the five-fathom depth to which the girl swam. Then he looked at her and grinned. Rachelle's eyes grew large in the dim greenness; she made a face at him as Inhetep let go of her. Rachelle shot up to the surface and sped off toward shore. Inhetep followed leisurely, working along as if he were a fish, for he had sprouted gills. Magick. This was indicative of his relaxed state of mind. The Ægyptian almost never used his power so lightly. The girl had been truly surprised at the display. That pleased him.

"That was a dirty trick," Rachelle said as Inhetep came up out of the sea and walked to where she stood.

"You were warned," he countered. "I've had quite enough physical exercise for one morning.

In fact, I have now developed a ravenous appetite! Are you ready to join me in a morning repast?"

"Humph," Rachelle said, turning towards the villa. "Yes, but don't change the subject. That was an unfair thing you did."

"No more unfair than you, a devotee of sport and physical activity, pitting yourself against a sedentary old heka-binder." It was so outrageous a statement that Rachelle barked a scornful laugh, and Inhetep grinned in self-derision. "Cease bickering with your master," he commanded without force or authority. "I won the contest, and now you must serve me for another day."

Rachelle lowered her eyes. "Yes, master," she intoned humbly. Then she gave him a dark-eyed look which would have withered a basilisk. "Tomorrow is another day," she said, and marched off, back straight, toward the bath at the left of the main building. Setne shook his head in admiration at her beautiful form as Rachelle strode ahead.

Hair still damp from the saltwater, Setne and the girl sat on the villa's little terrace watching the sea traffic—small boats and tall-masted ships to and from Valentia—as they enjoyed a simple breakfast. The Ægyptian invariably drank sweetened tea. This morning he had juice from Valentia's famous orange groves. Setne barely touched the crusty little loaf before him, but Rachelle made up for the wizard-priest's lack of morning appetite. Fruit, milk, bread with marmalade, smoked eel, and tea were spread out before her.

"You should eat more," she scolded Inhetep. "If you would exercise more and eat more you wouldn't look like a stork."

Setne scowled as if he actually took her words seriously. True, he did rather resemble a long-legged bird, but never one so homely as a stork! "And if you would spend more time in study and learning, young lady, you might have something better to look forward to than a lifetime as a sword-carrying bodyguard," he replied with mock seriousness.

"You seemed happy enough with such inconsequential skills when we were in Thessalonika, and—"

"You were nearly slain that night!"

"There in the warrens of the medina in Marrakech, I recall being of some small assistance too. . . ."

Inhetep harrumphed. "So? Have you forgotten how I had to rescue you in Milano? Had you been able to perform the simplest of Preternatural unbindings, death would not have hovered so near your pretty head!"

"Thank you," Rachelle said simply. Then she called, "Carlos, I am still famished. Bring me a pair of those eggs baked in cream!"

Inhetep was at a loss to know if the girl had

thanked him for saving her life or for his inadvertent compliment. He decided to drop the matter for now. Setne would pick it up again later, as he always did, when the opportunity presented itself. He ordered fresh tea and settled back to watch Rachelle devour still more breakfast. Inhetep had found the girl when she was but six or seven years old, a Phonecian or Shamish waif taken prisoner in the course of warfare between Ægypt and Pharaoh's neighbors to the east. Too young for service in a bordello or sale to a harem, too scrawny and sickly for manual employment, Rachelle had been placed on the slave block almost as a joke. In truth, there had been softly uttered jests and rude titters when the wizard-priest had purchased the little child. Five silver crescents he had bid—overbid. The slaver had immediately banged his gavel, snatched the coins, and shoved the child at the shaven-headed Inhetep, fearing that he was mad and would renege.

He had meant to be rid of Rachelle immediately. A few weeks at his own small villa to the west of Thebes to put a little flesh on her and make her presentable, then he would hand the girl and the manumission certificate over to the temple of Maat. Education, training, and work would have made the little slave girl into a priestess with no small degree of social standing in a dozen or so years. Rachelle had had different ideas. Inhetep had rescued her, so she was his no matter what. None of the magister's plan had any bearing on the matter.

A month and she was still as scrawny as ever and as wild-looking, too. Inhetep had returned from the east and reprimanded his household staff for failing to have the waif presentable for dedication to the temple.

"She is impossible," the chief of his staff had said earnestly.

"That one is a hellion!" the elderly house-keeper had agreed. "Send her packing now."

That was sufficient for Setne to take charge of the matter personally, yet somehow the waif had prevailed. Instead of being sent off to a temple, Rachelle wound up getting instruction with the children of higher class in the small temple of the nearby village. Inhetep had tutored her as well, and a few years later Rachelle had gone off to formal schooling, but not as an aspiring priestess of Maat as Setne had proposed. Rachelle had talked the wizard-priest into sending her to the great temple of Neith in Sais. Neith was the feminine deity of warfare, the Lady of storms and fighting. Rachelle went off as a little girl and returned a few years later as a sophisticated woman, a trained warrior, skilled hunt-ress, and keen thinker.

"Almost twenty years now," Rachelle said as she swallowed a mouthful of eggs.

Setne started, staring at her. "You haven't ac-tually learned . . ."

"No. I need no truck with spells, silly old dear." She answered the hanging question with a satisfied grin. "You are as easy to read as an unrolled scroll."

Of course. The Ægyptian relaxed. For a moment, he thought he had been slipping. Perhaps he was readable—he obviously was—but only to the girl. She was correct, and twenty years was sufficient time for his old friend to learn to read expressions, interpret body language, associate words, create an educated guess. It approximated mind reading. "You're mistaken as usual, amazon," Setne lied. "I was wondering if there might be something of interest in the count's personal collection of manuscripts and curiosities, that's all."

Rachelle snorted derisively. It was a habit she had picked up from the wizard-priest. "And I'm a dainty concubine of the Imperial Ch'in!" she retorted. Then Rachelle arose from the little table and strode off. "I will be in my chambers practicing my negligible arts. Please disturb me only if you need someone to rescue you."

Inhetep made a rueful noise, a clucking which might stem from either disappointment or a point scored against him. Rachelle would know which. He watched her walking into the villa. She dressed like a man, but her slender body's feminine lines were not disguised. Rachelle was as tall as many of the local men, but never would she be mistaken for one. The blue-black curls, finely featured face, and superb curves certainly qualified her for inclusion in even an emperor's harem. She had perfect manners, could sing well, and played harp and mandolin, too.

Beauty, etiquette, refinement, knowledge, and quick wit assisted her greatly in difficult times. Foes typically mistook her qualities for softness, weakness, vulnerability, but Rachelle was as deadly a foe with bow or sword as any amazon. She could out-wrestle and out-fight most men half again her weight, for she was a devotee of the art of unarmed combat, which applied the force of the attacker against himself. That, after initial schooling in the Grecian forms of such combat, made her nearly unbeatable by any opponent not likewise trained.

"Why does she remain with me?" Inhetep murmured aloud.

Carlos, hovering nearby in anticipation of the Ægyptian's departure from the breakfast table to pursue whatever it was such strange men as himself did to occupy their days, came close and bent towards Setne. "I crave your pardon, lord, but I didn't hear your command clearly."

"I said you should clear this stuff away," Inhetep told the Iberian. "I am finished."

"Very good, lord," Carlos intoned. "Will there by anything further?"

Setne waved him away, lost again in thought. Should he actually go to Count Patros' nearby castle? Or should he simply spend another leisurely day here? There was some letter writing to do, and he had not finished the treatise on antipathic dweomercræfting written by the woman who claimed she was Queen of the Romney or some such. What was her name, anyway? No matter . . . Inhetep's thoughts drifted back to Rachelle. Her stubborn refusal to be anything other than his guard had proved to be a benison from the gods. It had seemed quite the opposite at first.

He had been jibed about sending the homely little slave girl to school. The folk of Ægypt were very liberal in most attitudes, especially regarding sex, and they thought Inhetep was currying a wholly unattractive girl toward becoming a concubine. There had been no use in answering any of that. The huge eyes set in the sharp, thin face, Rachelle's cleverness, and her absolute devotion had made Setne's decision regarding her. With education and training and manumission, Rachelle would be accepted as an Ægyptian. Regardless of her plainness, the girl would find useful work in some ecclesiastical organization or with one of the various government offices. Even with only marginal talent for magickal practice, clerics were in high demand. He had tried, but despite his best efforts and her own willingness to try to please her benefactor, Rachelle had shown absolutely no ability whatsoever for any form of magick. None! The wizard-priest shook his bald pate at that thought. Almost everyone had a modicum of talent, which training and study could develop, if only to a very minor extent. Still, she had excelled at virtually everything else set before her as a challenge.

Someday soon, Setne would have to find a suitable husband for her. It was just that he did still need her. That had been proven to him time and time again over the last few years.

As an ur-kheri-heb, a great priest and wizard too, Inhetep was unusual in Ægypt, and outside of Pharaoh's realms the combination was as rare as a black pearl. The governor of the Abydos Sepat, one of the sixty-four districts into which the kingdom was divided, had requested Setne's services just as Rachelle had returned from Sais. He had gone, of course, taking her with him. After all, what else could he do? Desert his foster child upon her homecoming after so many years? The service had been important—dangerous, too. In the last desperate stages of the affair, Rachelle had been involved and proved the usefulness of her recent training by acquitting herself with no little bravery. The felonious officials and their hired killers had been slain or captured, the governor cleared of the false charges, and Inhetep sent back to his home with commendations and a sizable purse of gold.

"I didn't even get a thank you," Rachelle had pouted.

"Female slaves are seldom thanked," Inhetep explained wryly.

After a bit of consideration, Rachelle had told him, "It is time I accepted my freedom, Master Setne, but I have a single condition you must agree to if this is to be." Setne had been suspicious but finally consented. "As long as I wish, I am to be your servant, your guard, and your associate, if you feel that is appropriate." It was foolish, but the matter was concluded thus.

The work he had done for Governor Ptah-tetta came to the attention of many others thereafter, and even Pharaoh had need for Inhetep's "unofficial" services. For the last several years, he and Rachelle had been all over the realm and its tributaries, and other nations as well, to suss out crime and its conspiracies, to hunt down enemies of the state. The detection work was interesting and occasionally very rewarding financially. In fact, he received such an enormous sum for solving one particular case, that he was excluded as a member of the *Uchatu*, the Pharoah's secret service. But Magister Inhetep Setne could not cease being an investigator. For the last five years, he had traveled Yarth—at least the lands of Afrik, Azir, and Æropa—doing much the same as he had done before, but now as a private individual.

Ostensibly it was to learn more of his magickal art. Certainly, Inhetep had no need of money as long as he didn't squander the wealth he had inherited and the gold he had subsequently accumulated. In truth, he and Rachelle might have lived two lifetimes without want, traveling and living in state. The Magister had a thirst for arcane knowledge, but he had an even greater thirst for adventure undertaken in the name of truth and justice. Not derring-do exactly. The wizard-priest was addicted to solving mysteries, especially puzzles which involved crime.

Thus, each place he and the girl went was one which offered some unusual bit of lore. Inhetep's reputation as an arch-dweomercræfter who solved crimes, uncovered spies, and brought criminals to justice, always preceded him. That was sufficient to guarantee that the Ægyptian was called upon to serve in such capacity wherever he and the girl happened to go. Five years of traveling from city to city, twice that number of detection commissions, and now at last a real holiday. Here in Valencia there was neither serious arcane knowledge to be found nor latent mystery. This was fun, relaxation, escape. . . . In a short time, they would take a ship for Cadiz where certain ancient parchments were rumored to be held in a secret collection. Then it was on to Atlantl, a place of renown which Inhetep and all Ægyptians held in honor, despite the degeneracy and dissolution which had overtaken the once-great kingdom. Whatever came thereafter was up in the air, so to speak.

Perhaps it would be portentous to go on to the western continents; perhaps the time would be ripe for a visit to Hind and the far Orient. . . .

Lemuria? No, he had no desire to see that great
island in the Titanic Ocean, for the ways of its
people and their magickal pursuits were totally
alien to even the cosmopolitan priest-mage. Setne
caught himself there. Only a week of idleness
on the seashore in southeastern Iberia, a time of
relaxation with his trusted friend and confidante, someone almost his daughter—no, more—
but better not to dwell on that! How refreshing
to be housed in a charming villa, to see the
mountains, orange groves, the sea, the quaint
town of Valentia, to receive invitations from all
the nobility and wealthy citizens of the area.
What more could he ask?

"A whole lot," Setne said aloud, as he turned
and strolled toward the nearby garden. "I must
admit it. I am bored silly."

Just then Carlos emerged from the villa. He
spied Inhetep and flapped his arms as he ran up
to the Ægyptian. "Save us, save us, lord! You
know magicks. Save us!" the tubby little fellow
gasped.

"Whatever are you dithering about?" Inhetep
snapped, irritated at being disturbed from his
reverie. "Speak more distinctly," he ordered, for
despite a fair grasp of Iberian, Carlos was chat-
tering in a nearly unintelligible fashion. He re-
peated his words, and Setne reassured him, "I
am passing able to direct the unseen powers, but
just what is it you want to be saved from?"

"My cousin, Paulao, the one who is the coral

dealer in Valentia, a very prosperous and honorable man," the flustered servant explained carefully. "It is he who warned me, and I, in turn, now alert you to the danger!"

Inhetep exercised his will and remained calmly patient. "Just what danger?"

"The three men, lordship. The three men!"

"You must have some more specific information than that, Carlos."

"Ah, but of course. My cousin described them as great, tall—almost as tall as you from the way he described them."

"And?"

"And these three tall men, men as gaunt as death itself, Paulao told me, were just in Valentia inquiring about you!"

Setne was mildly interested now. "They asked for me by name?"

"Well, that I do not know, because my cousin said only that they were directed to this villa by an old busybody, who overheard them asking about a shaven-headed priest and offered them information as to where such a person could be found for their money. She is certainly a witch," Carlos reported with satisfaction.

"She did what?"

"Why, she took their coins, surely, then told them how to find this villa!"

"This is intriguing," Inhetep said, pondering the question of who might be seeking him out here in this backwater. "What threats did they make?"

The small man's eyes grew large at that. "Ah, venerable Magister, who knows what horrible things lurk in the hearts of foreigners—yourself excluded, naturally, magickal lordship," he hastened to add. Seeing no anger in the coppery face of the Ægyptian, Carlos continued. "Men with such looks—strangers, hollow-eyed spell-workers, surely—are never intent on doing good! Why else would they consult with a witch? Is there a feud which you are involved in? A vendetta, perhaps? You must save yourself and we who are here to serve you—perhaps leaving now would be best. . . ."

Managing to change the derisive laugh to a discrete clearing of his throat, Setne looked the frightened Iberian squarely in the face. "Most unlikely, Carlos, most unlikely indeed. Contrary to that, I believe we will prepare a little reception for these three gaunt men you say are coming." Carlos started to protest. Inhetep silenced him with a look. "See that the rest of the household is alerted. Have ices, cold tea, hot coffee, and some sweet cakes ready. Place chairs in the veranda, three facing west, two opposite them. Hurry!" The servant started to run off. "Wait! Tell the Lady Rachelle to attend me instantly. I'll be there in a few minutes."

"It is done," Carlos fairly panted, looking confident and worried all at once. At that Inhetep did actually laugh.

"At last! Something to break the monotony," he said to no one. Then, whistling tunelessly under his breath, the wizard-priest went into the nearby villa, long-legged strides covering the distance faster than had Carlos' running. "Let's see what death has in store!"

3

ANUBIS, SON OF SET?

Despite the warmth of the noonday sun, the men wrapped themselves in hooded cloaks of dark blue wool. Only their faces were visible, pale ovals shadowed by the deep cowls of their garments. The three seemed to glide along the dusty track between the groves. The rutted road led only to the villa on the shore of the Mare Librum.

If they saw the peasants who served the villa fleeing through the trees, the indigo-clad men showed no sign of it. When they reached the door of the residence, the central figure nodded, and the planks of the door gave forth a sonorous noise, as if someone had rapped on them with a billet of wood.

Rachelle opened the portal. "Salutations, wayfarers," she said to the three strangely garbed men. She spoke in the language known as Trade Phonecian, the lingua franca of Yarth. "Is there something you wish?"

"We seek an Ægyptian, a priest and magus of

some renown. His name is Inhetep. He is here."
The middle figure of the group spoke, and the
last sentence was not a question but a statement
of fact. There was neither deference nor challenge in his tone—no respect, no threat. "Now
we will enter," he said firmly. His Trade Phonecian was heavily accented.

"Perhaps," Rachelle responded, without moving from her position squarely in the entryway.
"Please be so kind as to throw back your cowls
first. I must also know your names in order to
properly announce you. Only then will I give you
three permission to come in."

It seemed as if the central figure was about to
voice some protest, but the man on his left made
a slight bow and tugged back his hood, and so
did the man on the right. Pulling back his own
cowl, the middle stranger said, "I am Aldriss."

Rachelle looked at the man on the right. "You
are . . . ?"

"Tallesian," he said in a harsh voice.

"And . . . ?"

The other man gave a small smile as if sharing
some secret with the girl. "You may call me the
Behon."

For a few heartbeats Rachelle stood unmoving,
head cocked to one side, eyes fixed on the three
men. They were lean and pinch-faced. They
were indeed men as gaunt as death. "Follow me,
and I will announce your presence to Magister
Inhetep."

She led them through the villa and back outside to the place Setne had chosen. The sun wasn't quite at its zenith, and its rays streamed over the wizard-priest's shoulders where he sat quietly awaiting the visitors. Rachelle announced each of them; Inhetep said nothing in reply, so the girl led them to the three chairs opposite the Ægyptian. Then she seated herself just to his left hand, eyeing the pale strangers.

"You are the one called Inhetep?" Aldriss inquired. It was almost a statement.

"I am he," Setne answered. "You are a bard, aren't you? From the Isles of Avillon—specifically Lyonnesse."

"How do you know that?" the man asked, startled.

Inhetep cocked his right eyebrow. "Your fingers. Harping and playing stringed instruments causes callouses, does it not, Aldriss? Besides, your comrade Tallesian is unquestionably a druid—he wears that proclamation in the beaded chain beneath his robe. The one claiming himself the Behon must then be a sage, a worker of dweomers of some considerable heka from the blankness of his aura. It is therefore clear that you three represent the political power of your state—noble, ecclesiastic, and magickal."

The Behon cleared his throat. His two companions looked inquiringly at him. "That is astute reasoning, Setne Inhetep. I had hoped for nothing less. We are, as you have discerned, men from Lyonnesse come to seek you out."

"I see." Inhetep turned to the girl. "The servants have deserted us, I fear. Please be so kind as to bring the refreshments I ordered from Carlos, my dear Rachelle, for I believe we will be conversing here some time." She hesitated, so the priest-mage reassured her. "Don't be concerned about my safety. These three men may appear threatening, but they mean us absolutely no harm—at this time, anyway. I'll be quite safe in their company until you return." Rachelle's mouth was set in a moue of disapproval, but she stood and went into the building. "While we wait, gentlemen, may I suggest you doff those woolen robes? This climate is not suitable for such apparel, and there will be nobody here to observe us, I think."

There was a little laughter from all three at the last remark. The men did as suggested, revealing white gowns worn beneath the heavy blue outer wraps. Both Aldriss and Tallesian were muscular of build but quite wiry. The Behon was merely thin. "We have searched for you for some time now," the druidical member of the trio said as he arranged his robe over the back of the seat. He straightened the amber beads and seven-rayed sun and rowan tree of gold which proclaimed him a druid of Mur Ollavan, the City of Sages and chief temple seat of the druids of Lyonnesse.

"Yes, I thought it would be the rowan shown atop the sun," Inhetep said as he watched the druid's action. "Tell me, which is the tree held sacred by Albion, yew or oak?"

"The yew, Magister Inhetep. The Caledonians bear the oak, while the folk of Cymru venerate the elm, and those of Hybernia the ash tree."

"Thank you for the enlightenment. I shall not forget."

Rachelle returned to the little courtyard laden with a big tray bearing cold tea and orange-flavored shaved ice in ceramic cups, guarded against the heat by a little lid on each. There was also a carafe of strong coffee and an assortment of small cakes and biscuits covered with nuts, candied fruits, and glazes. She placed the tray on a nearby table and began serving the four men, beginning with the gray-haired one who was identified as the Behon.

"The coffee, please. Now I see that this is more than a pretty face and strong arm," he said, accepting the proffered cup but declining any other refreshment. "I would that I had such an associate," he said to Inhetep.

The other two were more liberal in their selections. As Rachelle was seeing to them, Setne responded, "And why not? But surely, there must be someone in a city so populous as Camelough for training as apprentice. . . ."

It was the Behon's turn to show surprise, albeit he allowed only a mild bit to show. "So you are aware of who I am."

"It would be a fool indeed who failed to recognize the direct successor of Myrlyn and chief sage and magus of Lyonnesse. Who other than the ovate could be in such company as the master bard of that kingdom and its archdruid? So then, I am most honored to serve as host to three great men."

"I am grateful for your not mentioning my name, Magister. You of all people are aware . . ." and the Behon allowed his words to trail off.

"You do me too much credit, Ovate. I am but a simple priest, a servant of the Wise One, Thoth, who knows a few little tricks and cantrips. I understand the power of the true name; Isis herself was able to utilize Ra's to gain her surpassing skill in heka by such means," Inhetep said, then paused to sip a little of the tea brought to refreshing coolness by means of an enchantment he had placed upon a vessel belonging to the villa. "Please don't confuse my undeserved reputation solving crimes with a special skill in dweomercræfting. The two are quite removed, you understand. More tea, gentlemen?"

The Behon smiled broadly this time. "But of course, Magister. I most assuredly do comprehend. And no, I have still half a glass to finish. Aldriss? Tallesian?"

The bard opted for a second of the sherbet; Tallesian made sport of that, but himself had both more of the sweet, minty tea and another cake. It was plain from Rachelle's expression that she was wondering how those two men stayed so gaunt while eating so ravenously. "Perhaps as you do," Setne supplied under his breath. Rachelle quickly looked away from Aldriss and the druid, hoping that those two and the mage with them were not reading her as easily as was the Ægyptian.

"As I stated, august sirs, I am quite honored to be your host. At the same time, I am quite at a loss to understand why three of Lyonnesse's noblest men seek out a poor Ægyptian priest, one without so much as a local shrine to attend, on holiday in the wilds of Iberia. Will one of you be so kind as to enlighten me?" He looked at the Kelltic mage as he spoke, but he seemed to be aware of the other two at the same time.

Rachelle knew that trick of Setne's well. He would pick up many signs from secondary persons while seeming to concentrate on the chief member of any gathering. Aldriss, the bard, was eager to respond. He fairly wiggled but watched the gray-locked ovate for permission, with fingers seeming to stroke an invisible harp as he did so. That one would make an epic of whatever was to be said, the girl knew, for the fame of the Avillonian bards surpassed all others in Æropa. A quick glance at the druid, Tallesian, told Rachelle that he was more reserved but hardly less eager to speak. He sat erect, tense and ready.

Then she saw a slight motion from the Behon, a finger twitch signal. Both of his companions settled back and looked at the Kelltic master of dweomercræft.

"If I may, Magister Inhetep, I will attempt your request. My friends will fill in anything I've missed when I have finished."

"That is splendid, Behon. Say on." Setne now positioned himself so that he could observe all three of the strangers.

"One month ago there was a terrible killing in Ys. . . ."

Inhetep frowned. "Come, come my good magus, be more direct and forthright! In a place such as Ys is said to be, there must be a dozen murders a night."

"The reputation of the city is overstated. There aren't that many murders in a day and night there. So . . . no matter. This one was different. It involved the arch demonurge of the Academie Sorcerie d'Ys."

"I see. Hmmm . . . Isn't the fellow's name Fontainnoir?"

The Behon was secretly pleased that the Ægyptian had missed the mark. "Very nearly correct, Magister Inhetep, very nearly. The *Haut Omniurge* of the college was Bertrand *Frontonac*."

"You speak in the past tense. Interesting. I had thought that the fellow in question had committed murder, not become the victim of such a crime. To slay a sorcerer of such power takes the most insidious plotting or a skillful foe. Was it political? Personal grudge?"

"You strike to the crux of this affair, Magister," the elderly sage answered. "It was a shocking murder because it had been announced beforehand. Frontonac knew, took precautions, and then derided the unknown enemies who had announced his death."

Inhetep seemed quite unmoved by that statement. "I'll interrupt no further, good mage, if you will set forth the complete picture from the beginning—and I mean what occurred well prior to the demise of the demonurgist Frontonac."

"You know about the others?" Aldriss exclaimed.

"He does now," Tallesian quipped laconically.

The Behon sighed, settled back, and sipped a little of his now tepid drink. "The thing started a year ago," he finally said, looking upward a moment as if to mentally sort out the details before proceeding. "The first victim was the Eldest Spaewife." Setne was about to interrupt, but the gray-haired magus held up his hand. "I know, you need the background of that, too. Someone calling himself the 'Master of Jackals' was responsible. A king of Skandia, Rogven Iron Eyes, of course, received a demand for certain things prior to and after his principal heka-wielder was assassinated. Even I am uncertain as to exactly what the list included, but there was certainly money involved. Rogven, not known for his open-handedness, let alone timorous nature, demanded that the unknown blackmailer meet him in combat. Instead the Eldest Spaewife, the king's chief dweomercræfter, was murdered. They found her one morning soon after Rogven's refusal. The woman had been literally torn to shreds within her sanctum. The whole place was coated in ice ... bloody ice!"

"The protections?"

"Each still in place, all castings laid active, nothing else disturbed," the Behon replied. "If that could occur under the very roof of the ruler of the nation, and to the most powerful spellbinder in the country, what hope did Rogven have if the so-called Master of Jackals decided to slay him? The answer being plain, the king paid over the demanded things."

"A year past, you say?" Setne murmured. "There has been no rumor of the occurrence ... not even a whisper in the Greater Nexus."

"Rogven has done his best to see to that, but it is certainly worth pondering. Something far greater than the King of Svergie, powerful as he may be, has worked to suppress the information."

"A year ... Of course, I have been otherwise occupied," the wizard-priest mused, "but still ... This is most disquieting. Is there more?"

Tallesian nodded. "Much more. You have heard only the beginning." He glanced at the mage, who nodded his assent. "The Grand Duke of Livestonia, himself something of a demonurgist, was evidently threatened a short time after

that. He ignored the Master of Jackals and paid
the price. There is a new grand duke in Riga.
That was announced ten months ago. Next came
threats to the Northerners—Talmark, Russ, Kalevala, Finmark in succession—dreadful old
Louhi of Pohjola raved about threats from someone. Only rumors exist, but it seems they paid
whatever blackmail or tribute or ransom was demanded. The League of Hansa was not so wise.
Their three chief leaders were murdered in succession, which proves the stubbornness of the
Teutons and the deadlines of the Master of Jackals. It seems nothing can stop him."

"Come now, druid!" Inhetep interjected. "Isn't
that a trifle overstated on the face of the
evidence?"

"You haven't heard the whole yet," Aldriss
the bard supplied. "Last month, the most powerful sorcerer in Brettony, perhaps in Francia as
well, proved unable to protect himself against
this assassin—his agent, that is. And now—"

"And now I shall resume the tale," the Behon
said firmly, cutting off his associate. "The time
has come to do something about this matter. The
person or organization masquerading as the Master of Jackals must be discovered and brought to
justice."

Rachelle couldn't resist crying out, "You three
have come all the way from Lyonnesse to ask aid
of us—I mean, Magister Inhetep? His fame has
spread to the very fringes of Yarth?"

The Behon looked nonplussed, and it was Setne himself who came to the rescue of the sagacious mage. "We who bend dweomers and magickal powers to our will have a means of knowing about one another, so to speak. I doubt, dear girl, that the average citizen of Camelough, for instance, has ever heard of me. On the other hand, we also have means of knowing just who isn't around any longer. That is what intrigues me. I should have known about the deaths of such magi—"

"So should I have known—at least by means other than courier reports. There is nothing, a blank," the Behon finished with a shrug.

Tallesian was hopeful as he spoke next. "There is no denying that you are most difficult to locate, Magister. It took much mundane searching and questioning to discover your whereabouts."

"That's the power of the Ægyptian thaumaturgists for you!" Aldriss asserted. "No offense, learned Magister."

"No. Of course not. I have a question: Were all those murdered of the Black Arts?"

The Behon shook his head. "We thought of that. There is no telling about the Northerners, but the grand duke was at best a dabbler in the energies of evil, and the masters of the Hansa were most certainly not inclined toward anything but profit and gain from trading—"

"And then there's the most recent threat," Tallesian inserted.

Setne noticed the frown the ovate bestowed
upon Tallesian and directed his question to the
Behon rather than the druid. "So this Master of
Jackals has sent further demands?"

"To Lyonnesse."

"I thought as much," Inhetep said with a tinge
of self-satisfaction. "I am puzzled. You surely,
Behon, have sufficient heka to discover something about this whole matter, do you not?"

"I am unable to," the gray man said, looking
old and tired as he admitted it. "No casting will
discover who is behind this thing. Magick of all
sorts brought to bear on the scene of the murder,
the corpse, the witnesses reveals absolutely nothing. It is as if it was all done by some strange
power, some *science*, unknown to this world."

"I need to know everything possible about the
affair in Ys where Haut Omniurge Bertrand
Frontonac was done in," Setne snapped. If any
of his visitors noted his recall of the demonurge's
full title and name, they passed it off as excellent memory. The Behon narrated the full story
as it had come from Camelough's spy within the
Academie Sorcerie. Because the bard had been
trained for recounting from memory, Aldriss
supplied many details the magus overlooked, and
even Tallesian had a few bits to add. "What's
this business about black jackals?" Inhetep finally asked when the whole tale seemed to have
been related.

"A pair of watchmen admitted seeing a pack

of them—wild dogs, they claimed at first, but admitted later that they were strange-looking. Their descriptions fit only jackals—bigger than normal, though. Anyway," Aldriss went on, "these two guards saw the creatures first, just before midnight on the eleventh of the month, outside the gate to the college. There were a number of others who saw them too, and several boatmen and fishers swear that they saw and heard things like seawolves, only they were sea-jackals, swimming in the waters of the academy's shore."

"Who is now under threat of death?"

"That," the Behon said firmly, "must wait until you agree to come with us to Lyonnesse."

Setne glanced at Rachelle. Her expression showed eagerness. "No, thank you noble sirs, but I must say no. You see I am on holiday—a holiday promised for a long time and finally delivered. I cannot break my word on this matter. . . ."

"Holiday? Ridiculous!" said the bard. "How much longer is your blasted vacation to last?"

"Oh, at least two weeks, I am sure. Isn't that correct, Rachelle?"

"Well . . . Perhaps you might consider a hiatus. . . . she replied, without looking at the wizard-priest.

"That is a possibility to keep in mind, but there is another matter I am curious about. You three have certainly noted your opinion of my ability to solve problems such as this one, yet I am far from being either the greatest dweomer-

cræfter or the most able criminologist. Tell me
what caused you to come seeking me all the way
from your own island?"

"You are far too modest, Magister Setne Inhetep," the Behon chided. "If you aren't one of
the most able practitioners alive, you are no
Ægyptian." At that he paused. Inhetep might
have flushed a little, but his own natural color-
ation would have hidden it.

"I am most surely a man of Ægypt," Setne
admitted.

"You folk have thousands of gods," Tallesian
chimed in, "but despite that confusion, your
priests are remarkable in their potency! Why, if
what Myf—the Behon has said about your magicians is half true, it's a wonder Ægypt doesn't
rule the world!"

"We started once but found it rather a larger
calling than we were able to answer for a pro-
tracted period." Only Rachelle laughed.

"The point is, Magister, that you are a wizard-
priest who stands above a nation filled with great
ones wielding heka, as you say, magickal power.
That I know for myself," Tallesian blurted. "The
community of dweomercræfters places your art
in an esteemed position as well. Not even the
murdered sorcerer, Frontonac, for instance,
would have challenged you to open contest from
what I hear."

"There is more, Magister Inhetep," the ovate
firmly said. "Not only are you a priest and wiz-

ard of exceptional sort, but you are knowledge-able in matters pertaining to crime. Perhaps there are more influential and potent priests and wizards. There might be investigators and detectives more learned in the field of criminology. Neither the one lot nor the other combines what you possess. Does that explain why we have come so many leagues, spent so long, hunting you down?"

The hawk face turned towards the bard, Aldriss. "Not quite, for I sense that your comrade here has something he wishes to add."

"That's so," the man said. "There is certainly an evil force cloaking these hideous murders. It is all but impenetrable, but we have clues."

"Clues which brought you three in search of Setne Inhetep."

"Just so," Aldriss agreed. "The jackal is one. Black jackals, too, of monstrous size. The others are of such a nature that I am not at liberty to detail them. That will come if you agree to undertake the case and protect—never mind. What matters is that the Master of Jackals is certainly linked to your native land, Magister!"

"Ægypt?"

"None other. All of the evidence points squarely to your own country and one of its most powerful deities. . . ."

"You can refer only to Lord Anubis, I presume."

"That assumption is correct," the Behon affirmed. He looked squarely into Inhetep's green eyes. "And we know that Anubis is the son of Set!"

Rachelle gasped at the near sacrilege. "You are full—" she began. Setne lifted a hand, moved a finger, and the girl subsided.

"Let that pass for now, Rachelle. Suffice to say, I accept your request. We will accompany you on your return journey to Lyonnesse."

4

DEATH AND EVIL

"The overland route is shorter, so why do we take a ship?" Rachelle was annoyed at the prospect, for she was not a good sailor.

Aldriss stood at her elbow at the rail of the little sloop, hanging on every word the beautiful Levantine girl uttered. Before Inhetep could respond to her question, the bard took Rachelle's arm and explained as he steered her towards the prow, "First, the constant progress of a ship exceeds the rate of overland travel. Then again, the roads in Iberia are poor. There are bandits and all manner of feral things in the hinterlands, too. Near the Pyrannes, the mountains which divide this kingdom from Francia, it gets even worse, and then beyond things become worse still. There is comfort and safety only near the cities or great strongholds."

Setne listened and watched surreptitiously but didn't interfere. The Kellt was busily pointing out landmarks along the coast as the ship weighed anchor and began its voyage westward.

First, of course, they had to head south, then west beyond the Pillars of Herakles, then northward to the Isles of Avillon. This was a bad time of year for sailing, but there was no help for that. It was safer and faster than trying to ride through the various kingdoms of Iberia and through Francia and then cross the Channel of Avillon, or the Albish Channel as some called it, to reach Lyonnesse's southern shores. He turned to the Behon and Tallesian, who were conversing in low tones a few paces distant. "The winds will be foul, most likely. Can we freely employ countering forces?"

"Odd that you should mention that, Magister." The elderly magus smiled. "Tallesian and I were just considering the question."

"We think it a poor idea," the druid told Setne. "If we wish to keep our whereabouts, and yours, secret, then we mustn't disturb things too much. The castings we might employ would certainly lessen our chances of going unnoticed."

"I concur," the Ægyptian said. "Yet I assumed that we have stringent time constraints. How will we avoid endless delays in the Lantlan Ocean—especially near the great bay?"

The Behon nodded. "The Bay of Aquitania can be very dangerous in this time approaching the Winter Solstice. Fortunately, we have our bard, and his particular power is usable, for it is not connected to arts such as ours—not directly, anyway. Although each bard, skald, or troubadour has his or her own signature, and their manipulation of heka traceable and identifiable, it is unlikely to occur."

"You mean it won't be noticed?" Inhetep inquired.

"It isn't because it won't be noticed," the druid replied, "but because it will seem minor and different to any other sort of practitioner seeking information from the heka currents, directions, and flows."

Inhetep seemed uncertain. "We have no great spellsingers in Ægypt, albeit many castings are employed with the aid of chants and the like. What little I know comes from the Grecians and Latins. They contradict what you have just told me, Tallesian."

"That isn't surprising. With all due respect to all older cultures, the Kellts are the commensurate bardic folk. Even though the Skandian, Teutonic, and Frankish peoples work their best to rival us, their skalds and troubadours are still unable to rival the bards of Avillonia. We slip magical energy away so softly and quietly that only one who intimately knows the bardic art can have any inkling of just what power is being drawn and directed. Isn't that right, Behon?"

"Quite so," the ovate agreed. "Only the rhyme-singers of the furthest north, the folk of Kalevala and Pohjola, might know when a Kelltic bard is at work and what is being done by whom."

"How so?" the wizard-priest queried.

"The great ones in Kalevala, for instance, are what one might call wizard-skalds. If any heka-cræfter is able to meet the Ægyptians on their own terms in the art of magick, it is those great practitioners of Soumi—Kalevalan, Finn, Lapp or otherwise. It is similarly true, despite what Aldriss will ever admit, and Tallesian too for that matter, that those weavers of dweomers are certainly more than on a par with the greatest of our bards."

The druid harrumphed. "Perhaps, perhaps . . . But in days of yore, it was a different story. The young ones today are not what bards once were!"

"True," the Behon said. "Perhaps Cairbre, Finn, and Ossian were greater than the Waino . . ."

Inhetep had been keeping an eye on the two who were still chatting together near the bow. "Well, my fine Kelltic philosophers, then I think you had better round up your able bard and set him to work. Otherwise, he might dawdle the whole of the journey away," Setne added with a little testiness. Tallesian and the Behon still remained gaunt and pale-looking—magickally assumed guises, of course. Aldriss, on the other hand, had allowed himself to return to his natural appearance—young, muscular, with fair skin, flashing white teeth, and bright blue eyes. Too handsome, too foppish in his ways, the shaven-headed Ægyptian thought sourly. No. He had to be honest with himself. It was that the bard was

too forward, self-assured, and altogether too flir-
tatious with Rachelle!

The Behon smiled upon seeing the black look
Setne shot toward Aldriss, and Tallesian murmured something apologetic under his breath as
he went forward to fetch the bard. Fortunately,
the girl remained near the front of the sloop
when the two Lyonnessians came back to join
their leader and Inhetep. "You need my services,
then?" Aldriss asked brightly.

"It's you and yours who need mine," the
Ægyptian reminded him in reply. "I believe your
liege, the Behon, has some instructions."

"That is correct, Aldriss. We must have a very
fast passage. That can be assured only through
your vigilance and harping."

The bard stood straighter and squared his
shoulders. "It is an honor, and one I will truly
fulfill in keeping the charge, Behon." Then Aldriss grinned to each of the three in turn, saying,
"But, of course, in such a calm sea as the Mare
Librum, there'll be no need for my skill, will
there? Three days to the Pillars of Herakles in
all likelihood. If you will excuse me then, I think
I should return to where Lady Rachelle is waiting, for I have been recounting the history and
wonders of this land, and of Lyonnesse Isle."

Without another word, Aldriss turned and rejoined Rachelle at the bow rail.

Without seeming to notice Aldriss' departure,
Setne eyed the waves, looked up at the sky with

its scattering of puffy little clouds, then fixed his falcon-like gaze upon the Kelltic mage. "Pray tell me, Behon—you too, wise druid—all about these famed bards of Avillon's Isles. I am sorely lacking in this field of knowledge. To liken the elder ones to the great Vainomoinen is ample demonstration of their powers. Can you enlighten my ignorance?"

The two needed no further encouragement. Inhetep was an excellent listener and had near perfect recall. When it was evident to the Kellts that he was truly interested in hearing about their special form of spell-weaving, that singing of the bard, there was no silencing them. The weather was fair enough, the winds right, and the ship plowed along on her circuit of Iberia's southeastern coast. It was three days to reach the place where the sea met the mightier waters of the Lantlan Ocean. During that whole time the Ægyptian learned of bards while the bard, Aldriss, spent his time amusing Rachelle.

Three days later, they finally passed the Pillars of Herakles and came out upon the long swells of the gray-hued Lantlan Ocean. Rachelle still spent a good deal of the time near the foremast where Aldriss now played and sang to aid their passage. One afternoon the tall Ægyptian wrapped himself in a cloak borrowed from the sloop's captain and joined them.

"Are you thinking of taking up the harp, Magister?" the bard asked when Setne began setting down notes on a papyrus roll. "If so, you must learn to play notes, not take them," the fellow jested.

Inhetep smiled thinly. "No, no," he disclaimed. "I have never before seen a master spell-singer such as yourself in action. Perhaps I'll gain enough information this way to present a paper on the subject to the University of Innu—my own alma mater, as they say in Grecia—sometime in the future. Am I likely to meet others such as yourself in Camelough?"

"There's precious little chance of that," Aldriss said, grinning.

"I had thought as much," the wizard-priest said. "Well, never mind me. Do continue with your tune, and don't forget to keep the dweomers you spin thus on the unexceptional side."

"Now that'll be the truly hard part," Aldriss responded, "for one such as myself usually leaves a mark of virtuosity even in so simple a business as calling fair winds and keeping storms at bay."

"I can appreciate just how much wind a chap such as yourself can generate," Setne said as he casually peered up at the taut sails. "Why, the canvas overhead is fairly stretched to bursting!"

It was the bard's turn to look sour, but he couldn't be sure that the remark had alluded to anything other than the breeze which he had harped up to drive the sloop north toward his home. A note of irritation crept into the strains, but he played and sang on.

Despite the efforts which Aldriss put forth, a storm came up which would have demanded a major expenditure of supernatural power to suppress. The captain furled most of the sloop's sails and ran before it. The ship made safe harbor in Galicia, but they had to lie at anchor for three days before the stormy seas quieted sufficiently for them to set sail again. They had not, however, had to significantly alter their course. The following wind was stiff and would carry the sloop to Lyonnesse, making the lost days almost insignificant. Between the magick of the bard's spinning and good fortune, the five wayfarers would soon be in the port of Caer-Mabd. From that town, it was only a single day's ride to the capital, Camelough, the Behon explained.

"You haven't spoken of the involvement of your gods in the terrible business," Tallesian mentioned as they came within hours of their destination.

"Terrible business?"

"These murders and the blackmail behind them," the druid said a trifle crossly.

"Oh, now I comprehend your meaning," he responded in offhanded manner. "You see, I wasn't sure because of the erroneous assumption you made."

"Just what do you mean, Inhetep?" the Behon

interjected. "His comment sounded quite proper to me."

"It might have, but that's due to your own incorrect assumption. If you must know, Anubis is the son of Osiris by Nepthys, once the wife of Set and sister to Isis, Lord Osiris' chief consort. Anubis is no more involved in these murders than you or I, and I question strongly the possibility of the dark-minded Set having any part, either—although he would not be above all this and would certainly love to discredit the Guide, bring Tep-tu-f down from his high place, but . . ."

"But what, Magister?! Tep-tough? What is it you mean?"

"That no entity of Ægypt—nor even one associated with the Near East—is involved here. That is most obvious. What magick or hekau do any such ones have in the frozen north? Your own isles? Stony Ys? So few honor them, even know of the gods of my land, that they have but minor force in such places. Yet it was you who spoke of the great magicks which masked these crimes. Anubis is the Lord of Jackals, but your Master of Jackals is naught but a trickster in that regard, of this I am positive," Inhetep added. "For now, I'll say no more on that subject. I must see all of the materials you have, study the clues."

Tallesian was not ready to let the matter drop, and the fact that the wizard-priest denied any connection between Anubis and these murders and extortion did not clear the matter in his mind. In truth, the Behon looked skeptical as well. It was time to reveal some new information. "Do you know there are secret cults of a strange sort in the Teutonic lands? Brettony and Ys itself? There are undoubtedly such hidden shrines and devotees even in Camelough."

"Doesn't every land have its fringe elements?" Inhetep countered. He was obviously becoming bored with this conversation.

The ovate decided to add his weight to the discussion. "What my associate is driving at, Magister, is that there are cults honoring your Ægyptian deities, specifically a triad of them."

Setne turned so quickly that he startled his two companions. He towered over them as would a king cobra readying an attack. "What's that you say?!"

"A whole network of secret shrines have been discovered," the Behon supplied blandly. Then, in a voice heavy with meaning, the magus went on: "The three gods are none other than Set, Sobek, and the jackal-headed Anubis."

"You should have told me that long before now," Setne said in a level tone. His face was expressionless, unreadable, but there was a distinct chill in his voice, a message reinforced by his posture. "Had I known that, I would have insisted we put in at Ys to investigate these so-called cults and interrogated any worshippers who could be found."

Tallesian nodded. "We thought as much. That's exactly why we didn't mention it until we were about to dock in Caer-Mabd. You see, we are urgently needed in Camelough. There is no time for such side excursions as you would have insisted on."

The tall Ægyptian sat back in his chair. The cabin seemed smaller and more cramped, as if the wizard-priest had swelled to fill it somehow. Both of the Kellts understood the effect. Inhetep was drawing energy from the others and directing his powers toward some focal point. There could be no question as to what he was concentrating on. His words affirmed that fact. "There is an hour or two before we actually drop anchor. Please tell me everything now, and don't withhold any facts this time. Otherwise . . ." Setne allowed his sentence to end there. The meaning didn't require articulation.

There was no hesitation. Both men rapidly told of the findings of multiple investigations into the secret shrines and the triune cult. Set was recognized immediately, even in the hinterlands, as the Ægyptian lord of darkness and evil. Sobek, crocodile-headed friend of the dark one, was a natural accompaniment to the former. Anubis, however, was a strange third. "Our sages say that the Lord of the Jackals has a dual nature," the Behon finally said. "Might not he actually be the son of Set? Isn't it possible for the nature of a deity to change, to manifest itself in ways not before known? Before the struggle between Osiris and Set, it is said that most of your people held the red-haired god as admirable and beneficial—at least to themselves."

"Yes. Yes to both of your latter statements, that is. But no, the initial statement is incorrect. There is no question as to the parentage of Anubis, and his place is the twilight of the shadowy world, the Duat, where Osiris rules as king, just as it is in the realms of light and of Pet, the high sphere, where Ra reigns supreme." Setne seemed grim as he went on. "Once Sobek was also one of more wholesome nature. It is possible for the greater entities to realign themselves, for they have will as free as our own. Perhaps it is no longer mistaken to consider Anubis as the offspring of the master of Evil, for if the jackal-headed one has allied with Set, then he has become the spiritual child of darkest iniquity."

"I had thought you would approach this with such open-mindedness, Magister Inhetep," the Behon said with a note of compassion in his voice. "We are aware of your devotion to the ibis-headed Thoth. His relationship is that of Balance, though, is it not? We do that no harm when we condemn one of the Twilight Nature and Shadowy Darkness—the high standing of Anubis therein, his involvement . . . It is no reflection on the deities of Ægypt, Magister, but a sad commentary on but one of its number." The Behon looked into Setne's eyes. "It is up to you to discover just what machinations are afoot here. Then perhaps you can have your righteous gods intervene."

"Perhaps, perhaps," Inhetep murmured. "First, we will go to Camelough. There I will examine all of the bits of evidence you have, just as was promised me. Then I will decide what other steps to take. Death is not evil, not in the natural scheme of things. Evil does not necessarily bring death—or even use its fell and bony hand. Life is often more malicious than its cessation. There is much to learn, many things which must be analyzed and understood, before it will be possible to draw meaningful conclusions."

"One conclusion of a meaningful sort is at hand," the voice of Aldriss caroled. "We are about to drop anchor in the fair harbor of Caer-Mabd!"

All three turned and stared coldly at the bard. He hardly noticed because his spirits were so high. The Avillonian bards were truly only at home in their own isles, and clearly Aldriss was much affected by the sight of his native land. "Lady Rachelle is busily gathering your gear, Magister Inhetep. I'm off to do the same with my own now. Tallesian, Behon, aren't you going to pack up for immediate disembarkation?"

It was practical advice. The wizard-priest excused himself to see if there was anything he needed to do to assist the girl, and the three men of Lyonnesse likewise attended to gathering up their few possessions. Caer-Mabd was a thriving town of almost a hundred thousand people, the largest port in the country and second largest population center after the capital. Camelough lay a little over forty miles distant—a day's hard ride by horseback, and two days walk or travel by cart or wagon, though the fast coaches made it in one day because their teams went almost as swiftly as a single man on horseback.

Only a few minutes after the anchors had been dropped, the party was quickly whisked to shore and away from the port in a fast-moving coach.

"It is too bad," Rachelle remarked to her mentor. "I would like to see a little of Caer-Mabd, and I know you are always curious about strange cities. Is this matter so pressing that we couldn't spend even an hour or two? Some of the shops I glimpsed displayed very interesting wares."

He turned and stared at her, his hawk-like nose raised for a moment as if pointing at the girl. She looked only slightly haggard from the voyage—a surprising thing for one so poor a seafarer. "I can thank the bard for that," he said. Rachelle gave him a puzzled look. "I am merely noting how well you managed the long days aboard the ship on our journey here. Aldriss worked minor miracles ... but that is not a response to your query. The Behon is our employer, in a manner of speaking. He desires our immediate presence in Camelough, so we go hence to that place. I, too, would normally enjoy a day or two seeing sights. Perhaps on our return. Would you like that?"

"Very much." She smiled. "Perhaps we can find a native to guide us."

"Have you anybody special in mind?"

Rachelle smiled again. "Let's wait until the prospect is actual," she sweetly told her hawk-faced associate. Then she turned and looked out the window as the coach bounced along toward the royal seat of the great kingdom of Lyonnesse.

The Behon and Tallesian were silent and tense. It was evident that the nearer they came to Camelough the more worried they became. Even the bard was nearly silent, only occasionally humming under his breath as he stared into nothingness or gazed out at the scenery rolling by. These three were definitely part of the affair, and the one calling himself the Master of Jackals meant to exact his demands in the city for which they were heading.

Jackals are basically nothing but moderately clever animals, Inhetep thought. Cunning, perhaps smarter than a typical dog or wolf, but never close to a human. The information garnered from witnesses in Ys, however, seemed to point to jackals—far bigger specimens, creatures the size of enormous wolves, which behaved with almost human intelligence. Then there were the supposed sea-jackals. Why all that

showy business? After all, in the end it simply
came down to a flawed summoning of the air
elemental, so that instead a demon came and
slew the so-styled Haut Omniurge.

Frontonac had actually gone to Ægypt once.
Setne recalled meeting him in Innu. That was
thirty years ago now. More. The priest-mage had
then been but a fledging practitioner, studying
the laws of dweomercræfting. The Bretton had
been a respected, if dark, invocator even then,
and the half-dozen candidates studying to become kheri-heb had been brought out to hear him
speak on the subject of the Pandemonium and
the command of negative heka. It was a great
demon, indeed, that could kill the master sorcerer Frontonac with such ease. Greater still the
one who managed to cause it to come rather than
a prince of aerial nature! Skandia, the hyperbo-
rean lands, the Hansa masters, Livestonia, Ys,
and now Lyonnesse. Save for the realm of Norge
and empty Lappia, its path might appear to be a
circle drawn round a point—Brabant, Flanders,
Albion, or further north . . . ?

"You seem most thoughtful, my lord," Rachelle whispered to Setne. "Is there something I
should know? May I assist in any way?"

That sounded more like his faithful assistant,
and the Ægyptian smiled a little. It was more in
mockery of himself than for any other reason. "I
analyze even my own thoughts, Rachelle," he
said quietly. "But I am pondering this entire

matter now, for soon enough we'll be up to our necks in it. There is more to learn. Tomorrow morning, early, when we are fresh and rested."

"Now?"

"You have been trained, seen much, and what is known about the Master of Jackals and his murderous ways you have heard as I did. Please mull over the whole business. Look for anything unique, anything unusual taken in context of the whole bizarre nature of it, and search for some inconsistency. Before retiring, you and I will meet privately and compare our notes."

Her face was stony as she replied, "Of course. And thank you, Setne, for your confidence in me."

"You're welcome—but I always rely on you, Rachelle," the wizard-priest added.

The girl shook her head a little, making her dark ringlets bounce even more in the rattling carriage. "No. You include me as a sounding board, a bodyguard, a useful agent at times. This is actually the first time you have asked me to think and share my opinions on an abstract level."

"Bless me, Rachelle," Inhetep murmured, looking away and then back at her as he thought about what she had just said. "You are right! It must be that this is the first time we have actually had so much time to consider information before having to take action."

"Really? Well, shaved-pate, as you are the one

GYGAX

renowned for your thinking capacity, it must be as you say. Now, I had better cogitate, if you don't mind."

"Remarkable," Inhetep said before turning away. "My amazonian warrior plays with words as she does weapons. Such fine puns she displays! I believe that now either I am in for trouble, or else the Master of Jackals is doomed. . . ."

"Both," Rachelle whispered.

5

JACKAL'S MIND

"Why aren't we housed in the castle?" Rachelle asked petulantly. "Is it because we're foreigners?"

"It's because I specifically requested rooms in a quiet place," Setne explained firmly. "Anyone in the royal castle is under constant scrutiny. We need privacy and freedom from observation."

"Oh, but it seems so dreary here, and there's no opportunity to . . . to . . . You know what I mean!"

Inhetep was tempted to smile, but he decided not to anger her. "Rachelle, we will have ample opportunity to socialize with the court nobility after the problem of this murderous 'Master of Jackals' is solved. Let's put our minds to that."

"I'm sorry, Setne. I guess I am still a foolish little girl at times," Rachelle said with sincerity. "Of course you're right, and we need to be as unobtrusive as possible. This small inn is perfect in that regard. What is it you'd like me to do?"

There was the Rachelle he was used to! Setne began to outline the case as he saw it up to then, asking the girl to follow his own analysis point by point with her own. They agreed on the major features. The one masterminding the extortions and murders was certainly very powerful.

The targets were the great rulers. No victim could be revivified, and that meant a great deal of magick was used in the killings. From what they knew, no duplicate means of murder had been used. The demon in Ys differed from the other "weapons" as markedly as each instrument of death employed previously. The murder had been expected, yet it occurred despite all precautions. Once accomplished, the victim was always beyond any means of magickal restoration to life. Thereafter, the surviving individuals concerned had evidently complied with the demands of the killer or killers and paid over the ransom, tribute, blackmail—whatever the extorted payments might be called.

"We need to know exactly what was demanded from each victim," Rachelle said.

"That's just about impossible," Inhetep replied. "If these folk would agree to speak of the matter at all, most would certainly refuse details such as that. State secrecy, loss of face, and fear that the assassin or organization calling himself or itself the 'Master of Jackals' would take reprisals—all mitigate against our gaining such information."

"The power involved in each murder is also unknown."

"Not entirely, Rachelle. We know that there were aural readings in two cases, at the Academie Sorcerie d'Ys, and the report from Gothenburg in Sverige seems reliable, too. In the first certainly, and the second probably, we have unquestioned Entital energy, heka of the most powerful sort."

The girl frowned. "You said that Set, let alone the good and noble Anubis, are not the perpetrators of these crimes. Now you say that the highest magicks were used. Isn't that admitting you are wrong?"

"It is always possible to err," the wizard-priest said without humor, "but all entital force doesn't spring from the pantheon of Ægypt, let alone the Font of Wickedness or the righteous Lord Anubis. We face a killer able to summon great beings, or to actually draw heka from the greater planes. That doesn't contradict my assertion that the Master of Jackals has no connection to Anubis—or even to Set, save in evil-doing."

She pondered that a moment, then nodded her understanding and agreement. "So we have virtually no information as to who is responsible, what the motive is, or how the murders are accomplished. And since there is no possibility of returning the victim to life, we can't learn the killer's identity. What do we go on?"

"The connections between the crimes. There must be more than mere greed involved, I think. The pattern circles this area: northwestern Æropa." Inhetep stood up and went to his leather trunk. He rummaged around, drew out a flat case, and from that extracted a large parchment which was folded into sixths. "See here," he said, showing Rachelle the beautifully inked map of the continent. "Here is where the first murder occurred—Gothenburg. There is Pohjola, there below it lie Finmark, Kalevala, and the rest. Now south and west, and we come to Riga, capital of Livestonia, where we know another appearance of the Master of Jackals occurred. Next the cities of the Hansiatic League . . . here, here, and here." Setne pointed out the dots as his finger moved westward.

"And there is the Bretton peninsula of Ys," Rachelle supplied. "There is a crescent-shaped pattern."

The Ægyptian's coppery skin shone in the vaguely iridescent rays of the witch-lamp as he pointed out a place. "Not quite, my dear girl. See here? There are a few gaps in the circle."

"Circle? I see only a portion of a ring."

"From Ys to Camelough, and there is only the place I pointed out already and the Kingdom of Caledonia."

"Then the Master of Jackals will strike in . . ." Rachelle paused a moment to peer at the chart. ". . . Brabant, Flanders, or the northernmost of the Five Kingdoms of Avillon."

Inhetep gave her a look of doubt. "That assumes that I—we—will fail here in Lyonnesse, and that our slinking villain will then be at large to work his evil elsewhere."

"Oh, sorry, Setne," Rachelle mumbled abashed. "It came out the wrong way. What I meant was that the criminals *plan* to strike one of those three places next."

"Apology accepted." Inhetep smiled. "I wasn't actually serious, for I got your meaning. However, I am not so certain about your theory. You might be correct, Rachelle, but the gap seems altogether too convenient to be accidental. Let's suppose instead that this Master of Jackals provided for the possibility of being traced down in just such a manner as you and I have done now. Wherever he moves next there will be a gap. Think of our dilemma should the grand count of Flanders next receive the attention of the killer!"

The girl looked at the Ægyptian's sparkling green eyes. He was enjoying this challenge. "Worse still," Rachelle countered, beginning to get involved, "what if the Jackal Master moves his base of operations?"

"That's a dreadful prospect, girl," Inhetep fairly growled. "No need to worry about it yet, though. He hasn't yet finished here in Camelough. Tomorrow morning early we meet with the Behon and whomever sent him to bring us here. We might actually have an idea as to who our extortionist-killer is thereafter—and how to put the fellow out of his nasty business."

"Sensible." Rachelle yawned. "I'm worn out, and tomorrow is certain to be a demanding day. Time for me to retire," she informed Setne, heading for the door to her own bedchamber. "I'll awaken you at dawn," Rachelle added over her shoulder.

"For once, amazon, I won't object to your early rising habits," the priest-mage replied affably. "We must be in the palace at the eighth hour for breakfast."

Aldriss came to the inn to gather Inhetep and Rachelle for their short trip to the castle, which was the royal seat of the kingdom. Setne was very quiet, not even querying the bard as to whom they should be prepared to meet inside that palatial stronghold. Rachelle made up for it by doing all the talking. Astonishingly, Aldriss was not his usual loquacious and charming self. Instead, the Kellt responded in clipped sentences and monosyllables. Rachelle continued on airily without seeming to notice, until the ten-minute journey by closed carriage was over and the three descended into a small inner courtyard somewhere inside the extensive fortress. "Please come this way, Magister, Lady Rachelle," the bard told the two strangers.

"Where are you taking us?" Rachelle demanded.

"There is a private salon just beyond the foyer here," the man said with strained patience. "Tallesian, our Royal Archdruid, and the Behon are already inside, so please let us go in."

"But of course!" Rachelle exclaimed with a reproachful tone. "Why do you keep us standing here while you talk?"

Setne thought he heard the bard grinding his teeth as he opened the door for them. It struck the Ægyptian that Aldriss and the amazon warrior girl must have had some disagreement while aboard the sloop yesterday. But that explained only a portion of the tension. Aldriss was evidently nervous about this meeting. The room they entered was a high-ceilinged chamber with old wood paneling, a thickly carpeted floor, and various paintings and tapestries decorating its stone walls above the polished wainscoting. In the center was a long trestle table with four chairs to either side and a larger, padded armchair at the head. Two footmen in plain russet garb assisted them to chairs opposite the Kelltic spell-workers, as a third servant, also without device on his livery, seated the bard. Inhetep was across from the Behon and nearest the head, with Rachelle to his left across from Tallesian the Archdruid. Aldriss was at one place further down on the priest's right. There were only six places set, so as soon as the royal representative appeared, the meal—and the discussion—could commence.

"I trust you both were comfortable and rested well at the Prince House," the Behon said politely.

"Thank you, lord. We were very well cared for."

"I, too, thank you," Rachelle murmured, eyes fixed on the door through which their host would appear.

An uncomfortable silence settled upon them, broken suddenly by a hammering from beyond the inner portal. One of the footmen snapped to attention and opened the thick door. The three Lyonnessians jerked up out of their chairs and looked toward the open doorway. Setne and the girl were halfway out of their seats when the personage entered the salon.

"Please be seated, noble practitioners, lady," he commanded in a brisk voice as he strode up to the table. A servant flew to the table's head to pull the chair back for the man. "This is an absolutely confidential meeting. It hasn't happened, if you understand my meaning." He sat imperially on the embroidered cushion of the great armchair, a seat which moved as if by magick to accommodate him. "Being thus," he continued, "I grant leave to dispense with due formalities. You may address me simply as 'Highness,'" the man told Setne without smiling. He nodded toward the three on his right. "That includes you as well, of course."

"Yes, Your—Highness," the Behon murmured, and his associates bobbed their heads.

The man must be the crown prince of Lyonnesse, Inhetep surmised. He was too young to be

King Glydel, second of that name to rule the
isle, for the Ægyptian knew the current monarch
of Lyonnesse had held the throne for over
twenty years now. The ruddy-cheeked aristocrat
at the head of the table was only nearing thirty.
King Glydel had ascended to the throne at that
age. Here was Prince Llewyn, then. Despite his
pomposity and seemingly autocratic bent, Setne
thought him a very tough-minded fellow and
knew from reputation that the prince was a warrior of considerable accomplishment. What
Prince Llewyn had to say would be carefully
worded—and would bear close attention. There
were a half-dozen men serving them now, taking
care to wait according to precedence. The
prince, then the Behon, Setne, the Archdruid,
with uncertainty taken care of by simultaneous
placing of viands before Rachelle and Aldriss.
The wizard-priest was no stranger to such situa-
tions, and because he had banqueted with Pharaoh, the emperor of Byzantium, and a number
of lesser monarchs as well, Inhetep was able to
display perfect etiquette even as he took the
measure of the noble prince and listened carefully to what the man said.

A half dozen serving men placed dishes before
them. Prince Llewyn began eating immediately,
and the others then followed suit. "Eat slowly,
Sir Aldriss," the prince admonished. "I'll not
finish so soon as to leave you ravenous."

There was humor in his voice. So he wasn't

quite as Inhetep first thought! "Highness . . ."
the Ægyptian began. Prince Llewyn tipped his
head to indicate that his guest could speak. "I
am most honored that you have come in person
to breakfast with me. Am I to assume that you
are afterwards going to enlighten me as to the
. . . disturbing matter regarding jackals?"

"The Behon has spoken well of your magickal
repute, and other sources have told me of your
assistance in matters involving spies and criminals. I have small interest in the hierarchy of
those employing dweomers, Magister Inhetep.
Yet I have a feeling that I am the one who should
be flattered by your presence, not vice versa, especially considering your prowess of investigation as demonstrated on Pharaoh's behalf. Be
that as it may," the nobleman said flatly, putting
the royal mantle squarely back on his shoulders,
"it pleases me to have you here and to see you
so eager to take on the duty you have accepted."
Llewyn ate a few more bites and then waved a
hand. The servitors moved rapidly to clear away
the almost untouched food. Rachelle looked a little startled, and the bard actually uttered a low
groan.

So much for royal promises, Inhetep thought.

"Ah now, there you've gone and—"

"Tut, poet! Don't presume on your high office
to admonish a prince!" he scolded Aldriss, this
time with a bite to his words. Then softening
somewhat, he added, "Your silver tongue will

get you far more than you missed here, that I know. Even my trusted butler opens the pantry and buttery's whiskey spigots for you, Aldriss."

"That's so," the fellow admitted, flashing a smile at the prince and around the table. "And I find I am craving your pardon once again, Highness."

"Granted. Behon, dismiss the servants."

There was no commotion. The magus simply looked in their direction, confirming the orders of the crown prince of Lyonnesse. In truth, even that was quite unnecessary, for the men had heard clearly their lord's order and were moving quickly and quietly to obey. In a minute, the five men and Rachelle were alone in the salon. When the servitors had exited, Tallesian bolted both doors to the room. The prince gestured to his chief mage, and the Behon brought forth a short wand and began an almost silent casting which magickally barred the portals. That act was then followed by a spell of privacy, so that the entire salon was warded against any sort of eavesdropping or observation, whether by some normal means or through magickal ones such as clairaudience, clairvoyance, or scrying of any sort with mirror, bowl, or crystal ball. As that formula was completed, a thick layer of soot-hued fog furled into the room. Its ebony cloud covered walls, ceiling, and floor, but left the six in a clear and unclouded space as if they were in the eye of a storm. Setne was quite surprised, for such was a most unusual precaution considering the other two which had been taken. It was obvious the royal prince trusted not even the stone walls of his palace.

Both the bard and the druid were sitting on the edge of their chairs as Prince Llewyn reached into his short robe and drew forth an object. "This is the only clue we have as to the Master of Jackals," he said slowly, with the object hidden in his grasp. "Tell me, Magister Inhetep, have you ever seen anything like this before?" The prince's fingers uncurled, and there in his palm Llewyn held an obsidian figurine of the Ægyptian god, Anubis!

Rachelle gasped. Setne remained expressionless, even as something more disconcerting occurred. As Prince Llewyn displayed the figurine of black stone, its tiny eyes of inset ruby seemed to catch fire and grow larger. Twin beams of hot crimson light shot forth to a point just above the table. As if in a spotlight, there appeared a figure—a man robed in red and wearing a jackal mask, which covered the whole of his head. The magickally projected figure spoke, the voice coming as a soft whisper in the ear of each person: "King Glydel, you are my slave," the hissing voice said with mockery and self-assurance. "There is no need for me to inform you of my powers, to relate the fate of the spaewife Olga or a fool who was once called Karl. You already have knowledge of them, and the others too, who failed to pay tribute as my slaves."

"This is incredible!" Rachelle said loudly, her face hard with anger.

Inhetep touched her gently on the arm. "Yes, but let us listen," he said without taking his eyes from the projection.

"Listen well, or else I will strike down your most trusted servants, your sons, even you." The image seemed to mushroom as the perspective changed to show a close-up of the person's head. It was impossible to tell whether the speaker portrait was male or female, for the whisper and the mask precluded such knowledge. Besides, magick could easily alter perceptions. The unmoving lips of the black-and-gold mask, red eyes glittering as if alive, and sharp fangs which gave the impression of snarling attack and sneering mockery all at once, were the focus as the Master of Jackals spoke again.

"You or your son, Prince Llewyn, will be attending the Annual Council of the Five Crowns held after Beltaine. While there, you will announce to the others that you now recognize Set as the Great Lord of Lyonnesse, and that they too must do so. If any balk, inform them that the armed might of your kingdom will come down upon them.

"You must meanwhile pay tribute to Set and to Lord Anubis. One thousand of your golden griananas are to be packed in a stout bronze chest, one just large enough to hold the coins, no bigger. That chest you will have taken by ship to the middle of the Hybernian Sea and dropped overboard. If you do not comply with this small demand, I will strike down your Gwyddorr." Setne shifted his eyes from the archdruid to see Aldriss' face. The bard was pale and shaken, for he was the Gwyddorr, so styled in official Lyonnesse. The phantom figure continued. "Then you will pay twice the tribute I now require of you, slave. You have until sun's ebb to bow to my will. Then the druid dies. Each week of delay thereafter will bring fell death to another of your council—nobles, priests, or mages—and payment of an additional tribute of one thousand grianaanas, and no lesser coin.

"As to the proclamation of Set as Lord of Lyonnesse, you have until Beltaine to comply, and immediately after the council you must do so throughout the land. Failure will bring doom to your male children and yourself. You must show your intent, slave of mine, by yielding up to me the *Wheel of the Tuatha de Danann*. Be ready. When I tell you what to do you will have only one week to comply.

"Now go about your petty affairs. Say nothing of this to anyone or I will smite you down for the sport of it. I am the Master of Jackals, and Great Set is my companion."

The fire died in the statuette's eyes. It was as if someone had shuttered a lantern. The projection vanished simultaneously. A depressed silence filled the salon. The prince looked at Inhetep. "Well?"

"Odd," the Ægyptian said noncommitally. "Odd and intriguing." Setne had found false notes in the performance, but the wizard-priest was unprepared to articulate his suspicions. In fact, he felt he was a long way from that point. "This gold coin called griananas, what value has it?"

Aldriss supplied the answer. "It is *a grianana,* Magister Inhetep. The sun-wheel coin of official state business of Lyonnesse, although there are some in circulation elsewhere, of course. The grianana is made to equal the Atlantlan orb— an ounce of virtually pure orichalcum," the bard added by way of explanation. "One of either sort of coin is equal to three thousand of your Ægyptian bronze dinars."

"Surely you have more to ask!" Crown Prince Llewyn was agitated.

Setne nodded, face stoic. "But certainly, Highness, yet no small detail can be overlooked. I will now, with your kind permission, ask the questions you expect of me."

"Proceed."

"Who did this thing's words address first, your . . . king?"

That seemed to unsettle the prince. "No," he admitted slowly. "One of my servants intercepted it before it reached my—the king."

"As I thought," the copper-skinned man said in clipped voice. "It came a month ago. You paid over the gold?"

"Yes. I saw no choice, for Tallesian is indispensable. It bought time, too. Never will the kingdom give over its own gods in favor of Set!"

Inhetep smiled a little. "No, that would be unthinkable. Does King Glydel know anything of this matter at all?"

The prince shook his head sharply. "No, and why should he?" Llewyn asked defensively. "Six months is ample time to suss the matter out, find the culprits, and have their heads!"

"Perhaps, Highness," Setne murmured. "Yet one thousand of your triple-gold grianana are certainly not so trivial as to escape the attention of the king—"

"Griananas," Aldriss interjected. Llewyn shot him a dark look, and the bard shrank in his chair.

"I managed it so as to cause no shortage in the royal treasury," the young prince told the Ægyptian.

"And who is privy to the matter?"

"Besides those here assembled? No—" He bit his words short when he saw the small smile of incredulity on Inhetep's face. Prince Llewyn cleared his throat, sat straighter still, and in his most imperious voice added, "Nobody—save certain nobles of other kingdoms of Avillon, that is."

Setne inclined his head toward the royal
prince, his shaven pate glistening a little in the
subdued light of the magickally shrouded salon.
"As I thought, Highness. You say that the sovereigns of the other four kingdoms know of this?
That each has likewise received such an object?"

"How did you guess that?!" the Behon demanded, forgetting his place.

"A small thing actually," Setne said with apparent humility, but his statement cut off the
rebuke the prince was about to utter. "Even one
of moderate wit would realize that to make the
evil Set the over-deity of all Avillonia, each of
its five royal houses would have to be forced into
compliance. That means five of these figurines
were delivered: to Albion, Cymru, Caledonia,
Hybernia, and this one before us to Camelough,
capital of Lyonnesse." The wizard-priest held
out his hands, palm upward in a gesture of help-
lessness. "That much is easy, the rest another
thing altogether.

"Be that as it may, I am as much at a loss to
explain this as you. I fear that what I have seen
gives me no clue as to this so-called 'Master of
Jackals,' or his plans and purposes, than any of
you." Setne duplicated his gesture of uncertainty, but then asked, "Why do you suppose you
were given six months? The other victims seemed
to have been struck down—or complied, or
both—in but two months or less."

The prince stood up, glaring at his councillors

to assure their silence. "That is as obvious to me as the sending of five of these filthy little idols was to you, Magister Inhetep! This Master of Jackals is now frying bigger fish—Lyonnesse and the other four great kingdoms. Don't you see? He has given us a half year to establish the yolk of the filthy Eastern deity upon us all!"

"Filthy? I cannot but concur, lord," Inhetep said coldly. "Yet I find I must strongly take exception to the remainder of your remark. Now," the Ægyptian said, rising and looming over the tall prince, "I believe it is time that Lady Rachelle and I withdraw. It will not be possible for me to offer further assistance."

"Wait!" commanded Crown Prince Llewyn.

"As one ecclesiastic to another, pray remain," Archdruid Tallesian added.

The Behon likewise spoke, "Inhetep, I second that request as one scholar to another."

Rachelle looked at the bard. "What, Aldriss, have you nothing to say in this regard?" she asked mockingly. She turned to Inhetep, seeing him rod-straight and expressionless. "I am by your side, my lord ur-kheri-heb. None will challenge our departure." There was veiled menace in her lilting contralto.

"I must accept the blame for hasty words. I meant no offense and ask that you allow me to withdraw any which cast aspersions on your great land, Magister," the prince said as if through a closing throat. His pained expression showed that he was very unused to such apologies.

The Magister sat down. "Then I can only accept your graciousness, Highness. I will ask a few more questions . . ."

"Do so by all means," Llewyn urged.

"Which of the other four kings have full knowledge of this affair?"

The heir to the throne of Lyonnesse made a little sign, and the Behon responded to the wizard-priest's query. "Each of the crowned heads of Avillonia is similarly protected from dangers as is King Glydel, Magister Inhetep. The steward for young King Finn is handling the matter in Galway. The Laird Campbell is likewise standing betwixt this fiend calling himself the Master of Jackals and King Malcome of Caladonia. In Cymru I have spoken personally to Archmage Trigg, who is the chief advisor to King Owen, and he has assured me that the whole is well in hand. Only King Dennis of Albion is directly involved." The chief judge of Lyonnesse paused and looked at Inhetep, silently awaiting his further questions.

The Ægyptian switched subjects. "What of this wheel?"

"The wheel, as you put it, is the most powerful—"

"Of course, of course, man!" Setne broke into the Behon's lecture with a sharp-edged voice. "There isn't an apprentice of dweomercræft or

novice cleric in all Ægypt who isn't aware of the
Nine and Ninety Celestial Artifacts! I am asking
what you have done about the demand for it by
the murderer."

"Oh," the Ovate said with subdued voice.
"Prince . . . ?"

"Nothing!" Llewyn spat in answer. "That sort
of demand cannot be granted."

Inhetep looked skeptical. "Even at the risk of
many lives—your own certainly among them?"

The prince shrugged. "To yield that would
place the whole kingdom into the palm of the
Master of Jackals' hand," he said without force.
His face showed as much uncertainty as did his
evasive answer to the wizard-priests's query.

"So the Jackal wishes to control Lyonnesse by
means of possession of the Wheel of the Tuatha
de Danann as well as the imposition of Set. . . ."

"Yes," the Kellts said in chorus.

"Similar demands have been made to the other
rulers of the Five Crowns?"

"Well . . ." the Behon began.

"Exactly," Prince Llewyn snapped. "We are in
contact with all concerned. The fiend has demanded from each of us the great magickal objects which enable sovereignty."

Inhetep stood up for a second time. "Allow
me, please, to examine this purported statuette
of Anubis." Llewyn nodded; the other three had
no objections save cautionary murmurings. "No

need to fear. I shall exercise utmost discretion. Besides, this chamber is triply warded."

It was time to see what was on the Jackal's mind, Setne thought, as he stooped near the little figurine. He drew forth an enspelled lens and inspected minutely the carved stone. It was onyx, and the jet hue of the jackal head was as natural as the pale, milky color of the figurine's kilt. "This is incredible!" he announced. The workmanship was masterful, the stone perfect, and the carving that of only one origin. "It *is* Ægyptian!" The faceted eyes were probably from Hind, and the inlaid gold must be checked to see if its foreign admixtures discounted it coming from his native land, but Setne felt that would not be the case. He put away the crystal lens.

"Are you finished?" the prince inquired.

"No. I must see . . ." Inhetep replied distractedly as he drew forth several other small items. Without saying more, the wizard-priest began to lay castings of discovery. The aura of the figurine, its enchantments, powers, even its history and possessors were subject to such magickal inquisition. The object shimmered with halos of oddly hued radiances, but only to Setne's vision, for the others there able to discern aural lights had not empowered themselves to do so. This was the Ægyptian's work. Inhetep saw the emanations of evil as an indistinct cloud surrounding the statuette. Malign power and danger. The

thing was charged with many forms of heka—
the energy of stone, attendance by the supernatural and, greater still, that of the uttermost
nethersperes. It was very old. How many millennia? Inhetep was uncertain, but over six thousand years had slipped past since the carving of
this work. It had been done by a faithful young
cleric of Anubis, passed to an official—Setne saw
an overseer, a governor of one of Ægypt's many
sepats. There followed next a beautiful woman,
a high-ranking military officer, then a succession
of foreigners, the last of whom was a merchant
who passed it to another—an Ægyptian. There
followed many nondescript impressions. Then
the reading became hazy. Power of another sort
had been imposed, and it was the energy of a
sahu. That meant the figure had been entombed
with some mummy only a few hundred years
after its fashioning. There was a brief light, as
if it had been brought forth from the tomb and
might again have recorded impressions, only
magick interposed. This time it was a deliberate
obscuring.

"Come on, Inhetep! What is it you see?"
Crown Prince Llewyn demanded.

"Too much and too little," the wizard-priest
told him. "I will have to employ less subtle
means," he informed the five who were watching. It was not a request. It took only a few second to begin the incantation, and soon the power
of words and ritual brought a nimbus of golden

THE ANUBIS MURDERS • 97

sparks to dance around the little figure. Suddenly the amber luminosities were sucked into the statuette, and as they were absorbed the figure became larger and less distinct. Inhetep gasped in surprise. He stepped back a pace, for the mask of the Master of Jackals had suddenly solidified out of the haze of the enspelled object.

"You!" The sound hissed from the mouth opening. "Servant of Thoth, get thee from this place! You will not oppose your own gods, will you? Heed, Setne Inhetep, and I shall place you in a noble position. Disobey, and you will be cut down as these infidels will be soon should they fail me. That is what the mind of the Master of Jackals reveals to you. You may seek no more," the voice hissed evilly. There was a rush of wind, a loud clap, and all magick was gone from the salon. So was the figurine.

6

UNDERGROUND SECRETS

There were only the two of them now, Setne and
Rachelle, and they were back in their suite of
rooms in the Prince House Inn. It was near evening, and Inhetep hadn't moved from his chair
since they had returned just before noon. "Setne,
I'm hungry," Rachelle said conversationally. She
had been trying to stay unobtrusive and keep
busy, while the wizard-priest meditated. Inhetep
made no response. Rachelle sat down across
from him and tried to fix her gaze on his green
eyes, but the Ægyptian was looking slightly upwards with a fixed stare indicating that he saw
nothing. "O Greatest of Ur-kheri-hebu, O One
Whose Wisdom is as Thoth's . . ."

"Stop that nonsense!"

The words seemed to come from behind her,
but Rachelle knew his trick of ventriloquism.
The hawk-faced man was irritated at being disturbed and was trying to get her to go away—or
else strike up a conversation with a vase or bed-
post. Rachelle had to smile, for he had duped

her into that sort of thing a few times in the past. The wily spellbinder would use his voice-throwing ruse, then cause some petty spirit of the æther or similar origin to occupy the furniture and converse banally with whomever spoke to the confining object. Some of these forces were tricky and inventive, and the conversation might go on for an hour or more. "That's a useless ploy, bald-pate," Rachelle said firmly, still looking at Inhetep. "I want to talk to you, not some dumb spirit, and I want to speak now!"

"A dumb spirit would not converse at all, and you are speaking, I believe," the magister said with acid tones, still gazing off into space.

"Setne Inhetep, you pay attention to me this instant!"

Inhetep sighed, shut his eyes a moment, then looked at Rachelle and smiled. "Very well, guard and mistress of my household, you have my humble apologies and complete attention," he said sincerely, even though a portion of the Ægyptian's mind was still engaged busily with the problem of the statuette. "What service may I perform?

"I am hungry," Rachelle snapped.

"Am I to cook our supper, then, or would you have me conjure up some enchanted fare?"

Rachelle made a moue. "You know very well that isn't what I want, Setne. There is a small banquet tonight at the castle. *That's* where I wish to dine this night!"

"But of course," Inhetep said effusively. His long face was wreathed in smiles, and he arose, swooped, and before she knew it the girl was on her feet and being propelled toward her chambers. "Certainly, dear Rachelle, it shall be as you wish. I confess I have let the matter slip from my mind, but there—you've reminded me! Do put on your gown and be ready in an hour. I wouldn't have you miss the festivities for the world," Setne added as he shut the intervening door.

She thought it highly unusual behavior on Setne's part. He was never eager to attend functions of such nature as court dinners, doubly so when he was working on some criminal problem of a mysterious nature. Thinking that perhaps she had managed to select the perfect time to make her demand, the proverbial weak moment, Rachelle went about her preparations. She was happy and pleased. In less than an hour, wonder of wonders, she returned to the big parlor between her rooms and those of the wizard-priest. "What are *you* doing here?!" Her voice carried a note of real surprise.

"You look as lovely as a princess of Færie," Sir Aldriss said with a sweeping bow of greeting. "Pray forgive me if I startled you, but I assumed that when Magister Inhetep requested I call for you, he had made the arrangement at your request."

"Arrangement? Request?" Rachelle was filled

with annoyance, which would grow into anger if she allowed her emotions free rein. "No matter, Sir Bard. I must ask you to pardon my . . . happy surprise. Of course I expected to be taken to the royal banquet this evening, and my astonishment was provoked by seeing you, dear Aldriss. I had not hoped for anything other than some common escort, shall we say."

The chief bard beamed. "You will fairly have the court abuzz when they see you on my arm, lady. Shall we be off, then?"

"In but a moment, sir. Did the magister say where . . . ?"

Aldriss looked slightly annoyed, then an expression signifying the return of memory spread over his handsome face. "Ah, how could I be so forgetful? Here is a note which the worthy priest-mage left for you. May I open and read it for you?"

"No, you may not," Rachelle replied sweetly but with steely edge in her tone. "It will be in Hieratic Script—can you read such writing?" Without waiting for a response, she took the hastily proffered square of parchment, broke the seal, unfolded it, and read the contents:

Better you go alone, Rachelle, for I have an important clue. Each of us can thus be working on this very thorny problem. Watch over all there this night to ward against attack, magick, etc. Always be wary of anything

unusual which occurs at the banquet. Record such events for my return, and we shall discuss them then. Expect to be gone for some hours, so don't wait my return.
Always, Lovingly & Dutiful, Regretfully, etc.
Setne Inhetep, Magister

She was a little puzzled and very disappointed that the wizard-priest hadn't seen fit to take her into his confidence. Just where was Setne going? And for what purpose? He'd be in danger, Rachelle was sure of that. He *should* have taken her along on his foray. And such a strange note. . . . Bother this soiree, anyway!

"What troubles you, dear Lady Rachelle?" Aldriss asked solicitously.

She turned and smiled at him. Rachelle hoped the expression wasn't too thin. "It is nothing, Sir Bard, nothing. Quite the contrary, for Magister Inhetep has been kind enough to give me the night free from duties!" She laughed a little to emphasize her pleasure at the prospect.

"This way then, please, Your Ladyship. It is a fine evening despite the chill of winter. Our coach awaits." Moments later, the carriage was rolling away from the inn, its four matched horses heading for the palatial castle at a fast trot.

The gilded coach's departure was observed by a lone figure shrouded in the shadows of a nearby lane. When the carriage had passed from his sight, the man turned back and disappeared up the near alley. A flickering lantern revealed his face for a split second. It was a hard and ruthless visage whose scars and battering nevertheless could not hide his Phonecian heritage. The fellow was no taller than average, but his wide shoulders and big hands indicated that he had known much labor and hardship. Mercenary? Perhaps. Seaman? Certainly, if the rolling gait was considered. Cutthroat? Who else but one of that sort would roam the unlit byways of Camelough?

"Whiskey!" he demanded from the barkeep. The strange man had followed lane, gangway, alley, and passage to get to the tavern. It was far distant from the royal seat of Lyonnesse, and the most infamous of the many low dives in the city's slum district, Scathach. Foreigners, thugs, thieves, and all manner of riffraff lived and died without ever leaving Scathach's few square miles. But likewise, many of those in the district came from distant parts, other kingdoms.

The barman hardly noticed the stranger. Many came into the place. Most were no better looking than the Phonecian, and some were worse. "Whiskey," the sallow-faced barkeep said, as he slammed down the earthenware pot containing about three ounces of raw liquor. "That'll be ta spurs, killey," he growled to the scar-faced man.

The Phonecian produced a fat disc of silver from somewhere, so that the coin seemed to appear magickally beneath the barman's fingers.

"The change o' thet drake is yers," he informed the proprietor, "if ya kin tell me suthin'," the Phonecian growled back in near-perfect Lyonnese gutter dialect.

The barkeep was suspicious. Those twenty-three spurs—the difference between the two bronze coins he'd demanded and the silver drake the stranger had slipped him—could mean trouble. On the other hand, the sum was about all he made on a typical night. He eyed the scarfaced man. "What air ya askin'?"

The fellow with the battered countenance tossed off the whiskey in a single gulp. "Aaah . . ." he said slowly. "Anither, an' one fer yersel', killey," the Phonecian added. As he spoke, he made another of the silver drakes appear on the bar. "I'm seekin' atter Eastern curs, so ta spake."

The barman gaped at the second coin. "Noon i' these parts 'ave stray mongrels," he replied non-committally. "Jest what's special so's ta recognize an Eastern one?"

The scarred face broke into an evil grin. "Come on now, killey. Big, black ears, and from the place where all the gods 'ave animal 'eds," he chuckled softly.

"Well . . ." the barman responded slowly, glancing around furtively. It was early yet, at least two hours before midnight, the time most regulars came along Rushlight Lane and the Two Cups Tavern. The pair of silver coins gleamed in the barkeep's sight. The foreigner seemed all right. . . . "If you were to go over to Shoddyway an' around ta the Duke's Cellar, I'd wager on seein' summat that's o' interest to you," he told the Phonecian as he scooped up the two drakes. They barely clinked as he asked hopefully, " 'Ave anither whiskey?"

The stranger nodded, but this time he conjured forth only a big copper piece. The tot of liquor was splashed into the heavy cup. He waited for it to be filled as full as before, and the barman grudgingly obliged. "Me thanks," the scar-faced stranger grated. " 'Tis a quiet place—too quiet, so's I'll be rollin' on."

"It'll be right lively 'ere in an 'our, killey," the barkeep said, turning to fetch the jug containing his best whiskey from the shelf behind the bar. He'd give the Phonecian a free round—prime the pump, so to speak. Then perhaps the man would start to produce hard silver again. "This one's on the hou—" but he cut his statement short, because the scar-faced foreigner was gone.

The man's broad shoulders and his scarred face were quite sufficient to discourage would-be assailants, and even kept whining beggars at bay. One look told these street rogues that the Phonecian had a ready weapon, quick hand, and hard heart. Rushlight Lane wandered left and right in shallow curves, south from Roundabout Gardens all the way to Dray Street near the southern wall of the city. About two-thirds of the distance along the crooked lane, the edge of

the Scathach cloth and garment district shoul-
dered the byway. Shoddyway was wider and
straighter than Rushlight Lane, but if anything
it was more dangerous, because more of the deni-
zens of Scathach gathered along its length after
night fell.

When a young tart stopped him near Vixen
Court, a gaggle of her older professional sisters
looked on and laughed snidely. "She'll be scam-
perin' back right smart soon now," one slattern
remarked, having seen the man's hard eyes.
"Lookit 'at!" another hissed. Not one of the five
or six whores could believe it. The inexperi-
enced little doxy had actually scored! The broad-
backed tough was handing her coins, and without further ado the saucy trollop had slipped her
arm through his and was wiggling on down the
street.

"You'll be sarry!" one of the older ones jeered
after her. Another cried, " 'E'll beat yer arse!"
but the calls were ignored.

"Damme!" the leader of the group muttered
as the couple disappeared around a corner. "I
swears I saw gold when that barstid 'anded over
payment!"

Her friend was derisive. "Naw, deary. All's ya
seen was some new brass, an' 'ats the troof."

She was wrong.

"I don't care where we're goin', lovie," the little strumpet said. "At your pay, we can go wher-

ever and do whatever ya likes! But jest where are we 'eaded for?''

"So ya likes a little gold drachma, do ya,'' the Phonecian said, phrasing it as a statement, not a question. He saw the tart's thin hand go to her breast, fingering the coin she'd placed inside her blouse. The drachma was a smaller coin than the golden drake of Lyonnesse, about half its weight and value. It was nonetheless a handsome sum, for it equalled no fewer than five hundred of the common coins of everyday existence, bronze spurs. She noticed his glance, hastily removed her hand from the cheap cloth, and nodded. "Good,'' he said. "You an' I are goin' to pay a visit to a temple—a special kind o' one.''

"Whatcha mean?'' the girl asked suspiciously. There were some very strange places in Camelough's seamy sections.

"Don't get yer arse in an uproar now, cutie.'' There was a trace of humor in his voice. "All's I 'spect is that ye'll be takin' me to the place where they 'onors jackals, so's ta speak.''

She looked relieved and bored at once. "Sure, dearie. I bin ta that temple, as ya calls it—it were back in summer when it were first begin.'' She shrugged and looked at him. "Ain't nuffin' goin' on there. Lotta talkin'—jus bullshit promises about makin' us per folk rich and alla while takin' coins as contributions. What say we goes ta 'Attie's Paradise instead. They gots all kinds—''

"Later," he growled. "First ya takes me to see the place wi' the animal-headed statues."

"Ya bin there already?" The man assured her that he'd only heard about the funny-looking idols, so the tart led on. "It's below the dive called the Duke's Cellar," she explained. "We'll go inta the back way, they'll pass us through, an' then it's down the stairs inta the Ratshold."

"Whazzat?!" the Phonecian demanded.

"The Ratshold?" She made it sound like "Ratz-awld." "Come on, lovie, ya knows! The subcellars an' tunnels an' drains an' all that lot belows the 'ole city 'ere. Alls ya killeys knows 'bout that. Where'll else ya 'ide out?"

With a pat on her skinny bottom for reassurance, the scar-faced man said, "It's news to me, cutie. I ain't familiar with yer Ratshold 'cause this 'ere's the first time I bin ta Camelough."

"Nawrr . . . !" The little whore shook her head in wonderment at his lack of sophistication. As she steered him through a narrow gangway leading to the back of the Duke's Cellar, she wondered if this was a mark to be rolled. Too tough, she decided, but because of his inexperience, she figured he might be good for more coin—maybe even another gold drachma. She was smiling at him as they went into an alcove-like back entry, then along an even narrower and darker corridor. The Phonecian listened as the girl identified herself, told the guard that she'd brought a wealthy stranger along to pay his respect to the "liberator," and they were passed through a heavy drapery of old cloth. They stood before a worn staircase of stone. The brown illumination from a pair of old candle lanthorns flickered along the steps, which wound down about twenty feet, perhaps more, where the second light pulsed dimly below at the stairway's curve.

Muted voices were discernable from down the steps. They were accompanied by reed pipes, some form of brass strings, and a gong. There was another thick hanging to pass through, then the couple stepped into a vaulted basement, a subcellar of ancient construction whose stones and crude bricks might have been mortared in place centuries, even a millennium ago. Sputtering oil lamps of the sort used in Phonecian cities, or Ægypt for that matter, barely illuminated the huge, echoing space. The eerie light was made stranger still by the room's adornment. Just as instructed, the whore had brought him to the temple of animal-headed idols. The enormous statue of an ass-headed man with a muscular body clearly represented the chief deity of this secret underground temple. It had glass eyes of ruby-red hue and held strange objects in its plaster hands—a loop-handled dagger in the right, a long rod with spiked top in the left.

" 'At's the so-called god they say's the big 'un," the girl whispered confidentially to the broad-shouldered foreigner. " 'Is name's Set."

"Know the names 'o them others?" the Phonecian inquired sotto voce.

She shook her head. "The killeys 'ere claimin' ta be priests an' all are always tellin' us about this un and that, but how's a girl to remember all them stoopid foreign names?"

They moved to the center of the back area now, well away from the entry but not quite to the rows of benches. The tart had hissed that those seats were reserved for those who were believers—chumps who actually forked over coin and paid homage to these weird gods from far off. "Them's Ægyptian idols," the man told her. She didn't respond, except to shrug. He listened intently to the voices murmuring in the background, quickly identifying a chanted prayer to Set. It came from the ranks of idols flanking the central one. Some low-level magick was in use, whether to convey the sound from actual devotees elsewhere or to create it through enchantment. The same was true of the accompanying instruments. Despite the dim illumination and the heavy smoke from incense smouldering in pots near the altar, the scar-faced man was able to identify the other statues. To Set's right were Anubis the jackal-headed, the hippo-goddess Tuart, and four strange, chimerical figures. Crocodile-headed Sebek was near Set's left, along with five other unknown depictions of entities. Each bore a perverted *ankh*-dagger and some form of scepter or rod. The form of each idol was typical of those of modern Ægyptian make.

A trio of women in cowled robes suddenly appeared in the front of the underground temple, filing out from behind the ass-headed statue of Set. Two shook sistrums as one came forth and swung a thurible before the idol. The fumes washed around the statue of the evil deity, rising slowly in the heavy air of the subceller. Then a priest-like figure robed in red and wearing a mask in the shape of a jackal's head stepped forth.

"*Set is Master!*" the masked cleric boomed.

"The Red One is Mighty," came the intoned response from the cluster of worshippers seated on the benches. The cleric began anointing the statue with some unguent as another dozen of the faithful—more dregs of Scathach—entered and took seats.

"*All will serve Set, even as these great ones of Ægypt do,*" the mock-priest called from within his metal mask. Again the assembly responded. A litany of praises and claims followed, until the man finally stepped forward, raising his voice even louder.

"*You are lowly now, but when Set rules this land called Lyonnesse you will be as nobles!*" He paused as the congregation made noises of agreement. "*Through his son and servant, Anubis, the great Set will grant this to you and me. As a jackal, Anubis steals through the night; as a wolf, the son of Set*

*slays all those who oppress you, who deny us all
our right to the luxuries and wealth they horde for
themselves!"*

The roar of the crowd echoed through the
vaulted basement. There were now at least fifty
gathered, and more were streaming down into
the temple.

'I 'adn't 'erd 'ere was so *many* buyin' this rubbish!" The girl said in disbelief.

"Shut yer dirty yapper," threatened a big fellow standing near them in the rear. "Yer the
rubbish, doxy, 'lessen yer listens and takes 'eed!"

*"All over this city, throughout the kingdom, yes,
even into the realms around, is the might of Set and
Anubis spreading. Soon the power of the red one
will triumph over all false lords and oppressive ones.
There will come men who will lead us—you, me,
all of the outlaws and poor and common folk. We
will dethrone kings and place new leaders upon those
thrones. Then Set will rule our land and we will
be free."*

Another wave of cries rang through the crowded
temple.

*"The time is near. I know it for truth. You must
know it and tell all trusted folk of it. Once we asked
for your alms, for great Set was weak in this land.
Now his might waxes. We do not ask coins from you
any longer, no! We give you them!"*

There came choruses of shouts for such largess, calls to Set and Anubis to strike down the
nobles and king, and a near-riot of enthusiasm.

"When you take coins from the son of Set, you acknowledge his power, the greatness of Set and Anubis. Yet you must also believe, tell others, and make ready for the time of slaying. We know it is soon. A great priest from the land of Ægypt now walks in Camelough itself!"

There were mutters of disbelief, quickly hushed.

"Yes, there is such a one, and he has come to demand the oppressors cease their rule. I know this, and now you do. Pity our brother whose name is Setne Inhetep. It is written that his words will not be heeded. They will kill our brother, and then will we rise up and avenge the martyred one. And our leaders will be at our head, as Set and his son, Anubis, are leaders of all lords."

The sound of the gong rocked the chamber, hanging and reverberating for a long moment. The assembled faithful shifted and murmured expectantly. The three priestesses disappeared.

In their place appeared two burly men in pseudo-Ægyptian garb of red-and-black striped cloth. They huffed and strained as they carried a metal-banded coffer out and placed it before the masked priest, who waited until the pair were in position a few feet behind him before speaking again. *"It is time to accept Set's blessing! Let none with false hearts remain here. If you are faithless, the great one will know, and fierce jackals will come forth and tear those unbelievers to shreds! I will pray to our masters now. All not worthy must depart as I do so, for Set will read each one's heart. Then will come his blessing."*

The jackal mask inclined, pointed towards the ass-headed idol, and an indistinguishable chanting issued from inside it. There was an uneasy shuffling in the crowd, and a handful of people exited. "Shouldn't we be leavin' too?" the tart urged. The scar-faced man shook his head but gave her a little push in the direction of the curtained doorway to the stairs. "Be on yer way, lass, if ya 'ave a mind ta do so. Ya've erned yer pay as far as I'm concerned. As fer me, I be one who believes—in a manner a speakin', that is, so's it'll be me 'ere an' ya out." The exchange took only a few seconds. The young whore seemed uncertain, but the threat of being torn to shreds was too much for her, despite curiosity and the hint of largess about to be distributed. She went.

The masked cleric tugged upon the handle of the coffer's lid. It opened slowly, and even in the poorly lit basement, its golden contents were discernable from far back in the temple. There was a collective gasp. *"First, our lord Set gave us only bronze coin,"* the priest boomed. *"Few were here to receive that blessing. More were on hand to gain the coppers which next came. But last week, there were fine silver pieces for you who serve Set and Anubis. The hour of the tyrants' doom is almost here: Now the red one grants us rich gold!"* The crowd began to cheer, but the leader cried, *"Wait!"*

The noise subsided until the sound of breathing could be heard. The priest dipped his hands into the chest, raised them, and a score of glittering disks cascaded down. *"Set withholds his blessing!"* There might have been something similar to a mutiny then had the cleric in the jackal mask allowed the shouting and rage to grow. He raised both arms and thundered, "SILENCE!" At that same moment, a pair of monstrous black jackals, animals larger than the biggest wolf, stood where the two assistants had been, and flashes of red electricity, crackling bolts of miniature lightning, flashed through the air overhead between the pillars and arches of the subterranean vault. The crowd was awed, all eyes on the mock-priest.

"We have in our midst an opposer. Here before Set and the mighty Anubis stands one who would see them thrown down and dishonored!" There were hisses and growls. Men and women, tough and dangerous, peered around as if hoping to recognize the foe by sight and tear him or her to bits before the gigantic jackals came among them. Besides, that act would speed the distribution of the gold "blessing" from Set which winked at them nearby.

"You can not detect him," boomed the masked cleric. *"It requires the mighty eyesight of Set, the unerring nose of Anubis, to suss the enemy out."*

There was an uneasy stirring at those words, and each person there tried to put a little distance between himself and any stranger nearby. Someone in the assembly shouted, "Set yer wolves on 'em!" It was an unintentional pun which made one or two in the big chamber chuckle softly. The Phonecian was one. There were glares at the offenders from all sides. The scar-faced man seemed oblivious to such threat and looked only at the angry priest on his dais there in the front portion of the temple.

From the entrance area there came a thud and the sound of metal on metal. *"That was what I awaited, faithful servants, brothers and sisters. This place is now sealed tight and barred fast. The enemy cannot escape! Now I will point him out to you, and each may assist the jackals of Anubis in execution of the common foe!"* The crowd growled assent, eyes fixed upon their masked benefactor, the priest whose hand would serve out the coins. With great drama, the man held forth his right hand toward the statue of Set, and the idol's ruby eyes shot forth bloody-hued light. As if it were palpable, the priest filled his hand with the light, withdrew it, and held it out for all to see. He appeared to be holding a transparent, glowing sphere of ruby. *"Watch where the mark of mighty Set goes. The one it strikes is the one who must be slain!"*

Shouting thus, the mock-priest hurled the ball of red brightness out into the chamber. At the same instant, the hundreds of gold coins in the coffer shot up into the air as if they were the waters of a geyser and began to rain down throughout the underground temple. Pandemonium broke loose.

7

HUNTER AND HUNTED

"I haven't the foggiest idea what might have happened, Inhetep," Sir Aldriss said. "Are you quite certain she hasn't gone off to see the sights of Camelough?"

"Absurd! As much as Rachelle enjoys visiting plazas and shops, she would not depart before dawn without informing me or leaving a message."

They were together with the druid, Tallesian, and the man known as the Behon, in the royal citadel of Lyonnesse. Setne Inhetep had insisted on speaking with the three of them just a little after sunrise.

Tallesian noted that the wizard-priest looked drawn and tired. Small wonder, he mused, given the girl's absence. "The ostler knew nothing, you say?"

Setne didn't look at the druid as he responded. "That I did say. Aldriss, tell me again what you two did last night!"

The bard looked mildly annoyed but complied, sighing. "We left your inn about the first hour of the night and came here until the festivities ended some four hours later. I then escorted Lady Rachelle back to her chambers. That was perhaps the second hour of the late night. The night porter let us into the lodging and actually into your suite as well—seems she had lost her key. Anyway, I bid her a good night there at the door, and the porter and I returned downstairs. Then the coach conveyed me here."

"I saw you in the game room at the end of the second hour—Tallesian, too," the Behon chimed in to remind Aldriss—perhaps to prove to Inhetep that the story was true.

"Yes, of course you did," the bard said affably. "We had a tot together, and then I retired."

"The porter agrees, Behon," Setne informed him rather acidly. "I am not questioning Sir Aldriss' veracity. I am quite sure of that matter. I am merely trying to pin down the time when Rachelle . . . disappeared."

"Disappeared?"

"Just so, magus. She has vanished, whether of her own volition or due to foul play remains to be discovered, but discover it I shall."

The chief judiciary of Lyonnesse stood up. "Come, you two," he called to Aldriss and Tallesian. "We brought Magister Inhetep here, and now he fears he has lost his trusted lieutenant. We must assist however we can in tracking down Lady Rachelle, or we are poor hosts indeed."

Accompanied by the three men, Inhetep re-

turned to the Prince House Inn. Questions were
asked of all the staff, but to no avail. Then the
wizard-priest had the hall outside their suite
cleared, and all four collaborated to discover
through magickal inquiry what had become of
the girl. They began first in her bed chamber,
but no impressions could be raised, and there
were no useful aural readings, either. The same
was true in her dressing room and the big lounge
between Setne's apartment and Rachelle's. To
be sure, they cast dweomered nets over the
Ægyptian's rooms, but the magick was as empty
of information as that done in the amazon's
quarters.

"Incredible . . ." the druid muttered.

"Not at all," Setne responded. "I gave her protections, and she utilized them. At least we
know that she wasn't under duress in this place.
She left of her own volition."

"How so?" the Behon asked.

"She would have broken the amulet of cloaking easily, and there would be strong readings
here," Inhetep said. Aldriss suggested that she
might have been taken by surprise and overpow-
ered before she could manage that. "You don't
know Rachelle," was the sardonic reply.

It was a different tale in the hall, however.
There were a myriad of readings in the common
corridor, but they managed to find what they
were seeking. The Behon lay a casting evocative
of things past, a magick which brought phantom

images into being. It was not particularly responsive to time, so the four men had to stand and watch for almost an hour before the invocation yielded what they desired. But at last, after innumerable passing of sundry other guests of the establishment, the four observers were rewarded. A heavily cloaked and muffled figure came again, as it were, to the door of Rachelle's apartment. It was certainly a man, and a tallish one, because Aldriss was actually near the portal and the phantom was taller by several inches. It knocked silently, and a transparent image of the girl opened the door. She smiled. The figure entered the room beyond, shutting the door behind itself.

"Damn my precious precautions," Inhetep exclaimed. "There's no way of telling what happened after this!"

"Who do you suppose the man was?" the bard drawled, looking at Inhetep. "The fellow might have been you from his height and the way Lady Rachelle welcomed him."

"Rubbish," the Ægyptian snapped at Sir Aldriss. "There was no means of actually telling the height or build of that visitor."

Both Tallesian and the Behon looked from bard to priest-mage. The Behon cleared his throat loudly. "Would you mind telling me when you discovered Lady Rachelle was missing?"

"Of course not. I returned here at the first hour of the morning—a quarter past four hours

of the clock, to be precise." Inhetep ticked off
the facts in a staccato fashion. "After changing
and laving and a brief devotion, I crossed the
lounge and rapped on Rachelle's door. That was
no later than one half hour after my arrival.
When there was no response, I entered her
dressing room and also searched the bed chamber. The remainder is known."

"Ahh. Would you mind telling me—us—where
you were until after the fourth hour and what
you were doing?" asked the Behon.

Inhetep straightened and looked down at the
Kelltic magus, who was probably the most powerful man in the kingdom after the king and the
crown prince. His face was disdainful, his voice
cold. "I was investigating the case which you
and your associates induced me to undertake,
Behon. I spoke with people, observed, and otherwise did those things which must be done in
such matters as extortion and death threats and
murders. Is that sufficient?"

"See here, Magister!" admonished Tallesian.

"No, druid, it is you who must see. I dislike
the inference in the question of my activities.
Let us place the accountability directly where it
belongs, sirs. This is your land and your city—
your problem, until I decided to assist. If Lady
Rachelle is missing, has met with foul play—
anything—the responsibility for the occurrence
is yours, and it is a matter for your police to
handle. She must be found and returned un-

harmed. Otherwise ..." Setne allowed the implied threat to trail off.

"This is intolerable, sir," Tallesian said with pale face. Aldriss was also quite livid at the Ægyptian's remarks. Only the Behon seemed calm and unperturbed.

"Otherwise, Magister, you will have suffered a loss such as that which threatens us three, our prince, and even the king," said the elderly justiciar. "I will personally see to it that there is a hunt for your lady lieutenant. It will begin this very morning and not cease until she is found." The Behon scribbled a message on a small sheet of cream-colored paper. He handed it to Aldriss, and the bard left the room. "Now, Magister, as to the inference—suspicion, to be blunt—let us be reasonable. Not knowing just who this Master of Jackals is, each and every one of us might be under suspicion. I know, I know," the man said to forestall objections from Inhetep. "You were employed by us to solve the mystery and prevent blackmail and murder. Yet we too must be exceptionally cautious now. Wouldn't it be extremely clever for the criminal to impersonate a crime fighter?"

The wizard-priest cocked an eyebrow and tilted his head, looking very like a bird of prey as he eyed the two Lyonnessians. "Really? It is a novel idea. Had it occurred to you that the criminal might have been impersonating me in order to kidnap Rachelle? That would account for her attitude when the muffled man called earlier this day."

"That is certainly a possibility. Nevertheless, you must admit, Inhetep, that your unwillingness to account for your own movements is dreadfully incriminating," Tallesian said stiffly.

"As for that, you may rest assured that when the time is right I can and will give exact details, to the minute, mind you, as to where I was and what I was doing during the time one of your citizens here in Camelough tricked Lady Rachelle into captivity—or worse. Now, however, I must find that villain and punish him!"

"Not so fast, Magister Inhetep. I must remind you that we have laws here. Your presence in Lyonnesse is as a guest, and guests must obey just as citizens do," the Behon huffed. "You are hasty in your assumptions, too. I believe we must clear up the matter of your own alibi before you trundle off in search of the perpetrator, so-called. There are a dozen men investigating the matter at this moment, so your participation can wait. I must now insist you come with us. We'll go to the police headquarters at Penkeep and set things straight there."

"Unacceptable, my good sir," Setne snapped. "That allows the criminal too much time. Every hour that passes doubles the difficulty in locating him and my associate."

"What you think is not unimportant, Mag—"

The Behon froze in mid word. Venerable Tallesian was also absolutely still. Neither could speak or move because the wizard-priest had spoken words of power, uttered *hekau* in Ægyptian terminology. To be more exact, Inhetep had used magickal energy drawn from the furthest Planes of the multiverse, power employed by deities, in fact, to remove himself from the stream of time. Both men were far too able and protected from ordinary dweomers to have allowed Setne to employ some lesser force to paralyze them. But they could not prevent him from shifting himself thus, at least not without preparing ahead for such magick. "That should suffice for now," Inhetep said. He stalked away down the corridor of the inn's second floor, went down the steps, and passed by unmoving people on his way to the entry doors. He seemed to move as if under water.

Actually, the tall Ægyptian was being careful to go slowly, for a mundane person being outside the confines of the fourth dimension created a dangerous friction. Running when so removed from time would surely result in spontaneous combustion. Even Inhetep the wizard-priest, the most able ur-kheri-heb ever to have come from the realm of Pharaoh, was not capable of altering the danger of timeless existence.

Although he concentrated carefully on his progress, Setne was unconsciously keeping track of his heartbeats. The magick triggered by his utterance would persist for a limited span, as it operated in all the dimensions, time included. Seeing that there was nothing of interest in the frozen tableau of the inn's lobby, Inhetep moved steadily toward the door. He had about two or three minutes left before the dweomer snapped and he was back in the normal time stream of the world. The effort of removing himself from time's effect had drained Inhetep of a considerable portion of his energy, his ability to utilize heka. So great a magick demanded enough personal energy to channel the entitative-source power, the magickal energy flow of the greatest force. Only a desperate situation would bring him to utilize the power, and in Setne's mind the situation was indeed desperate. Perhaps he couldn't blame the Behon, a justiciar and judge—counsellor and policeman, too—from taking every precaution. Perhaps . . . But there was no doubt in his mind that Rachelle had been lured away and was now being held. The reason was unclear, but the culprit, at least indirectly, had to be the Master of Jackals. The power of that one to go undetected and untraceable was phenomenal. If he was not able to begin the search immediately, Inhetep was convinced that the enemy's magickal abilities would preclude any chance for rescuing Rachelle.

Setne dispelled the picture of the girl from his mind. He was ill at ease with the sudden change in attitude on the part of the Kellts—Aldriss, Tallesian, and the Behon. They had traveled a thousand miles to locate him, yet now they shifted from regarding him as the sole hope against the machinations of the Master of Jackals to a possible suspect in Rachelle's disappearance. Did they consider him an agent of the Master Jackal? The sinister mastermind himself? Unlikely ... A ruse, then? Their own lives were threatened, the royal family as well—that gave sufficient motive to be thorough, cautious, trust no one at all. Something nagged at Inhetep's mind as he pondered this, but he couldn't be sure what it was. He was missing something. It would come to the surface eventually. Right now he had to worry about staying free and active.

Perhaps a minute remained to him. Setne had gone in his slow-motion pace away from the inn, turning a corner and taking a route which gave him the best chances of escaping the hunt which would commence very soon. The three men who had been with him would take a moment to realize what had happened, and then one of them would use magick to alert the authorities under them of the Ægyptian's escape—of his flight from questioning and suspicion of complicity in a matter of gravest import. Police and plainclothes agents would be swarming the streets of the city, particularly in the vicinity of the inn, in a quarter of an hour. "Ample time for—" He cut his vocal thought off short. In that instant, he understood the thing which had been bothering him: one of the unmoving figures just outside the hotel was a man he had seen last night. The fellow must have been there to watch Inhetep. It was too late to go back and investigate that now. The energies which lifted him out of the flow of time were sinking. The wizard-priest knew he had only a few seconds left. Should he be seen as he was, there would be no avoiding capture. A tall, copper-skinned and bald-pated foreigner was noticeable in even so large and cosmopolitan a city as Camelough.

Setne ducked into a narrow passageway between two large buildings. He would use yet more magick to disguise himself. Under normal circumstances he would have had a whole gallery of different personas to assume, each so natural and different as to be virtually undetectable— except by a dweomer specifically employed to discern true form and magickal alteration. But because of the recent use of hekau, and because of his need to be swift, the Ægyptian had only one choice. The air rippled around him. Where a tall Ægyptian had stood a heartbeat before was a shortish Phonecian whose battered and scarred face gave the impression of menace and an unsavory background. Not at all what is best, the altered Inhetep thought to himself. That face would arouse the suspicion of any law enforcer— save that they would be looking exclusively for another fellow altogether for the next few hours! He continued along the gangway, heading directly away from the inn and the royal citadel.

*   *   *

Damn! He felt tired and hungry. The fatigue could be remedied easily with a draught from a little flask of restorative, enchanted stuff he always carried. The hunger was another matter, for he needed to sit down and eat a full meal as the tonic worked. He took a swallow of the liquid, stoppered and replaced the flask in his girdle, and searched for a haven. How many might recognize him in this form? Not enough to worry about. The "Phonecian" had been seen closely by only a half-dozen people. The barkeep, the young whore, and a handful of those who attended the "service" of Set. Double that number had seen him from a distance or in conditions which precluded recognition and positive identification. There was an exception to all, but Setne decided there was no use worrying about that now.

After another few streets and lanes, Inhetep espied a public house. The neighborhood was plain and the buildings somewhat rundown here in one of the city's marginally middle-class sections. He smiled, knowing no one would think to look for him there. He entered and took a table under the suspicious eye of the proprietor, then ordered a large breakfast from the waitress—the owner's wife or sister from the look of her. His initial course, a big bowl of steaming barley porridge boiled in milk and swimming with plump little dried currants, was thumped down in front of him almost immediately after he had completed his lengthy list of required comestibles. He had thought how Rachelle would have been laughing at him for ordering so much—more than even the girl usually ate. The strain of using entitative powers for magick depleted spirit, mind, and body, of course.

"If ye don't object," the sour-faced waitress said, daring him to object by posture and tone and expression, "I'll be collecting the payment for t'all of yer fare now—nine spurs in coin of the realm."

Inhetep considered teasing the harridan into accepting a silver coin of foreign mintage instead of the bronze Lyonnesse ones, but resisted the impulse. Instead he reached into his tunic, took out a small purse, and carefully fished out a copper harp, a coin worth five of the bronze ones, four spurs, and then, but slowly, one more of the bronze coins. "Here's the whole of the reconin', lass," he said in a gravelly voice suitable to his impersonation. Then he put his finger on the last bronze spur. "Ya gets thissun too fer yersel' if ya hustles m'food ta me."

She wasn't impressed, for it was no more than an ordinary gratuity for good and efficient service. Of course, that was rare in this place, but the usual customers expected nothing but what she delivered. After eyeing each coin and feeling them to make sure they weren't counterfeits, the waitress took them away saying, "Ye'll get the rest when it's ready."

Grinning down at his porringer, Setne devoured the thick gruel and thought about what he must do now. The situation in the underground "temple" had almost been deadly. Inhetep had felt the magickal probing and known that someone, not the masked priest, had discovered that there was a very unusual "worshipper" present. He had to remain put. Any movement would have betrayed him, and he needed to detect the enemy and test his skills. Had the spell-binders there known that the "Phonecian" was none other than Setne Inhetep, ur-kheri-heb of Thoth? He doubted that. His own wards against aural reading and identification by thought reading or magickal detection would have prevented easy discernment of that. Penetration of all the shielding the magister employed would require either much time or very potent dweomers. "Ahhh," he sighed, polishing the spoon as he ate the last of the porridge. "Service 'ere!"

In short order, the remainder of the meal was thumped down upon the wooden table, the dishes taking up most of the small space. There was a fresh baked loaf, a small platter of smoked eels undoubtedly caught in the fall from the nearby river. Next to them was a dish of cold game pie—local pigeons, actually, for the most part—filled with eggs, vegetables, and mushrooms to give it proper volume. That was indeed satisfactory to his way of thinking. Lyonnesse folk ate altogether too little fruit and vegetables for the Ægyptian's taste. Butter, a jack of stout, and a plate with two winter pears and a wedge of local cheese completed the order. Despite his resolution, Setne added a pewter coin to the bronze one. That made his tip a spur and a half, for the coin with the leaf on its face was but half the value of the bronze one. There was a sniff from the sour-faced woman, but she took them both and stumped off. She'd ignore him now. Inhetep desired that very much.

Eating ravenously didn't prevent him from returning to his thoughts. He hadn't actually discovered the depth of the enemy's ability to probe his cover, but the sudden appearance of the two "megajackals" indicated that they were either fairly capable of ascertaining things, or prone to excessive display and force. The business with the coalesced light was out of the ordinary, too. That sort of casting required use of a great deal of heka, and considerable art, too. Supernatural light and monster-jackals . . . That indicated the subterranean temple was indeed close to the Master of Jackals' organization. The demagoguery indicated that something more than extortion and murder were afoot. Then there was the trifling matter of the masked ecclesiastic naming Inhetep fully and telling the "congregation" that he was a friend and fellow-rebel about to be martyred on behalf of their pseudo-religion. This was a matter which required much thought and further investigation.

The whole so-called temple was a fake. The idols had been made by someone very familiar with the Ægyptian pantheon and religious practices, possibly a renegade cleric from his own land. No matter. None were consecrated properly, most had been of deities nonexistent in Ægypt—or anywhere else, probably—and the "service" had been so much oggus-bogus. There was magick, all right, but those dweomers were of the sort to captivate weak minds and implant ideas. Those ritual effects were at work from the time the make-believe priestesses were on stage, so to speak. Setne quaffed off half of the thick brew. The eels had been quite salty. He poured a bit more down, then pondered the meaning of the whole charade. Thus immersed in thought, he hardly noticed the taste of the hard fruit and sharp cheese.

Given the astute nature of the foe, and their precautions against just such a thing as he'd tried last night, it was no wonder that the officials here (the Behon, for instance) didn't have any idea just how insidious a plan the self-proclaimed Master of Jackals was hatching. It had been a very near thing, for had the jackal-masked priest used that magickal light to mark him, Inhetep knew that he'd have been attacked by all present. Perhaps he could have used his own powers to escape, but everything would have been blown open—literally, perhaps—by that. It was sheer inspiration, his little trick with the coins. Rabble such as those assembled in the subcellar temple were totally unable to resist the lure of gold. When he'd placed an antipathy between the coin's metal and the stone of the floor upon them, the golden discs had shot into the air, of course, taking a position equidistant between the stone floor and ceiling, moving out toward the middle of the room because of the walls. Then, zap! Cancel the dweomer of antipathy, and the heavy coins rained down into the crowd. In the tumult caused by that, the priest had been distracted sufficiently for Setne to bring replication magick into play. The fool had eventually hurled the ruby-red globule of light, but as it sped outward it engendered a pair of twins just like it, the twins each produced twins, and so forth. None of these were aimed at the Æyptian. Each was uncontrolled and flew toward the nearest person. Inhetep had been marked by bloody illumination, but by then half of the others in the temple were likewise branded. Between lust for gold and blood, a melee ensued, with shouts of rage, cries of innocence, and all the rest so loud that nothing sensible could be heard in the din.

The jackals had been another matter. He might have taken care of them by summoning a great sphinx, for example. Even spirit-jackals— what those things were, feared such a monster as that, just as ordinary jackals fear a lion. That would certainly have announced to his enemy that the ur-kheri-heb was there in person. Not six practitioners in all the Yarth could conjure a great leosphinx at the drop of a word. Changing his structure from normal to semi-ætherial was risky, especially since the ones who had brought the "megajackals" to the temple could easily send those monsters into the same state in pursuit of their quarry, and he had assumed there would be wards and traps set for anyone trying to enter or leave the place magickally except via secretly established paths. No form of invisibility possible on short notice would fool the keen-sensed jackal-things, so Setne had had to improvise in the split-second allowed him by their attack. The instant the two impacted, the Ægyptian had changed himself into a replica of themselves. Their proximity, auras, odor, and even a bit of hair snatched from one's mangy hide had enabled the transformation.

The shift had cancelled the ruby light which had marked him, and as far as any onlooker could tell, there were three of the horrible creatures now, not two. Even the spirit-jackals weren't sure which was which. One bit at him, he bit back, and so did the other. The three whirled round in a frenzy of fighting, Inhetep recalled with a smile. Then he had nipped a nearby worshipper on his rear. That was sufficient for the other two. The megajackals fell to biting nearby folk with indiscriminate fury and lust for blood, their mentally given command to attack only the "Phonecian" quite forgotten. There wasn't a prayer of setting matters right then. Until the monsters were subdued, and order restored, the whole temple was a battleground.

The commotion resulted in the barred door being opened. They had no choice, for the folk inside would have died under the fangs of the spirit-jackals, and there went the carefully planned "brotherhood." The pretend-ecclesiastics—the priest in his jackal-mask, the priestesses, and some other individual, too—had rushed into the press. They tried to subdue the crazed beasts and get the normal worshippers out while keeping Inhetep in. Pretending to attack viciously, Setne recoiled, slipped belly-down between legs and running feet to get out the door before anyone with magickal power could intervene. He had bounded up the stairs on four strong legs, shot past a bug-eyed guard, and disappeared into the dark. He supposed that the two actual spirit-jackals had quickly been set in chase after the false one. Too late.

Magick to return to normal form—that of Setne Inhetep. More dweomers to wipe out all trace of the transformation and to prevent tracking by scent. That was over too swiftly for the pursuing beasts to stop. Then the Ægyptian made a point of sending himself elsewhere very rapidly. Now he could be seen far away at about the same time the chase was on in Scathach; there would be a different sort of hunt when the pack came up with an empty bag. Meanwhile, Setne had a lot to accomplish. The kidnap of Rachelle was a complication he most certainly didn't need! He had to locate the girl and rescue her first, and the Master of Jackals would have to wait.

"That's what they want!" he said suddenly aloud, taken by the obviousness of the whole event.

"What's yer trouble?" the surly waitress demanded.

Setne grinned his most evil grin. The "Phoenician's" look was more than enough to make the woman jump back and clutch at herself. "I'll 'ave yer waggin' worm of a tongue, I will, next time ya speaks thatta way, bag!" he growled menacingly. She fainted, and Inhetep strolled out of the place. He no longer cared if anyone remembered the Phonecian. "They know why I am here, what I am meant to do, and will stop at nothing to see that I fail," he said to himself as he stepped into the street. He saw a peripheral movement and managed to jerk his head aside in time. A thumb-thick bolt from a crossbow, reeking of venom, stood buried in the timber frame of the building. It was an inch from his ear.

8

HIGH ROAD, LOW ROAD

There was nothing to do but run. Setne ran as fast as he could, bobbing and weaving as he went. Another of the quarrels zipped by his head, its passage making a nasty humming in the air as if it were a live and hateful thing. He fumbled in his garments. The assassin was indeed using living missiles. No. More properly, the killer was seeking the Ægyptian's life with bolts enchanted to a state resembling that of life. These missiles would seek him out as would hungry mosquitoes, only their sting would be as poisonous as an asp's. Inhetep invoked the force of the talisman he had drawn from one of the little pockets inside his tunic. It was fashioned of hard, red stone—a carnelian shaped into a cobra's head. Even as he called forth its power, the wizard-priest continued his evasive running. Turning a corner, which he was certain was out of sight of the crossbow-armed assassin, Inhetep flattened himself against the wall and held the red-hued serpent form up before his face, as if he were peering at it.

Another of the buzzing missiles shot round the corner, the quarrel seeking him out as if tied to Inhetep by a cord. The thick shaft touched the talisman as it sped to pierce the Ægyptian's eye. Both bolt and stone evaporated in a little puff of smoke. "Rot you!" Setne cursed, aiming the useless words at the unseen attacker. There was no time for him to work up anything really effective against whomever it was, and the magick cast upon the little arrow had been so strong as to destroy his prized ward against poisonous attack! Without hesitation, Setne again began running, ducking into an alley, pounding along a covered passage, thus eluding further missiles and possible pursuit—for the moment.

His enemy knew him as the "Phonecian," and that meant that Inhetep was now in an impossible situation. If he shifted to some other guise, he would be draining yet more of his precious reserve of heka-power needed to survive the lethal assaults which were sure to be forthcoming. Yet he had no time to rest and restore his energy until he could manage to hide himself. In this form or his own, the Ægyptian would be recognized and hunted. Probably any other physical guise he took would likewise be identifiable to those who were seeking him. The forces being used against him were impossibly great; the foe was employing dweomers of a sort not possible to humans. To combat the threat, Setne had to get back to his own lodging, get to his belongings somehow, and arm himself for the contest. How to do so without being seen? There was an easy but obvious method. It was so obvious (and dangerous) that the wizard-priest opted to try it. The Master of Jackals and his thugs would probably dismiss the possibility of Inhetep trying it.

A little brown sparrow winged just above the tall rooftops of Camelough, arched upwards for a minute, circled, and then sped straight ahead, diving as it went. A sparrow hawk nearby gave chase, thinking to take the prey unsuspecting, but it vanished into an open vent in a gable, and the raptor gave a frustrated "kreeep!" The hawk flapped up and then shot down into an enclosed courtyard where it changed into a brown-robed man.

The rats in the walls of the inn scurried aside to make a wide berth for the big, reddish one that scuttled along their avenues. Something about it was unnatural, and it was too fierce-looking to approach. Ignoring poison and traps, Setne-the-rodent located the area of his room and found a narrow opening that he could just squeeze through. He peeped out with beady black eyes first, just in case. . . .

"Don't touch anything!" the blond man said to the pair of armed soldiers in the room. "It is dangerous to probe the effects of any mage, let alone a wizard-priest's things." The two guardsmen grumbled a little at the thought of not being able to filtch anything but were careful to avoid even the furniture. "You two, stand watch outside. Give the alarm if anyone comes in—or even if you so much as hear noise from this room! Clear?" Both soldiers assented. The man with straw-colored hair tarried in Setne's bed chamber, eyeing the various objects scattered about.

Even as a rat, the Ægyptian could sense that the fellow was a practitioner of some sort. The man was probing for auras and magickal emanations. The rat scurried beyond range. He waited until the blond police official left, then, he squeezed his rat form through the narrow opening. Setne performed the little dance and accompanying chitterings to negate the transformation, and if the pair of guardsmen heard the rat sounds, they ignored them. It took only seconds. "That's better," the wizard-priest whispered to himself as he stood once again in normal form. It was an easy matter for him, then, to lay a casting which muted all sounds in his chamber, even though it took nearly all of his remaining heka to do so.

In a matter of moments, the wizard-priest had gathered everything he needed, including his personal reservoirs of magickal energy. Then he changed his garments, slipped a few clean clothes into a small leather valise, and headed straight for the door, where the pair of soldiers stood guard. The magister was, frankly, in high dudgeon. Their backs were turned away from the bedroom as the two stood chatting idly, attention focused vaguely upon the entry to the suite. Inhetep stepped forward, touching each man on the neck with either hand. "You are alone together," he said softly. The cloaking spell existed only in the inner room, and the guards nodded as they heard the Ægyptian's voice. "You have seen nobody at all, have you?" Each man agreed with that, too. "Good!" Setne said with hearty comradery. "But you must be ready, because the next person to enter through that door will be the fugitive, Inhetep!"

"We'll knock him senseless the moment he comes in!"

"Be careful. The Ægyptian is tricky," Setne said, his hawk-face smiling. "He might appear as a woman—even your superior!"

"We attack anyway, don't we Flynn!" It wasn't a question, and Flynn nodded his concurrence with hard face.

Inhetep returned to the inner chamber. He rubbed his hands together, the coppery flesh nearly glowing in the subdued light of the room. Inhetep smiled broadly. "I do so love a real challenge! Well, my so-called Master of Jackals, you think to order the course of things, but I shan't comply. No, no indeed I shall not. You think to chivvy me about as a hare, or at worst have me running about seeking for Rachelle. That is what *you* wish. That is of no import, for Magister Setne Inhetep does as *he* wishes. We shall meet anon. Sooner than you think, too, Master Jackal. Until then, dear fellow, you might have a bit of care. You won't enjoy our meeting in the least bit when it comes."

The wizard-priest pulled a cowl over his head, kept his hands concealed beneath his commodious cloak, and whispered a few syllables. There was a rippling in the atmosphere, a faint soughing of air as if a wind blew into the room from some hot desert. Inhetep stepped ahead a pace and vanished. He was gone from Camelough, Lyonnesse—all of Æropa, in fact. He had used his arts to step from the room to his own private place in Ægypt as one would step from house to street. That took care of his immediate pursuers. The police and various minions of the government of Lyonnesse could blanket city and country looking for him. It was high time to seek answers to certain important questions. Then he might return to Camelough, or he might not, but he would locate both Rachelle and the Master of Jackals—undoubtedly the former held prisoner in the lair of the latter.

The enemy would certainly have sufficient powers available to scan the immediate past. They would see how the wizard-priest had entered the bedroom, taken care of sounds, guards, and then left. They would not know exactly what he had taken, how Setne had left, nor to what destination his dweomer had carried him. The Master Jackal, however, would certainly be able to eventually trace Inhetep's trail to this place. Setne cast a carefully screened trap just in case he was followed. He laid a spell of duplication, so that if anyone conjured themselves into this place—or sent some nasty visitor from a nethersphere to attack him—that casting would be deflected and shunt the intruder away from his sanctum. In the event it was a dweomercræfter attempting to visit him, Setne's magick would flip the other right back to his starting point. However, if it was a heka-binder sending a demon or the like to handle the business, the energy would shift. The assassin would then step instead into the immediate proximity of the one who tried to send the monster elsewhere.

"A nasty little surprise however it occurs," Inhetep said aloud as he completed his work. "Now I'm off to see about this impersonation of deities."

He exited the hidden room and entered his own study. No one was around because it was near midnight in Ægypt. That suited Inhetep, for he wanted neither company nor suspicion of his being there. Leaving the villa by a side exit, Setne slipped past a flock of geese. The least disturbance and the birds made more noise than ten times their number of dogs. The gaggle was silent. Then he strode into the wastes which ran westward from the village. His long legs carried him quickly, and soon his sandaled feet were pushing along in loose sand. A mile ahead was a small pyramid, one which was relatively new in terms of this ancient land, for it had been constructed only some two millennia ago by one of Inhetep's forebears, one Neteranubi-f-Hra, to be exact. It had been done ostensibly as the "Eternal House" of the ancestral mage, but in actuality it had another purpose altogether. The secret chamber in the heart of the pyramid was most magickal.

There are many means of moving from one reality to another, to journey from sphere to sphere, plane to plane. The "underworld" of Ægypt, the place of many of its most powerful deital and entital beings such as Osiris, Ptah, and Seker, is that nether-realm known as the Duat. Getting from anywhere else in the multiverse to the Duat is a very difficult matter, unless one happens to profess the Ægyptian ethos, accept one or more of their pantheon, and then dies. Setne qualified for two of the three conditions, but he had no intention of dying—at least, not soon! Neither had his great-great-great-umpteenth-great grandfather, Neteranubi-f-Hra. The pyramid had been constructed specifically to allow the passage of a living person from this world, called Yarth, into the manifold planes and their attendant spheres, called the Duat. There the strong and daring dweomercræfter might meet and converse with deity, fiend, serpent, and all manner of strange and mighty beings. Of course, that individual risked much, but that is the nature of the most powerful magicks used by mankind. In such a high stakes game, the rewards were great, but failure could mean death—or worse.

Inside the pyramid, safely through the protective traps and secret passages, Setne Inhetep began the family Ritual of Transference. At the proper moment, he spoke the word of power coupled with the place he wished to go in the Duat, *Amenti*. This was the key to the entrance of the planes of the underworld. Twelve great divisions existed in the Duat. Each was ruled by a deity, Osiris being nominal overlord of all, an emperor of sorts. This headship, such as it was, came as much by dint of force as anything else. Many of the planes comprising the underworld of shadowy nature were gruesome places, ruled by Evil, populated by monstrous beings. By entering the Duat in the heart of Osiris' domains, the wizard-priest avoided the terrible places both before it and deeper within the whole. But in Amenti was a judgment hall, as well as that place where the spheres of Osiris' own habitation began.

"Who would stand before the Throne and the forty-two Assessors of the Hall of Judgment?" demanded a savage-faced *neter*, a being of power and neutral disposition.

"It is Setne Inhetep, a faithful priest of Thoth, worker in heka, who seeks to pass," the Ægyptian responded to the challenge. Then he named the name of that Watcher, his Doorkeeper companion, and the Herald, too—all of whom kept safe the gateway to the Hall of Maati. "But I have not come except as a supplicant to speak with Lord Osiris, and Lord Anubis, and my own Lord Thoth, too, should he be therein. Living am I, and alive will I remain, Eyes-as-Piercing-as-Spears. My flesh is proof against the knives of the fiends, my shadow so strong as to grapple with serpents, my heart so fierce as to make pale the face of monster or demon hungering for it. Soul and spirit and double are threefold proof against any devil who would have at them. My name is proof against fiery uræi."

The strange and terrible ones before the tall doors opened them. "You may enter then, man. Know that you have but little time in this place, for living flesh cannot survive long here. Beware lest you have to return again for judgment!"

"I am conversant on all matters pertaining to that, too, guardian of this portal. If that should eventuate, you may be assured that the balance will not dip against me." Setne spoke the names of the doorposts, lintel, threshold, and door, then strode through the open entry without further ado, looking neither right nor left, and keeping tight control over his mind and body. One false word or step could be fatal. When he entered, he found the endless hall dimly illuminated and deserted. Of course, those who were outside wouldn't know of the conditions inside. There were two means of egress. One led to the Field of Reeds, home of those spirits who were true and just and sought an afterworld of twilight. The place was called Sekhet-Aaru and its viceroy was Menu-qet. The second gateway led to the place called Sekhet-Hetepet. That plane was directly overseen by Osiris. This place was but the first of many "halls" in Osiris' own demesnes, each such place a sort of quasi-sphere. In the multiple planes of Osiris' personal realm, there were also many other, larger spheres, places not unlike Yarth and places very unlike it. The Opener of the Duat, Anubis, could be anywhere therein, or even further off in one of the other planes of this portion of Pandemonium. Thoth might not be here at all.

When the mighty sun deity, Ra himself, journeyed through the Duat, he progressed only with the company of powerful beings to assure safety of passage. How could a mere priest and wizard of mortal sort manage such a trek should the ones he sought be afield? "Which portal must I pass?" he asked aloud.

From the shadowy depths of the hall stepped a darker figure. "You shall pass neither, ur-kheri-heb," a baritone growl informed him.

Setne started, his hand bringing up an ankh of copper as he whirled. "Oh! My Lord Apuat," he said, visibly relaxing. The wolf-headed deity was the friend and companion of Anubis and the "Opener of the Southern Way." That is, Apuat was a guardian for all good folk deceased and bound for this place.

"You are not welcome here, Setne Inhetep," the wolf-headed god said. He came closer, adding, "It is not for want of merit in you, servant of Thoth."

"May I ask you a question?"

Apuat nodded. "That you may do, for my sole command is to see that you do not enter the planes here."

"I need ask of you, then, my lord, what offense have I given to Lord Osiris?"

"None at all, albeit it was that Great One who sent me forth here to watch for you."

Inhetep was puzzled. "There is gross slander and falsity in the lands west of Ægypt that Lord Anubis has been made into a dark and vile tool of Set. . . ." The tall deity seemed unmoved, but Inhetep plunged on. "There is great power being used to mask this evil work, machinations which seemed directed to establish the red-eyed one as greatest in Æropa. Should he gain such energy from that, the whole balance of—"

With a hand outstretched to rest on the wizard-priest's shoulder, Apuat interrupted Setne's sentence. "It is as it is. Osiris has forbidden Anubis to speak to you, and even Thoth has chosen to withhold converse. It is not as it seems. I cannot say more about that."

"Set! I will seek out the Lord of the Lowest if need be." He looked at the wolf-headed entity whose visage belied heart and purpose. "Is that permitted?"

The fanged head shook slowly, almost sadly. "There is much power, and it would never permit your entry into the Eleventh Plane, to Jessert-Baiu where the Ass dwells." Apuat referred, of course, to Set's realm in the Duat, not to his domains among the stars. "The ship of Ra travels there with utmost difficulty, Setne Inhetep. You are not ready for such a journey. Yet, perhaps all of the gods of Ægypt depend on your work. Do you think it strange that deities must place their hope on a mortal?"

All his words were laden with hidden meanings. Setne was sure that Apuat was somehow constrained from revealing what he knew just as the others were. This was indeed something beyond murder and extortion, but perhaps there was also less to it than might appear. "Then I must locate the one foe, the liar who claims to be Master of Jackals."

"It is always wise to remember that what is falsehood today might be truth tomorrow," the wolf-head said slowly. "Your own instincts must guide you now, Magister Setne Inhetep. Let your five senses take you quickly to the heart of the problem."

Setne bowed. When he looked up, the hall had vanished, and he was again within the hidden chamber in the pyramid. He sat there for several minutes, reviewing and contemplating all that had just occurred. "So," Inhetep said at last, standing up and walking purposefully toward the hidden exit from the stuffy little chamber, "I think the abortive visit to the Duat was fruitful after all."

Outside and heading back toward his own home, the tall Ægyptian seemed to fly across the ground he walked so quickly. He whistled a little air as he went, a rather tuneless sound which would have told Rachelle, had she been there, that the magister's mind was working furiously on some plan as he went. Then the copper-skinned priest of Thoth vanished inside the low-walled villa which was his seldom-visited home. In the morning, nobody there would even know that their master had come and gone.

9

DEATH IN LONDUN

Avillonia. Three islands, five kingdoms, and a mixed people who had come to consider themselves one. One, that is, in terms of dealing with those from other lands. Perhaps they regarded the Brettons as acceptable cousins, the folk of Flanders slightly less so, and some of their other immediate neighbors, along with Atlantlans, Romans, and Grecians, respectable enough to deal with. Others, especially such neighbors as Neustria, Francia, and the Teutonic lands were filled with undesirable persons. If the people of such lands came to any of the Five Kingdoms, they might survive well enough in the larger cities. In fact, the capitals of the kingdoms of Avillonia had large populations of foreigners from all over Yarth. Caledonia and Cymru, the two smallest kingdoms, each had under two million inhabitants. Their capitals, Edinburgh and Caerdyv, the one with only some thirty-five thousand citizens, the other boasting sixty thousand, had foreign quarters with non-natives totaling about ten percent of their populations. The same was true for Glasgow and Cardigan, too, those cities being about as large as the capitals. Hybernia with between three and four million, Lyonnesse with between four and five—whose great capitals, Dublin and Camelough, respectively, each had one-quarter million or more souls—supported slightly larger foreign populations. Albion, the most populous kingdom of all, with over seven million, also had as its capital the largest city in Avillonia. Londun totalled over seven hundred thousand residents, and that census omitted all persons not holding citizenship. Almost a hundred thousand "strangers" dwelled in the city. Londun was not the largest city of Yarth, but it was certainly one of the twenty or so with populations near to or over a million.

Ch'ins, Hindi, Phonecians, Shamish, Yarbans, Atlantlans, Berbers, and even some number of Ægyptians were to be found in the foreign districts of the metropolis of Londun. Fully a half of the non-Avillonian population was made up of such Azirians and Afrikans. The balance were of a somewhat less exotic sort—merchants of Hansa and other Teutonics, Francians, Russians, Skands, Romans, Grecians, and Iberians, too. Nobody in the city paid much attention to these strangers, so it was surprising to all when a growing mob of Londuners began to pour through the streets in the Limehouse district. "Kill the POCs!" some screamed. Others began smashing

windows and pillaging. "Pocs" was the slang
term for all Ægyptians, an acronym derived from
"Pharaohs Own Citizens." The mob and riot
were soon taken care of, and only a dozen or so
deaths and three times as many serious injuries
resulted from the affair. Then the Lord Mayor
demanded to know why it had happened in the
first place. The Bow Street Runners went out in
force to find the answer.

Setne Inhetep could have given them the answer easily enough. He had left his own land
and had returned to Avillonia, if not to that very
district of Camelough, by magickal means. That
left obvious telltales, but the wizard-priest was
no longer very much concerned about that. He
went directly to a place in Hybernia, to the
dwelling of a fellow Ægyptian who was also
practitioner, albeit in only a small way. Onru-
hehept wasn't exactly thrilled at the Setne's arrival, but he was accommodating nonetheless.
Without using his diplomatic status, the official
managed to get Inhetep an audience with the
king himself. It was a brief meeting, but both the
Hybernian monarch and Setne were enlightened.
King Finn arranged for the priest-mage's conveyance across his land to the sea, where Inhetep
boarded a fast packet bound for Glasgow the
next night. In the Caledonian capital, the Ægyptian simply used bluff and his renown to gain a
similar audience with the monarch of the northernmost of the Five Kingdoms of Avillon. De-

spite precautions, Setne was assailed by thugs while in Edinburgh. But their attempted assassination failed because agents of King Finn were still trailing the wizard-priest and interceded, as it were, to set the attackers straight. A dozen corpses had to be disposed of, and the Royal Caledonian respect for Inhetep rose accordingly.

From the capital of Caledonia, Setne was conveyed by another official convoy to the seat of government of Cmyru, the city of Caerdyv. There he was likewise granted immediate audience with the ruler of that nation. That wasn't surprising, for by this time he was accompanied by trusted emissaries from both Hybernia and Caledonia. Owen, twelfth monarch of that name to rule the western portion of the biggest of the three Avillonian islands, ordered passage for the tall Ægyptian, so that Inhetep sailed from the capital city to Albion the very next day. Debarking at Bristol, and now purposely alone and without shadowing agents, the magister took various coaches eastward to reach Londun, that sprawling metropolis on the Thames, as quickly as possible. There King Dennis was holding court over Sunsebb Tide, as the winter solstice was called in Albion.

"Please tell your superior that Magister Setne Inhetep of Thebes is here on important business," the wizard-priest said in clipped tones to the lesser porter of the royal palace, a great complex of mansions and towers called the Citadel of Londun.

The fellow had a long face which grew longer at Setne's command. "As you wish, ah . . . noble Ægyptian sir," the functionary replied. He made the honorific sound shoddy, and his expression conveyed the likelihood that a foreigner such as the tall, hawk-faced Easterner with reddish skin and shaven head would receive only the attention of those curious to see an outlandish inferior. "Please be so good as to wait here," he added, waving the priest-mage toward a long, hard bench of carved oak much polished by the posteriors of similar supplicants.

Fifteen minutes passed. The lesser porter literally flew back into the plain antechamber where Inhetep sat calmly waiting. He was wringing his hands, a gesture between worry and anxiousness. "Your sincere pardon, Magister Inhetep," he said with utmost solicitousness. "The Lord Chamberlain himself will see you immediately."

The fellow had dallied. That was obvious to Setne. He'd probably stopped to chat with another petty official, pinch a serving maid, and then strolled to the office of the porter. That one had certainly had Inhetep's name on a list. Setne imagined the junior running off down a corridor at the harsh command of his superior, taking word of the Ægyptian's arrival to the porter's own master, the chamberlain. He saw the long-faced fellow in his mind's eye running breathlessly back to inform the porter that Sir Chauncey would personally receive the visitor. He stood up and looked at the man without expression.

"Dreadfully sorry about the wait," the assistant to the porter gulped under the emerald-green stare of the wizard-priest. He wondered if such foreign spell-cræfters could read minds easily, then hastily dropped the thought. With a bow, the fellow ushered Inhetep into a wide hallway and conveyed him to the suite of offices occupied by the greater officials of the royal household.

The major domo stood and extended his hand to the Ægyptian. "How may I be of service, Magister Inhetep?" he inquired politely. "It is, of course, an honor to receive a cleric and mage of your reputation."

Setne tapped his breast with a careless gesture, an acknowledgement of the chamberlain's greeting, but he ignored the extended hand. It was not customary in Ægypt, and the wizard-priest chose to stand on that now. With similar disregard for Western etiquette, Setne seated himself upon one of the several chairs near the table the man used as his desk, nodded as if recalling the chamberlain's query, and said, "I am here to speak with your liege, King Dennis."

"I see," the chamberlain said coldly, walking round so as to seat himself across the table from his caller. His face was a bit flushed. The Ægyptian's behavior indicated that either he was rude or ignorant or . . . something else. "Arranging a royal audience is a matter of some difficulty, and you have come so unexpectedly—"

"Have I, Sir Chauncey? Odd. As a former member of a service similar to Albion's, I had thought a spy system as efficient as yours would have known a day or two ago that I must be headed here."

The chamberlain's flush darkened and spread. "See here, Inhetep—"

Setne stood up, bowing. "Oh, have I said something out of place? I am unused to your court formalities, and I crave your pardon. Nonetheless, what I have come for is of utmost importance. Please conduct me *immediately* to King Dennis. He will understand once I have spoken to him."

"That is impossible. However, you may relate to me whatever information you have which *you* believe will be of interest to His Majesty. Rest assured, I will relay the gist of it to him in expeditious manner." Sir Chauncey paused and looked expectantly at the hawk-faced man opposite his desk.

With a shake of his shaven head, Setne refused. "Most unacceptable—and for your own sake, too, I must add, Lord Chamberlain. The words I have are for your sovereign alone. When may I speak with the king?"

Sir Chauncey set his mouth in a tight line. "As you wish, Magister. The next possible audience

is the day after tomorrow. Please be at the citadel on the stroke of eight."

"I understand," the wizard-priest replied.
"Thank you for your courteous assistance in this
matter."

"No trouble at all, sir," the chamberlain said
with sudden thawing to his cold tone. "Yes . . .
speaking of courtesy, is there anything I can do
to make your stay more comfortable? Have you
lodging?"

"There is nothing, thank you. There is a small
Ægyptian quarter in Londun, I believe. Several
acquaintances of mine dwell there, and I will
stay with one of them until the day of the
audience."

Sir Chauncey was still being helpful. "I say,
Magister Inhetep. At least allow me to get you a
chair and a guide! That section of Londun is
quite a warren. It's possible to get lost just trying
to arrive in the vicinity."

"That's most kind but unnecessary," Setne
said, with a smile of thanks to match the chamberlain's own cordiality. "I appreciate your offer,
and it is good to find you bear no animosity due
to my abruptness and persistence. You see, Sir
Chauncey, this *is* a most critical matter, and the
safety of the crown itself might be involved.
Anyway, I will be here as you instruct, and
meanwhile I shall find my way about town well
enough. As they say, we dweomercræfters are a
hard lot to lose."

"Yes . . ." the chamberlain replied with distraction. The words Setne had uttered regarding the safety of the crown had had a sharp impact on the man. "Well, until we meet again, Magister."

Escorted out and on his way, Inhetep walked briskly for several blocks, the cold winter air pushing him along. Having completed that constitutional, the tall Ægyptian sought out a public carriage, and after a few minutes found a small hansom typical of Londun. It was unoccupied, so he climbed in and asked the driver to take him to the foreign quarter—the place where Ægyptians were to be found, if the man knew where that was. "Near 'nuff," the cabbie replied, and whipped the tired old plug pulling the small cab into a sort of trot. Near the river warehouses in the Limehouse district, however, the man stopped the conveyance and asked for payment, saying, "Hit's gettin' too blamed dark ta see, so's I'll take m'fare now—place yer lookin' fer be only aways orff."

Sleet was beginning to fall, and the stuff was being swirled about by a freezing wind which blew in gusts off the nearby river. Setne hunched down in his great cloak and slogged ahead, taking the first lane to the left, then another to the right, and finally a twisting way of alley-width to the left again. No witchlights or other magickal illuminations were in evidence here. Such things were subject to theft, of course, for having a light of that sort saved a poor man much in the way

of candles, lamp oil, and the like. There was a
sputtering torch a little ways ahead, the flam-
beau set into a niche and semi-shielded from the
elements in order for its flame to lure passersby
into the drinking house before which it stood. A
sign there showed a double-faced deity sporting
eight arms which brandished various weapons,
and crude lettering beneath proclaimed it in
both Brytho-Kelltic and Vedic as the "Golden
Shiva."

There were darker shapes in the gloom and
sleet where Setne had been only a moment before. Without seeming to notice them, the tall
man stepped to the doorway to the tavern,
ducked under the low lintel, and pushed open
the door. Twanging strains of music, a hum of
voices, and red-gold light rushed out over the
hissing ice and blustering wind. Then the door
banged shut, and the alleyway was left to its dis-
mal self. Inhetep stepped inside and shook off
the crusted sleet, shed his damp cloak, and
found a seat near the carved bar. He smiled a
little. At least the folk of Sindraj, Hind, and Cey-
lon alike, appreciated warmth.

"Date wine," he informed the sloe-eyed wench
who came to his table. She brought a battered
pewter goblet of the syrupy stuff, and Setne
sipped it with a satisfied sigh. Perhaps it wasn't
very good, but it reminded him of home. There
were lamps burning low and a large fireplace
ablaze in the corner. Setne looked around the

large room and the clusters of patrons, perhaps two score in all. His gaze fell to the floor. Sure enough. In the center was a heavy iron grill, and nobody went near it. "Salamander?" he asked when the serving girl came by his table again.

She merely nodded. It was of no interest to her. "More wine, effendi? Perhaps you seek other things too . . . ?"

Four men had entered the place. "Finally," Setne muttered aloud. The dusky-skinned wench looked puzzled and hopeful. "More wine?" "Yes." "Other things?" "No," the Ægyptian managed somewhat distractedly. He was keeping careful watch on the four without looking at them. That required all of his attention, so Inhetep didn't see the shrug and flounce as the girl went to fetch more wine. Inhetep paid for his order and pretended to be absorbed in his drinking and the six musicians who sawed and toodled and thumped away nearby. Then he called the wench over to his table again. "How do I find the district where the Ægyptian folk dwell?" he asked loudly.

"I am uncertain," the Hindi woman said with a pout. That changed to a smile when Inhetep produced a pair of coppers, slipped one into the girl's hand, and told her to use the other to bring them both another drink. The wench then related several ways of getting to the area Setne had inquired about. "Oh, you are looking for the place where they have many shops offering the goods of your country for sale?" she asked in response to his words. "Then you need only to go along the next street aways. When you see the sign of the Gypsies—an eye in a ball of glass—turn to your right. In a little while you will come to the place where your folk live."

With that, the wizard-priest grinned and gestured toward the musicians. "Bring a full ewer of whatever they like and ask them to join me," Inhetep told the sloe-eyed maid. "If you are free, come and sit with me, too. With such a short way to go, I can spend much time here having fun." The wench went off to do as he had asked. One of the four men also got up and left the tavern. Setne was positive the man had overheard everything. Still smiling, the Ægyptian soon had the company of the band, the serving maid, and a couple of other women who had drifted over to the group. Setne put his purse on the table and emptied it. A dozen or more copper and silver coins spilled forth. "Now that should do for our thirst!" he said drunkenly. "Can any of you charming ladies dance?"

Within half an hour, there was a roistering party in full swing around the Ægyptian's table. Soon, in fact, several of his fellow-countrymen appeared as if by magick in the Golden Shiva. Although they were of common sort, Inhetep welcomed them as if the three were cousins. The musicians resumed their places to accompany the woman who was dancing for Setne. Then another woman performed and more folk joined the noisy throng. More silver came from somewhere on the magister's person, and greater quantities of beer, wine, and spirits arrived. "Is there a pair of strong fellows here?" the shaven-headed priest-mage cried. "I'll pay the winner of a wrestling bout four dolphosess. I want some entertainment of the rigorous sort!" Although several of the wenches volunteered other sports, Inhetep held firm, and soon a pair of stalwarts agreed to give it a try. A space was cleared for them as Setne set out four of the Achæan coins, silver disks each worth about twenty-five of the common Albish bronze coins. The match began—and in no time the contest brought bedlam to the tavern.

As several tipsy onlookers cheered the wrestlers, a third contestant leaped into the fray. Someone joined the trio in order to even things out. Then a tankard was hurled into the crowd, and a general melee commenced. At the height of the brawl, several people managed to escape the devastation. Beside a stray Hindi or two and a Phonecian gambler, the three Ægyptians who had wandered in left the tavern the same way, but with more energy than when they had entered. Anybody keeping track of the wizard-priest would not have wondered why he didn't leave when his countrymen did. Somehow the tall man had become embroiled in the fighting and was seen only occasionally in the sprawl, a shaven head here, a lean, coppery arm there. In fact, three hard-eyed men were watching Inhetep as he brawled. Naturally, they paid no attention to those who left hurriedly.

Outside, the three Ægyptians ran off toward their own quarter as fast as they could. There was no telling when the watch would arrive to break up the melee and arrest all they could lay their hands on. The cost of damages and the fines would certainly pauper a working man! It was no more than a half-dozen blocks to the part of Londun where the former folk of Pharaoh dwelled. Actual distance was difficult to measure in the slant and twist of street and alley. Halfway there, the men slowed to a brisk walk, breath steaming in the chill air. Only then did they feel safe in laughing and jesting about the whole affair. They headed directly for their own favorite drinking establishment, the Fattened Goose. "Where's Buhor?" one of them asked when they arrived. The second man shrugged. "Who can say? Perhaps he decided to go home—he hardly said a word after we left that stupid Hindi tavern." The first Ægyptian was about to go back into the street despite the cold and look for his friend, but then he saw a pair of sisters he knew. "Too bad for him," he said to his companion, pointing toward the women and winking.

Buhor was eventually dragged unconscious from the Golden Shiva. He had no idea how he

had become involved in the fighting, swearing
to the local magistrate that he could remember
nothing except talking and drinking with
friends. Unimpressed, the judge fined him heavily, and Buhor would have ended up in the work-
house had not some unknown benefactor paid
over the whole sum on his behalf. Meanwhile,
however, the three Albish men fared better—and
worse. The police were quick to defer to them
when one of their number presented certain cre-
dentials. "Search for a tall Ægyptian," that one
told the lieutenant in charge of the watchmen.
"He's easily spotted—shaven pate, hawk nose,
and green eyes. His name is Inhetep, Setne Inhetep, and he's wanted for questioning by the
Royal Palace." No trace of the wanted man
could be found, however, so soon thereafter the
three hard-eyed men had to report back to their
superior empty-handed. Nobody ever saw them
again.

The day after the disturbance in the Golden
Shiva, a mob attacked the Ægyptian district.
The Bow Street Runners found answers for the
Lord Mayor. It seemed that they were whipped
into a frenzy in secret cult meetings. Something to do with an Eastern god called Set-
Anubis and a traitor. A lot of silver and gold
was involved—the mob had been showered
with silver coins to encourage them to find and
kill the traitor. Gold was promised them if
they succeeded. Before further investigation

could proceed, however, the proceedings came
to a halt.

Word arrived from the citadel. The Royal
Chamberlain, Sir Chauncey, had been found
murdered. Beside him was a statuette of the
Ægyptian deity, the one with a black jackal's
head, Anubis. There had been a warning, too.
The Lord Mayor was charged with finding the
culprit, and one Magister Setne Inhetep was the
chief suspect. The Runners were in the right
district, so they simply switched from seeking
the cause of the riot to looking for the wanted
man.

For a week thereafter, all of Londun was
buzzing with the story. Broadsides reported
the tale in lurid and fanciful detail. The fol-
lowers of the underground cult of Set disappeared. There were massive searches in the
whole foreign quarter, and virtually every
Ægyptian, or foreign male over average height
for that matter, was hauled into one station or
another for scrutiny and questioning. The initial furor settled, but there were still whispers
of the strange business. Rumors persisted that
the whole matter was a plot by rebels and foreigners to overthrow the king and the Kelltic
gods, too. There was a good deal of indignation
among the good people of the city. All foreigners found it necessary to keep a very low profile. Those who went abroad made a point of

visiting local temples to pay their respects to the established pantheon of Albion. But no trace was found of the ur-kheri-heb, the Ægyptian wizard-priest named Setne Inhetep.

10

SETNE THE BLOODHOUND

Camelough stood on the high ground and even higher bluffs of the eastern shores of Lake Lhiannan. The big lake was fed in part by the waters of the River Newid, a deep and lovely stream navigable by boat and barge for several leagues above the city, and for miles and miles beyond that by smaller craft. A number of villages lined the banks of the Newid, appearing amid fields and woods almost as if part of nature's growth. These charming little settlements were the homes of local farmers and tradesmen, as well as those of a few gentry and even nobles from Camelough whose summer residences lay in one or another of the riverside hamlets. Thus, among the thatched cottages and narrow buildings could be seen stately houses with high walls protecting them, little castles on the shore, or moated villas. The size and construction depended upon the status of its owner and the size of his or her purse. Because of the mild climate of Lyonnesse, activity continued in these residences even during the depth of winter; some of the aristocrats rusticated over the Sunsebb holidays in their country estates, for the local shire knights and prosperous merchants were renowned for their wassails and festivities during the merry season.

Mild or not, the trip up the River Newid in an open boat was a cold one, with damp wind to accompany the chill night air. "How much further?" Setne demanded of the two broad-shouldered men pulling on opposite oars of his hired gig.

"At least 'nuther 'our, yer worship," the man at the tiller answered. He did so because the two rowers needed all of their breath to maintain the fast pace dictated by this strange man who had engaged them to row upstream in the middle of the night. "Wind's foul, ya see, an' the boys'll be needin' ta take a rest soon," he added.

"Never mind slacking off," the Ægyptian snapped. "You can change off with each other and get some respite that way. If you manage to get me to my destination before midnight, I'll give you each a pair of silver drakes."

Their destination was a collection of buildings and villas called Glaistig Pool. "Must be one hellsapoppin' carouse yer awaitin' ta gets ta," the helmsman cried loudly, so as to be heard above the wind and splash of water. His long-haired passenger merely grunted and jingled the coins. "Alright," the riverman growled, "we'll be swappin' duty on 'em oars. 'Ave yer coin all nice an' ready like.''

Inhetep wore a wig, of course. It was a common enough thing in his own country, and in past centuries such attire had been social convention even in Lyonnesse. These days, however, nobody knew of them—at least not commonly, and the three men working the boat were certainly common. Had the wizard-priest appeared with shaven pate, one of them might have connected Setne to the Ægyptian wanted by the crown officials. But none of them knew as they labored against the stiff breeze and strong current. When they rounded the bend near the villa Setne was seeking, he asked the men to put him ashore where a huge old willow tree jutted out over the dark water of the river.

" 'E's got eyes like a owl," one of the rowers hissed to his mate, for only after a minute of hard pulling did he see the tree the Ægyptian had described. The captain informed Inhetep, "Yer 'bout a mile from the dock o' Glaistig Pool, yer are."

"This will do fine, boatman," Setne said firmly. "My dear cousin's lodge is but a few rods away from this spot." There was a dwelling about a bowshot's distance, but it was neither the habitation of any of Setne's kin nor his actual destination. The less these men knew the better. As the skiff thumped against the bank, Setne carefully handed each man the promised payment, two sil-

ver drakes. Then from a small shoulderbag he
drew forth a squarish pottery bottle. "Here, my
good fellows. Something extra for your hard and
long efforts on a cold night. It's Hybernian whiskey, fine old single malt and full of warmth.
Drink a tot for me on your way home!"

"That we will, yer worship. Ta yer 'ealth!"
the boatman added, as he unstoppered the bottle
and took a good swig. "Aaarr, now 'ats whiskey!"

Inhetep watched as the gig and the three riv-
ermen disappeared back into the mists. The
whiskey was excellent Hybernian, all right, but
it was also dweomered so as to make one's memory a bit fuzzy. In a day, not one of the three
would remember the trip or the passenger they
had had in their skiff. Not unless they drank
only a little of the stuff, and knowing men such
as the river boatmen were, Setne was sure that
the whole quart would be gone long before they
made Camelough, ten miles down the Newid. He
gave a secret smile and turned to face the land.

Inhetep hadn't stayed in Londun after the day
of the riot near Limehouse. His being followed,
the mob, and then the murder of the Chamberlain told a plain story: the Master of Jackals was
intent on eliminating his opponent, and the
criminal would stop at nothing until the magister was dead, or at least held fast in some deep
dungeon where he couldn't interfere with what
the Master Jackal intended. First had been the
suspicion and assassination attempted in Cam-

elough, leading to Setne's being a wanted man in all Lyonnesse. Relatively minor attempts on his life followed. Then came the matter in Londun and the posting of a reward there for him as a suspect in treasonous matters, rioting, and the killing of a crown officer. It was too late for the mastermind behind the plot to do anything about his successful visits to the other three kingdoms of Avillonia—Cymru, Hybernia, and Caledonia. Setne knew that there would be similar warrants on his person in those realms, though, for the Master of Jackals was a thorough and bitter enemy. "We shall see who hounds who, Jackal," he hissed under his breath as he recalled the events. Then the tall Ægyptian strode into the darkness of a grove of trees, heading toward a walled castle-manor on the riverbank about a half-mile distant upstream.

The fact that there were so few clues and no trails to follow in the extortion and murders made no more difference to Inhetep than the fact that he had no path to walk along in reaching the building for which he was headed. "Perhaps the final goal isn't as apparent," he said aloud as he stepped over a fallen limb about halfway to the tall building protected by its high walls. "But I am sure who will serve as guide to that desired place." At the edge of the copse he stopped, staying well back in the shadows of the leafless trees, hardwoods which had all shed their greenery in the frosts of the autumn gone.

The high walls formed a right angle to the main building and a lower wing, so that inside there was a courtyard—and garden, too, probably of considerable extent. The curtain of stone was only about twenty feet high, with an octagonal tower at its corner. The squat construction was about ten feet taller than the wall itself, and a dim light showed from its upper portion, a lantern's glow from the arrow slits. Inhetep watched the tower for a few minutes. A yellow light washed out for a moment. Someone had emerged from inside. A dark form moved along a parapet inside the place, head and shoulders just discernable between the crenellations of the battlement. Despite its looks, the fortified manor was a functional stronghold. The sentries were obviously not particularly alert, taking time to warm themselves instead of continually pacing their posts, but that was typical of any such place not under threat of attack. The owner and guests holding their revel inside the great hall were not expecting unfriendly visitors. Yet if the sentries were slack, there were probably less fallible alarms protecting the manor.

It was necessary to approach the chateau more closely in order to discover what castings were in place to ward it from intruders. The wizard-priest stole forth as silently as a shadow. A quarter moon was shining, but scattered clouds alternately made the landscape dark then light as they crossed the night sky. Setne moved with the darkness, so that when the soft moonlight again illuminated the open ground around the dwelling, he was cloaked in the shadow of the tower. From there the copper-skinned Ægyptian used his special senses and a charm to find what magick guarded the walls and gate.

The weaving was so subtle that even Inhetep almost missed reading the castings aright. The protections were not the forthright sort of priest-cræft nor the bold sort typical of dweomercræft. The magicks woven through stone and wood and all around were a net so clever that most prospective intruders would view them as but weak wards easily avoided or removed by counter-spell. Energies were drawn in parallel, castings set so as to enwrap and at the same time support one another in a vertical manner. Dispel one, and those above and below would react. Then the varied horizontal forces could not be passed through without undesirable consequences. No negation would disarm these protections.

"I am not surprised," Inhetep thought to himself "Alarms, voices, quasi-spirits and goblin guards, spun into a web of deadly traps and killing magick too. Each is so laid as to be in harmonic sympathy with the other. Dissonance or discord will come if even the least is disturbed, but there is an answer . . ." And as that crossed his mind. Setne took from his girdle a little ivory tube wrapped with a filigree of silver, a minia-

ture flute, and began to play upon it. There was
no sound, at least as far as human ears could
hear. Yet there were notes, a melody of ever-
increasing complexity. A discernable darkness
grew before him. Had the sentries been able to
view it, they would have seen something like a
spot of pewter-gray appear on the stone wall.
The circle grew ae1from coin-size to the diameter
of a saucer, a platter, a targ, then a great round
shield. Still Setne played soundlessly. The
lightless circle was now nearly as tall as the
Ægyptian. Fingers moving rhythmically on the
tiny instrument, Inhetep paced slowly ahead.
Dogs began to bark and howl inside the little
fortress. Setne ignored them. He went into the
grayness, but it was no longer stone; it was
space. As he stepped slowly into the enchanted
nothingness, a faint fire sprang from his head and
shoulders, running along arms, body, and legs, so
that it appeared he was burning with a violet
blaze. After but a few paces, however, the little
lilac tongues of flame shrank, sparkled, and died
in a coruscation of deep purple motes as they
shot off into the sooty nothingness. With a last,
inaudible trill, Inhetep stepped through the solid
stone wall into the courtyard and ceased playing
the ivory instrument.

He was standing amid several flowering
shrubs, which screened the harsh rock surrounding the hall. The dogs ceased their yowling
the moment the wizard-priest stopped playing

the flute, but the sergeant-at-arms had already appeared in the yard with a handful of guards. They had torches and were armed.

"Corporal of the guard!" the officer called loudly. Setne crouched in the shrubbery made magickally green and blooming for the festivities. Light from the tower's open door spilled into the courtyard and over the greenish witch-lights set at intervals along the buildings. "Is all well?"

The soldier in charge of the watch cried out for his sentries to report. "East wall. All's quiet!" came a voice. "South wall," shouted another gruff voice, "and it's as dead as a blarsted graveyard . . . sar!"

"You get yer arse outta that tower, Clouter, an' makes double sartin that nuffin' disturbs the lords inside this evenin', 'ear me?"

The guardsman was irritated but didn't dare argue. "Them damned dogs was jes' tryin' ta sing along wi' the band playin' from inside, Sarge, but ol' Clouter'll stay sharp the res' of the night if it'll makes ya happy."

"Happy my arse, ya lazy blarster. I'll be back in a 'our ta check!" Sergeant and guards stamped around a little, giving a hasty and mostly cursory inspection of the area, then returned to the warmth and revelry of the main building.

Inhetep remained absolutely still. The corporal was standing almost directly above where he hid, and the man was peering down. Then Setne heard the sound of splattering about a yard away. It's a lucky thing you're not relieving your bladder on me, the wizard-priest thought darkly as the corporal finished urinating. Then the guard walked off, and Inhetep glided from the bushes and across the yard to the lower wing of the villa. Neither spell nor lock were set to prevent entry here inside the walls. The door opened at his touch, and Setne entered a dark, narrow hallway. It turned right, and a door to the left certainly led into the barn area where horses and carriages were kept and feed stored. This was the servants' wing, and it was virtually deserted now because of the revel in the great hall. All staff were busy caring for master and guests. At the end of the corridor, Setne selected a door at random and entered.

In the small room, evidently one belonging to an important servant, the wizard-priest discarded his dark, woolen cloak and high boots. He hung them on one of several empty pegs on the wall rack. Beside them he placed his wig. He was now clad in only his Ægyptian garments, but these were rich and decorated with gold and glittering gems as befitted one attending a noble feast. Instead of sandals, Setne drew on a pair of low, slightly pointed buskins, almost slipper-like in their lightness and flexibility. He rubbed his hands together in anticipation. "Now let the fun begin!" he exclaimed aloud. "No more hare to chivvy from thicket to thicket." He pulled the door open again and reentered the hallway. "In-hetep is now the hound who will be nipping the jackals here...." So saying, the tall man left the low wing and entered the main building.

The place was a mansion. Thick beams supported high ceilings. Polished hardwood floors and wainscoted walls were glowing under soft, dweomered lights that resembled the warm illumination of wax tapers. A servitor came hurrying around the corner. "I ... you ... is there ...?" the pretty little maid stammered, obviously flustered by the bald-headed, copper-skinned stranger, who was dressed as a noble. "Yes," Setne told the lass. "You may disregard whatever instructions you have previously received. I desire that you convey me immediately to the usher—there *is* an usher, I trust."

Now the girl was truly puzzled, but she had no thought of anything other than complying with Inhetep's command. "Oh yes, m'lord, there is most certainly an usher—Master Medwyn by name, m'lord. Do you wish to go through the grand salon? Or will you prefer a more discrete route?"

That made the Ægyptian smile. This was a highly perceptive and intelligent servant. "By all means, lass," he replied, "let's use the more quiet way, for what I have to say to Master Medwyn is most confidential—a sort of special surprise for your great lord, as it were." The girl nodded and led Setne through several small servant's passages and into the foyer of the main hall. There were two tall doors, closed, from behind which came the sounds of the wassail— music, loud voices, laughter. Before these portals stood a liveried man whose sash and gold chain bespoke his position as an officer of the staff, to whit, the usher. Inhetep waved the lass away, stepping quickly to the man on duty at the doors before he could ask anything of her.

"Please be so good as to announce Magister Setne Inhetep to His Lordship the Gwyddorr and the other guests within, Master Medwyn," the wizard-priest said smoothly. His tone was firm and irresistible. The usher had no thought of anything other than immediate compliance. He bowed, opened the two doors, and stepped into the massive room beyond.

Thump, thump! sounded above the party as the fellow used his staff to draw attention to his proud performance of office. The noise dropped off as eyes turned towards the entrance. A guest at midnight was most unusual indeed. "The August Magister Setne Inhetep!" Master Medwyn cried, embellishing Setne's style as was the wont of such functionaries. He began a sweeping bow but stopped short as gasps rose from the assemblage of revelers in the salon.

"No need for all that," the Ægyptian murmured in the general direction of the startled usher as Setne strode into the great hall and faced the two-score folk staring at him. "What?

Is a poor ur-kheri-heb of Thoth so important as to create an interruption in the festivities? Nay, nay, dear people! Please go back to your revelry, for I have come only to speak a word or two with your host; then, I fear, I will have to hurry off."

A babble arose from the guests. Someone shouted, "The very devil himself!" and a dozen guards leaped from their positions of attention around the chamber and rushed toward Inhetep, who stood unmoving. He folded his arms and smiled more broadly still into the confusion.

11

HIDE AND SEEK

Two of the soldiers were ready to drive their broad-bladed spontoons at Inhetep's chest even as another pair were approaching fast to reinforce that attack. From somewhere above, someplace hidden by pillar and drapery and decorative work, a pair of arrows zipped down to pierce the Ægyptian just as the spearpoints would. Their target was unmoving, a small crook held in one hand, the other crossed with a flail as if in imitation of some Pharaoh. Just as the steel tongues of spear and arrowhead were about to strike home, however, Setne's arms uncrossed. The spontoons were caught by the crook and swept aside as if they were straws, even as the many little tails of the sweeping flail brushed aside the speeding shafts as mere flies would be swept from their course by such an instrument. "Come, come, Aldriss! Haven't you instructed your guardsmen better than this? Surely they need know that such as they can do no harm to a real kheri-heb!"

Every guest in the hall was silent at those

words. The bard arose from his high-backed chair at the head of the banquet table. His aqua-blue and emerald-green velvet robe, all embroidered with silver-thread trim to betoken his station as the Great Bard of Lyonnesse, rippled and glittered as he moved. "You dare!" Aldriss roared. Yet his face was paler than normal, and there was a faint tremor in his voice.

"You mean to ask how I managed to pass through your enmeshing magicks, I think," the wizard-priest said as he walked slowly down to where the bard stood. Celebrants flinched and shied from the Ægyptian's approach—some because they thought him a vile assassin and plotter against their kingdom, others for reasons less pure.

"STOP!" The command seemed to thunder through the hall with unnatural force and clarity. The bewildered soldiers froze in their tracks, and the revelers likewise ceased their attempts to get clear of the coming confrontation. The snow-clad figure of Tallesian stepped from behind a thick column and cried, "I believe I had better deal with the murderous Ægyptian!" At that, guards and gentry alike unfroze and began fleeing frantically. The bard remained standing where he was, and for some reason the six musicians nearby likewise stayed put.

Inhetep, too, was motionless. He watched as Aldriss gave a small sign and the players began to perform, viele, harp, lute and the rest striking up a soft but moving air. From where he stood, Inhetep could see both of his antagonists. "This is a useless charade, druid," he said tonelessly as the fellow began to slide sideways, the first small motions of a conjuration evident in the movements of Tallesian's fingers and hands. "You, too, Aldriss the Gwyddorr. I have come for your prisoner. Free Rachelle now, and I will not be hard on you."

A radiance as bright as the white of the druid's gown appeared as a halo above Tallesian's head. It brightened into a silver intensity, then suddenly became ebon. The nebulous blotch then spat forth jagged bolts of electrical energy. Each was only as long as a man, no thicker than a spear shaft, but where their argent tips touched, stone blackened and broke, oak burst into blue-flamed incandescence. These flashing darts of deadly electricity flew from above Tallesian's head as fast as a man might snap his fingers. They rained upon the wizard-priest like a hail-storm. "Feel the fury of Dagda!" the druid cried, directing more and more of the lightning bolts upon the motionless Ægyptian.

Setne was ablaze, only it was not Setne. Where the wizard-priest had stood was a tall bennu, the phoenix-like bird whose very essence was lightning. The creature's beak darted here and there as a great heron might spear fish. The bright bolts of energy were as fish to the bennu, and the bennu was Inhetep. Then it ceased devouring the lightnings and flapped its rainbow-bright pinions. The sudden gust of air drove Tallesian back, his snowy gown whipping wildly about his body, then the druid fell. Almost simultaneously, the long-billed head turned, and the bennu spat back the stuff it had devoured. One bolt shattered the shalms and laid low the man who had been playing them, another sent the viele into ruin along with its musician. Four more in such rapid succession that the eye could not follow, and no more orchestra played to the bard's behest. Then the bennu again became Magister Setne Inhetep. "Did you think that I was so dull as to ignore the heka you would evoke with your musical henchmen there?"

The demand fell on deaf ears, for Aldriss was seeking desperately to bring forth alone the magick he had hoped to work through his band of chanters, those journeymen nearly bards themselves. They had seemed naught but minstrels to the party-goers, but it was evident that the Ægyptian had recognized them for what they were. Aldriss' tenor voice rose strong and sweet in a call for supernatural prowess even as he picked out accompanying chords on the little harp he had grabbed from his table. Suddenly the instrument felt cold and unnatural in his hands. Aldriss looked down and shrieked, for the harp had turned into a cobra, weaving and spreading its hood just above where he grasped it. The bard flung the reptile away and yelled, "May you rot in cold darkness, Ægyptian!"

Setne easily avoided the flying cobra. As if to further demoralize the Kelltic spell-weaver, the snake turned into a musical instrument again as it sailed through the air, and smashed to flinders against a stone column. "I would have no uræus treated so," the magister said mockingly to the unbelieving Aldriss. "Now lead me to where you have her held captive." The deadly threat was heavy in his tone.

"Never!" the bard snarled in reply, and with that he sat roughly in the chair behind him. When he struck it, the tall seat toppled over backwards against a curtain, and Aldriss was lost in a swirl of drapery and the overturned chair.

A quick glance showed the wizard-priest that Tallesian was still unmoving on the floor. He must have struck his head severely, for he now lay unconscious, allowing Setne to devote his entire attention to the fleeing Aldriss. Naturally the cowardly man wouldn't run far—not until he felt safe to do so. That meant the bard would head straight to Rachelle to take her hostage. Inhetep ran to the table and bounded over it, long legs showing coppery in the process, flowing kilt and short cape streaming behind as if he flew. Wrenching aside the thick curtain, Setne saw an alcove with three doors in its walls. A glance upward revealed a trapdoor overhead, and beneath his feet was yet a fifth means of egress. A concealed exit could be found quickly, but the chance of guessing correctly was not so likely. Each false way would be riddled with traps to slay the unwelcome pursuer, and even the correct passage would be guarded by deadly mechanisms.

Setne knew that sorcerers preferred the depths while most others sought height as a means of security. To the right the passage must eventually lead to warrens amid the interior walls of the manor, while the left-hand door would take one to the outer wall and whatever secret corridors existed there. The one straight ahead could lead up, down, or to a hidden chamber. There was a smudge of heat evident to Setne's heka-enhanced eyesight on that last portal, so he shoved it open and ducked into the low space beyond. A slight creak warned him, and he pulled back just in time as a weighted timber dropped down halfway to the floor. A skull could be crushed, a spine smashed by the force of its fall. Scrambling on all fours to pass under it, the wizard-priest entered a small secret room some eight feet wide and a little deeper. "How clever of you," he said aloud upon seeing the place, for in it were five more exits—two flights of stairs down, two going up, and a door straight ahead. "The telltale of your passage makes the multiplicity of choices useless when one can see body heat," the hawk-faced man cried aloud as he bounded up the leftmost stairway.

When the sound of Setne's running feet faded, another noise could be heard. Muffled thuds and stifled cries drifted from a portion of the wall along the passage the wizard-priest had just fled. A panel slid sideways. Aldriss stepped out of the cell which the open panel revealed with his captive, bound and gagged. Rachelle struggled, trying her best to give cries of warning through the cloth. "You be silent, bitch!" the bard hissed, "Or else I'll slit your throat here and now!" Rachelle ceased her noise. Should Aldriss fulfill his threat, she knew that Inhetep would be so struck by the sight of her corpse that his enemy could smite him with heka, perhaps mortally, as shock slowed the Ægyptian's reflexes. "Better," Aldriss said through clenched teeth. "Now move those pretty legs of yours quickly—run! I want us back in the salon where we'll set our ambush for your master." He gave her a shove, which nearly sent Rachelle sprawling on her face. The force of the bard's strong arm propelled her into the little passage, where she rebounded from the far corner and along the narrow corridor toward the salon as if she were a ball bouncing.

"Bravo!"

The cry made Aldriss start and jerk his head to the right. His worst fears were confirmed. The green eyes and sharp smile of the shaven-headed Ægyptian shone from the top of the steps. "You!" the bard gasped.

"That's right, bard, me. Did you really think

you could fool me with this child's maze?" He was laughing, but there was menace, not mirth, in Inhetep's voice. "I let you think me off on a goose-chase, so you would release Rachelle and come into the open. Your early cooperation in separating yourself from her was an unexpected but most welcome blunder. I had thought you would be more careful, and I would have to risk myself in a more close quarters situation."

Aldriss allowed the man to rattle on as his fingers found an acorn he had sequestered in his garment. The nut was charged with preternatural energy. The bard hurled it as hard as he could, slamming it into the stairs at Inhetep's feet. Aldriss shouted as the acorn burst and a shower of blazing sparks and thick smoke instantly screened the priest-mage from his view. With the sulfurous cloud obscuring his movements, the man dived down the passage into which he had pushed Rachelle, rolling and regaining his feet in a smooth motion. Perhaps the missile's magickal explosion and choking fumes would do scant harm to the accursed Ægyptian, but it gave Aldriss time to grab the amazon and use her body as a shield. His fellow conspirators could handle the wizard-priest once and for all.

But even as the last of the blazing tongues of flame were dying, Inhetep was in action. He didn't dare to send a counter-blast down the narrow passage after Aldriss, for Rachelle might still be in the corridor. Instead, Setne leaped down the steps and followed the fleeing Kellt. As soon as he entered the passage, the wizard-priest crouched so as to present as small a target as possible, traveling almost like an ape on all fours.

The bard was setting himself up to work great mischief on his pursuer, but he hadn't reckoned with Rachelle. When the girl saw Aldriss with his back to her, obviously readying to use some magick against Inhetep, she flung herself upon the man. She struck Aldriss behind the knees, and the man fell forward with a thud. At almost the same moment, Setne emerged from the passage into the salon.

"Nice work, my dear child!" he exclaimed as the girl struggled to rise from the tangle of the fallen bard's legs. "Here, I'll get you shed of those damned ropes," he murmured, pulling Rachelle upright. He used the knife from his broad girdle to cut the bonds from her wrists.

"Hmmmh, mmmth!" she said, wild-eyed and panting.

"Yes, of course," Setne said with a slight grin. "It was merely a matter of priorities. . . . He severed the heavy cloth strip holding the gag in place.

"Setne! I was beginning to wonder if you'd ever show up and get—" Rachelle cut off her words when she saw that the fallen bard had suddenly changed into a monstrous bear.

As the amazon looked frantically around for

some weapon, Inhetep used his little wand to good effect. Aldriss had arisen, his bear-form a towering threat of claws and huge fangs about to sweep priest and warrior into its deadly hug. Setne was suddenly a thing of spines, a ball-like hedgehog with quills two feet long. The bear's paws swept out heedlessly. There came a snapping as of dry twigs and rattling of spines. The blow knocked Inhetep some distance away. At the same time, there was a roar from the bruin; the striking paws were now pierced, each looking like a pin cushion thrust through and through with the barbed spines. The injured, bloody bear paws beat the air as Aldriss-bruin vented his fury and pain. Then the form shimmered, and instead of a brown bear there was a pit viper whose body was as thick as a man's thigh and whose length was greater than two tall men.

"Very wise, bard," Inhetep cried. "The serpent has no extremities to remain pierced by quills. I give you credit for your cleverness." The wizard-priest had himself returned to human form, his garments torn and stained by a splotch of red where the claws had done damage. He seemed little harmed, though, and even as the giant viper coiled to strike, Setne was busy with his own magick. Perhaps the sudden transformation would have given Aldriss the edge he sought, but the bard reckoned without Rachelle again. The girl saw the serpent readying to strike, and this time she flung a chair at Aldriss.

The missile didn't harm the viper, but the impact caused the deadly strike to miss its target by a fair margin. "Thanks!" Inhetep called to Rachelle, and then the magister became a huge, thick-scaled lizard whose long jaws sported scores of small, needle-sharp teeth. It was just the sort of reptile made to dine on poisonous snakes the size of Aldriss the Great Bard of Lyonnesse.

Of course, that left little choice. As Aldriss shed his viper-form, the coils sprouted feathers. In another instant, a huge marsh hawk stood where the serpent had been. "Keeaah!" the raptor shrieked in triumph as its wings beat the air. Aldriss was obviously going to fly from the contest now, content with escape, victory forgotten.

As the hawk rose so did an equally huge eagle owl, for Inhetep too had altered form to counter the bard's tactic. The two fierce birds met in the air, and with a storm of flying feathers, fought and fell to the floor. As the two struck, they changed again, Aldriss and Inhetep throttling each other.

"Enough!" The word of command came from Rachelle's throat as she held a sword to the bard's neck. Aldriss stopped his struggle.

"Now I recall just why I went to so much trouble to rescue you," Inhetep remarked as he arose and straightened his garments. "Admirable work, girl!"

Aldriss lay unmoving, glaring up at Rachelle and the tall Ægyptian with equal hatred. "Shall I finish this foul and treacherous kidnapper now?" The warrior woman put a little more pressure on the steel so that the blade's edge just barely cut Aldriss' skin.

"Great gods, no," Inhetep said with feigned shock, as if he thought Rachelle was actually about to sever the man's neck. "Master Aldriss will surely have a lot to say to us now, and I believe that his words will buy his life. Do spare it until we find out if my prediction is correct, Rachelle." The wizard-priest looked down mildly at the pale-faced bard. "You do have some things to tell me about, don't you, Gwyddorr?"

The girl held the brand hard against the bard's neck, but Aldriss was no coward. "You may rot in your foreign hell, Inhetep, before I say any-thing to you."

"Tch. I am shocked," Setne responded. "Yet I believe you will certainly admit that you are the one who kidnapped Rachelle, won't you?"

"She came with me of her own accord," the man snapped back. "I merely held her here after she had willingly come."

"He speaks but a half truth, Setne," the ama-zon said hotly. "He called on me that evening after the revel and said you had sent him to get me and bring me to where you waited."

"And you went like a lamb? Rachelle! Why didn't you heed the warning?!"

The girl looked puzzled, and so for that matter did Aldriss. "You warned her about me? How in—" He bit his query off short.

"That's right, Master Great Bard and murderous plotter, I did just that. But why did you ignore the caution, dear girl?"

"Well, I . . . I didn't get the warning," Rachelle admitted.

"Of course you did," Inhetep countered. "I placed it in the note I left for you about my not going to the festivities at the castle. Down the left-hand margin, as clearly as anything, I told you 'B E W A R E A L D R etc'."

"Oh." The pretty mouth was hesitant. Before she had opportunity to explain that, in her haste and anger at the wizard-priest, she had failed to pay attention to his note, Aldriss spoke.

"You are a filthy Eastern dog, Inhetep!" the bard spat. "I said from the first that you would be trouble!"

"Really?" Setne said mockingly. "And just who was it you said that to?"

"No matter to you, burn-skin, and your doxy either, for that matter. You'll find out soon enough, and then it will be too late!"

"Doxy!" Rachelle cried with fire in her dark eyes. "And you, doing your utmost to get me into bed, putting your hands all over me when I was tied and helpless! You . . . you . . . Now I'll show *you* what it's like to have unwanted attention when there's nothing to be done to prevent it." Her arm tensed, grip tightening on the sword.

"Easy, Rachelle," Inhetep cautioned. "Aldriss is going to explain just who he was warning about me—aren't you bard?" There was stoniness in the Ægyptian's eyes as he spoke.

If the Kellt saw danger in those emerald-hard eyes, he was either very brave or very foolish— or both, for he ignored the look. "Both of you are now as good as dead," Aldriss spat. "Think you that the Master of Jackals would let two petty ones such as yourselves upset his plans? Never!" There was such conviction in Aldriss's voice that a chill went flashing up Rachelle's spine. Even Inhetep drew back a little. "You are doomed now!" the bard cried, one arm shooting suddenly up and pointing.

Perhaps it was the oldest trick in the book, but Rachelle grabbed Setne and the two of them went sprawling away from where Aldriss pointed. This allowed their prisoner to regain his feet and mount a new attack.

"Fallen foes abandon action," Aldriss sang even as he stood upright. "Helpless, hopeless, stifling sanction. Fearful, frozen, pitifully palsied; Laid low, the fallen foe!" The last couplet completed his quatrain and bore the ring of the bard's triumph as he voiced the strain of the cantrip. Its power was slow to come, but the initial singing had sufficient effect to give Aldriss the chance he needed. Suggestion was strong, and the dweomer he spun by his lyrical chanting weighed down the two and made their movements ponderous and uncertain.

With grim satisfaction, the bard went on with his magickal singing. Setne seemed to be getting sloth-like, the long fingers of one coppery hand gradually disappearing inside his short jacket. "I ... reject ... your ... heka...." Inhetep was saying slowly as he fought to break the weight of the casting, which was enfolding them in its magick. He had just managed to grasp the energizing form of his golden ankh and had the amulet partially withdrawn from his garment as the bard finished the second quatrain.

Rachelle too was trying to break the power of Aldriss' singing by sheer will force. In truth, the amazon was moving more quickly than the ur-kheri-heb, rolling slightly away from the bard and about to come erect. The sword she had picked up was still in her hand, and Rachelle's arm was drawing back as if to hurl the blade at Aldriss.

"Useless!" the man shouted in triumph as he drew forth a figurine. "I call upon—" But that's as far as Aldriss got. Two red beams were issuing from the statuette when a Kelltic symbol of power manifested itself in the air directly before the unsuspecting bard. The bright fire of the wheel met the bloody rays. The spoked torus blazed and grew to twice its potency even as the deadly beams rebounded and struck the bard full in the face. Aldriss uttered a horrified cry that turned into an awful, rising shriek of agony, then his head exploded, and the fire of the raging magickal sign roared out and consumed him utterly.

12

MISTAKE

"Are you two all right?" It was Tallesian's voice.

"But I thought . . ." Rachelle began. Inhetep's touch caused the warrior girl's words to fade.

"We are well enough, thank you, but what did you do to Aldriss, druid?" The question had a sharp edge, and Setne's hawk nose seemed aimed at the man.

"Good—excellent! I feared the worst there for a second," Tallesian said with some heartiness and warmth. "I'd have acted far sooner, I assure you, Magister, save for doubt."

"Doubt?"

"Well, to be forthright, sir, I thought you a most dire enemy." He looked squarely at Inhetep. "When you came strutting into the festivities here, I was set to do my best to lay you by the heels. You knocked me down, stunned me in the process, too, I might add." Tallesian made a wry face and rubbed the back of his head, flinching a little from his own hand. "Quite a goose-egg there. Anyway, when I finally came round and managed to figure out what was going on, I saw you, and your amazon companion with a sword at Aldriss' throat. For a second or two, it was a near thing—going to use the last resort against you rather than that blackguard, who was supposed to be the Gwyddorr and my peer, you know."

Inhetep raised a hand, and the druid looked at him inquiringly. "I do appreciate your explanation, Lord Tallesian, but something you said . . ."

"What was that?"

"You referred to a 'last resort,' I believe. By that do you mean the sigil of energy you sent at the bard?"

"None other," the man confirmed, nodding vigorously. "Not at all sure what happened to it, though. It went all wrong at the end and—"

"Never mind. I thought it rather strange, too, for the thing went from one grade of power to another and seemed a nonesuch. Do you suppose it was an interaction with whatever Aldriss was trying to use against Rachelle and me?"

"Unquestionably," Tallesian concurred.

Rachelle couldn't understand why the druid had come round so suddenly to their side. "You were here celebrating with him, and you have evidently favored the ones who dared accuse my lord Inhetep of some crime—and after you yourself induced him to this island, too!"

"Come to the point, please, dear girl," the Magister urged.

"What made you blast your countryman and peer?" she demanded of Tallesian.

"Why, he was the one responsible for all this—he was the Master of Jackals!"

"Was he?" Rachelle demanded. "I never heard him admit to anything like that."

Tallesian seemed a little flustered. "He most certainly was about to try to kill you both, and he as much as admitted that he was the mastermind behind all this terrible business when he said he wouldn't allow the pair of you to foil his plot!"

"He asked if we thought the Master of Jackals would allow Rachelle and me to interfere in the plan he was part of," Setne said forcefully, picking up from where his companion had left off. "He neither admitted to being the mastermind—boastfulness was something Aldriss was known for, too, I think—nor claimed he had spun the web. But he did mention warning others."

"Others? Did he now . . ." the druid said reflectively. "Wish I'd have overheard that bit better. No help for it now; the blighter has gone beyond even your questioning, Magister Inhetep. If you ask me, though, I'd say that with his death we've heard the last of the Master of Jackals!"

The tall Ægyptian gazed at the ash-strewn place where the energy of the magickal wheel of force had devoured Aldriss. "You are likely to be correct about that, druid, although I think I will try to learn what I can anyway."

"By all means, Magister, by all means. While

you and your assistant are checking on that, I believe I should settle things here," Tallesian said, walking back toward the hall. "Bound to be a frightful commotion after all this row. Important folk to reassure, guests to placate, rumors to squelch, and all manner of things to set straight."

"Such as Magister Inhetep's guiltlessness?" Rachelle called after the druid.

"That, too," he called back, and then he was off to find the staff and guests who had taken refuge when the battle began.

"You think that Aldriss was actually the Master Jackal?" Rachelle asked when Tallesian was gone.

"Hmmm . . ." the wizard-priest responded vaguely, without turning to look at her. He was stooped over the place where Aldriss had stood, palms outward, fingers spread as if to catch vibrations. His green eyes were fixed in an odd stare. "As I suspected."

"Suspected? You suspected Aldriss of being the Master of Jackals?!"

Inhetep turned then and looked at the lovely face framed in its disheveled mop of dark curls. "I can't recall you ever looking more beautiful, Rachelle," he said with a smile. "I trust you weren't despairing of rescue."

"Oh, Setne, I'm sorry!" She stepped up and hugged the smiling Ægyptian with sufficient force to drive the wind from him. "There!

That's to let you know how grateful I am. And no, silly old shave-pate priest, I never once thought you'd fail me."

"I never did, of course."

"I didn't accuse you of failing, let alone—"

"Never thought *Aldriss* was the leader of the pack of jackals, I mean," Inhetep interrupted. "Too bad he was so totally destroyed, obliterated by some raging flux of entitative origin so as to make it impossible to gain anything here."

"That sounds very like the circumstances of the murders we were trying to solve, Setne."

"Yes, Rachelle, my dear amazon warrior, yes it does." He was about to say more, but just then a number of servants began to straggle back into the salon, the more important ones immediately beginning to fuss and direct the lesser staff in the clearing, cleaning, and tidying. "Never mind now. Let's go and find the druid and see what he has in mind."

Rachelle shook her head. "You do as you wish, great wonder of the ages," she said acidly. "Perhaps *you* haven't noticed it, but I'm barely clothed, and it's chilly in this draughty old pile. And I'm tired and hungry, too!" Rachelle turned and began walking away. "I'm going to find some suitable attire, and then I'm going to sit in the most comfortable chair I can find and eat as much food as those lazy servitors have left lying about and will bring to me."

Setne had to laugh. He hadn't noticed that she

was clad only in very skimpy undergarments. Partially because of the pressure of the situation just past, partially due to having seen her often in the nude, Inhetep had been guilty of a gross error. Worse still, he hadn't inquired if she were in need of food and rest, assuming her to be the iron amazonian guard, forever ready for anything. "Again, my dear Rachelle, I find you all too correct. I believe you're now safe enough here, even half-dressed, as long as you flourish that sword a little should any varlets come too close." He chuckled again. Rachelle made a face at him, a familiar and reassuring act to Setne, and stalked off. Setne thought one of the female guests at the villa would soon have yet more to complain of regarding her visit to Aldriss's retreat when she discovered her clothing missing. He was about to go in search of the archdruid when Tallesian came back into the salon.

"There you are, Inhetep. Manage to learn anything?"

"Did you see Lady Rachelle?" Inhetep asked offhandedly.

"Well, yes, of course. She passed me in the main hall just a minute or so ago. Heading for the staircase and muttering something about a gown, I believe."

"Fine. After what's happened, I don't want her getting into trouble again," the wizard-priest said, as if explaining.

Tallesian's face drew into a long expression.

"Understandable, Magister. I queried you about another matter, though."

"Did you?"

"The bard . . ."

Inhetep had a bland easiness in his voice as he responded. "Ah, that's what you meant when you asked if I'd found out anything. Not much, I fear, good druid. So little, in fact, that all I can do is make a note of it and hope that something discovered later will fit—this whole business is very much like those interlocking-piece puzzles the purveyors of amusements are touting these days!"

"Yet you *did* get a clue?"

"I said so, yes. No sense in talking about that now. What's your own view of things, Lord Tallesian?"

The druid shook his head. "Like you, Magister Inhetep, I have too little knowledge at this point in time to hazard a guess—save to reaffirm my conviction that you two are absolutely blameless, and that Aldriss was up to his neck in treasonous killings and extortions."

"So what is our next step?"

"That is quite easy. A barge will be calling for us here in a few hours. It will carry us downstream to Camelough for our evening appointment with the Behon and his Royal Highness. I think that in the meantime I'll retire to my bedchamber and get a little rest."

"There is a capital idea!" Inhetep said with a

yawn. "Now that you mention it, I must admit I'm near exhaustion from the night's work. Would you be so kind as to find some officer of the house to prepare a bed for me and another for my assistant?"

Tallesian agreed readily. "Of course, sir. Perhaps we should actually delay the return to Camelough a bit under these conditions, eh?"

"As you wish, Lord Tallesian. After all, you are the royal official and we are but guests."

"Guests? Well, now, seeing that the chief culprit in the matter has been found and destroyed, perhaps *honored* guests might be better used to describe your position," the druid said jovially. "If you will excuse me now, I shall see about locating the proper servants for you and Lady Rachelle."

After some four hours of sleep—certainly not sufficient but enough to take the dull weight of exhaustion from his shoulders—a soft-footed valet awakened Inhetep. "His Venerable Lordship the Archdruid has asked for your presence below," the nondescript fellow murmured. He drew back the heavy draperies to allow morning sunlight into the bedroom on the second floor of the castellated mansion. "The Lady Rachelle?" Setne inquired sleepily. The servant told him that a maid-in-waiting was preparing her bath at the moment, so Inhetep lay back and luxuriated on the down mattress for a bit longer. The valet fussed about, drew a vast cauldron-like tub of steaming water, then departed, adding, "A meal will be served in a few minutes, m'lord."

After some stretching and grumbling, Setne arose and stalked stark naked to the alcove which contained the lavatory, glad that the Westerners had recently adopted indoor plumbing—at least the aristocratic ones. After shaving head and beard, Inhetep tested the water in the huge tub and found it had sufficiently cooled. He like neither hot nor cold baths. This was the temperature of his own pool in Ægypt on a warm day, a bit below body temperature. A quick immersion, lathering and shaving the rest of his body, and he was ready for the day. Wrapped in an enormous towel, Inhetep found his clothing and emptied its many little pockets and hidden places. Then he used a cantrip to clean and freshen the cloth. "Magick has its uses," he murmured with a smile as he observed the effect. Even laundresses and valets using similar little dweomers tended to ruin fine apparel with soap, water, scrubbing, and pressing; and recently developed fluids for cleaning were possibly worse when it came to dyes and metallic embroidery so necessary for special apparel. Inhetep seldom trusted his own apprentices with the care of his better garments, and this particular costume was one of his finest.

"Are you still preening, peacock?" Rachelle's voice gave Setne a start. The girl laughed.

"Humph. Very humorous, I'm sure," the man

grumbled. "Have you no manners? A lady must knock before entering a gentleman's chamber." He continued to admire his handiwork even as he scolded her. "In fact, I believe that here a lady shouldn't even enter a—"

"You look like a stork caught in someone's laundry." Rachelle exclaimed. "Storks shouldn't preen. Hurry along, slow one. And as you well know, I am no lady but your guard, so I needn't knock at all. As to being a *gentleman,* I believe it wisest to refrain from further discussion of that topic...."

"Bah! You impugn my noble birth? Well, never mind such foolishness," he said quickly when he saw the glitter in her eye. "You seem most invigorated by your short sleep, Rachelle. Youth is a most wonderful benison in such regard." Then, without so much as another glance in her direction, Setne stalked to where he had dropped his underclothing, uttered another minor casting to restore it to pristine condition, and proceeded to dress himself. "Have you managed to learn anything from the staff?"

Rachelle shook her head. "No. The lot of them are very close-mouthed this morning. Someone has certainly instructed them to keep silent."

"Perhaps they were instructed," Setne commented, "or perhaps they are merely subdued after the events of last night. After all, their master has not only been slain but also held as the chief culprit in matters of treason, murder, and extortion. While they haven't the real details, you can stake your life on the fact that the staff and servants have a better handle on matters than seems possible. Certainly the officers of Aldriss' household are well schooled in being silent, but the help are gossiping among themselves now as quickly as their tongues can manage."

The warrior girl paused. "But I thought you were suspicious as to . . . well, you know!"

"That was wise," Inhetep said as Rachelle bit off her words and instead used vague generalities. Whether through spy-hole or via magick, whatever the two of them said here might be overheard, and not until the time was ripe should what they actually knew be revealed. "I think my uneasiness about this case has been unfounded. It was seemingly a little too easy and pat, the business with the bard," Setne told her with a slight droop of an eyelid. "But everything points directly to Aldriss, and if the investigation actually uncovers his co-conspirators and their network of petty clerics and thugs, then I'd say that the problem of the Master of Jackals has been laid to rest."

"Oh," Rachelle said softly. "I stand corrected, lord. I will no longer seek other suspects."

The ur-kheri-heb shook his bald-shaven head. "Don't be so quick, dear cohort! I said if all of the rest of this treasonous lot are found and brought to justice. If there is the slightest hint of any cover-up, then we'll be certain that the mastermind behind the murder and plotting still lives!"

"Speaking of living," the girl said earnestly, "*I* shan't be able to much longer unless we have something to eat. I'm absolutely starved after my imprisonment here—the devil of a bard seemed disinclined to feed me!"

With that the two went down to a smallish room which was a little distant from the kitchens, guided there by the nervous-looking major domo. "The Venerable Archdruid awaits your pleasure in the Oak Dining Salon," he murmured as he directed them to the place. Tallesian was there. Having finished his own repast some time before, the druid sat and sipped a dark brew from a cup, awaiting the Ægyptian and his companion.

"Will you have food?"

"But of course," the magister responded, helping himself to a small, golden-crusted loaf and a pot of butter nearby. "Some of that coffee you drink, too, good druid, for I miss sorely that amenity here in the West."

"It is rare in Avillonia," Tallesian admitted. "If the Phonecians were less greedy in their profit-taking, perhaps the stuff would be more popular."

Inhetep and the druid began discussing trade and the costs of imports as Rachelle set to with the serious intent of eating everything available.

One day, perhaps, her appetite might catch up with her, but not as long as her physical activity and metabolism remained high. She ate twice what the wizard-priest consumed even when Setne was hungry, but Rachelle's form showed not a trace of excess weight. She ignored Inhetep's glare as she ate another plate of crisp bacon and scrambled ducks' eggs seasoned with bits of fresh herbs and a sprinkling of some local cheese. Finished at last, she sat back and smiled at her mentor. "That was a very nice little breakfast," she said sweetly.

"More a noon feast," Inhetep countered with a sarcastic tone. "Is the boat ready, Lord Tallesian?"

"The barge? But of course, and now we should be on our way. Lord Inhetep, Lady Rachelle, shall we depart?"

"Magister will suffice, sir," Setne said as he rose and headed for the door.

13

ROYAL SCOURGE

The journey back down the Newid took but a short time. There must have been a considerable rain upriver, for today the current was brown and strong. It carried them swiftly to Lake Lhiannan, and to Camelough on the western shore of the lake. The barge docked at a rather out of the way location, not at the royal piers near the citadel's massive Lakegate entrance, and a closed coach waited at the steps leading up from the landing place. A swarm of armed footmen saw all three into the carriage. Although they wore no insignia, it was easy to see that they were soldiers—the royal guardsmen, undoubtedly. Setne observed that they were escorted most cleverly. A half-dozen horsemen who might be nothing more remarkable than out-of-work mercenaries going for a ride about the city went well ahead of the coach, while only a handful of horsed attendants accompanied the conveyance, two before, two to the rear. The Ægyptian looked at Tallesian. "How many agents are stationed along our route?" he asked so softly that none save the three passengers could hear.

The druid raised an eyebrow and made a wry face. "No keeping anything from you, Magister Inhetep. It's a bit more than a mile to the citadel from here, and we have placed a hundred of our best men along the route—just to be certain, you know. It is most likely that Aldriss was the one commanding the pack of jackals, but . . ."

"Most judicious, my lord," Inhetep said. "Far better to be a trifle overprotective than to find oneself again out-foxed."

Five minutes later they rumbled under a stone arch and along a deep passage through the wall surrounding the palace complex. They entered a small and absolutely private courtyard reserved for the royal household and those special visitors who were not to be seen coming to the citadel. Steps were rapidly set in place beside the carriage, footmen opened the doors, and the three descended. A silent officer of the guard bowed to the druid, then to the two foreigners. Tallesian recognized the fellow with a curt nod in return, then said to Inhetep and Rachelle, "Please follow Captain McFlood. I must go to make my report personally, but I'll rejoin you two in a very short time."

Rachelle was clad in finery filched from the villa. Although she looked the part of a beautiful woman consort of an aristocrat, Setne knew that somewhere beneath her velvet and lace the amazon was armed with all manner of weapons. Rachelle was most distrustful of the Lyonnesse after their accusations against him. That was excellent, for the girl would be extra alert in all respects, and that was most needed now. "Here," the soldier informed them as they stepped into a secluded lounge. "Please allow me to get whatever you need for comfort."

"This is quite sufficient, Captain McFlood," Inhetep told the guardsman. "If we require anything during the course of our wait, I shall summon a servant."

"The bell pull is here, Magister Inhetep," the soldier said. Then he left the two alone, departing with a stiff, half bow.

"Stuffy martinet," Rachelle snapped. The guard officer hadn't so much as glanced at her. That was most unusual, for Rachelle was used to being stared at by soldiers, especially when she was dressed as she was.

"He was impressed, never fear," Setne said drily. "He was radiating it profusely, along with worry about his position if he so much as made a single mistake. Orders from above command especial attention and utmost respect for both of us."

"So they are trying to make amends now," Rachelle said with satisfaction. "After the shameful way they treated you, Setne, that is the very least these barbaric Westerners can do!"

Further discourse on that subject was cut

short by the arrival of the Behon and Crown Prince Llewyn.

"Again, as when we first met, Magister, Lady, please do not stand on formalities. This time, however, you may use my proper form of name and title when addressing me—Crown Prince Llewyn or Royal Highness," he said seriously. "In any event, our Chief Druid will join us in a moment, and then we can put this whole nasty business to rest once and for all."

Of course both Rachelle and Setne had risen when the heir apparent to the throne of Lyonnesse entered, and when he had finished speaking both sat quietly. "Thank you, Royal Highness," the girl said carefully. Inhetep cleared his throat and shifted a little, then spoke.

"It is evident from our reception, Crown Prince Llewyn, that you have removed official suspicion from the two of us." His gesture brought Rachelle into the statement to make the point clear. "Likewise, I assume that you agree with Lord Tallesian's assessment of the situation. Blame is squarely placed upon the dead bard, Lord Aldriss."

"He was a shame to the grand title of Great Bard!" The Behon had come into the room silently as Inhetep spoke. "Of course His Royal Highness now fully comprehends the situation, for Tallesian made the facts absolutely plain to us."

If the man's serving as a mouthpiece for him

bothered Prince Llewyn, he didn't so indicate; in fact, he displayed not the least annoyance. Instead, he nodded affirmatively as the ovate spoke. Then he nodded to the Ægyptian. "You have put it succinctly, Magister Inhetep. Some few loose ends need to be tied fast, and then we will reward you and see that you are safely away to whatever place you deem a desirable port of call."

"I say, Inhetep," the Behon said, beaming. "What a wonderful life you lead. What with the beautiful Lady Rachelle to serve as companion and exotic places to visit, I'll wager you'll be glad indeed to bid farewell to this little island of ours." He punctuated the statement with a sigh. "Would that I were able to be so free of care and duty of statecraft!"

"Here, now, Lord Justiciar! Lyonnesse needs your counsel and dweomercræft at all times," admonished the prince. "Be not sighing for such adventures as our two worthy crime-solvers are wont to pursue."

Before the wizard-priest could respond to any of that interplay, Lord Tallesian entered the salon. "My Royal Prince, Lord Behon, Lady Rachelle, Magister Inhetep, I have excellent news!"

"So soon?" Setne murmured. Nobody seemed to notice.

"Tell us," Prince Llewyn commanded loudly.

"It is as you thought, Crown Prince. Although the stripling bards who served Aldriss have eluded the agents sent after them, a whole nest of vipers has been found and captured!"

"Now that's splendid news indeed!" the Behon enthused.

"What do you mean?" Rachelle asked. "Your words fail to convey anything of substance."

The man flushed a little but managed to flash a wan smile in her general direction. "At the urging of our wise and perspicacious crown prince," the archdruid said, "the police authorities went out and began rounding up suspects and cult members as soon as my communication reached here—early this morning. Already some three-score villains have been clapped into irons, and there are a dozen or more babbling their confessions even as we speak!" He looked at Prince Llewyn, then at the Behon, and finally glanced from Inhetep to the amazon warrior. "Now do I make myself clear, lady?"

"A little more, sir," Rachelle replied with serious tone. "Yet I still have many questions. May I have leave to ask them?"

"Certainly!" the crown prince snapped. "His Venerability Lord Tallesian will be honored to answer with full details," he said, staring meaningfully at the druid.

"Your Ladyship . . . ?" Tallesian ventured.

"Have you ascertained who the so-called Master of Jackals was?"

"Not with absolute certainty we haven't—not yet. We do have some conviction as to it being the bard, however, and this is surely going to come out as questioning of other conspirators continues. It is worth noting that we have received neither retribution nor threat of assassination since Aldriss' death."

"You think the Master Jackal would strike in retribution for the loss of one of his—or her—lieutenants?" Setne queried.

"But of course. That's quite in the nature of an assassin such as this fellow is—was, I should say. Think of all he did previously—failure to pay extortion was sufficient cause for foulest murder!"

Rachelle again took over questioning the druid. "What manner of men have the police managed to find? And just how are they connected to the false cult of Set, Anubis, and to the Master Jackal?"

"I have a list of some of the miscreants," the Behon volunteered. "If I have permission, Royal Highness ..." The prince nodded quickly, and the mage ran down the list of notes on a little scroll of paper: "A defrocked druid, these next five are simple felons of one sort or another, here's a thief of some considerable infamy, here's a dissident spellbinder I met once as an apprentice to the Fellows—don't recall which magus he was serving, and now there are noted two Albish priests and a man we think a spy for that government too ... interesting ..." He looked up for a moment as if reflecting, then recalled where he was. "I beg your pardon," he stammered. "I'll continue. The common run-of-the-mill criminals I've passed over, but even so there are another score of names to check here."

Setne inclined his head and spoke. "That is impressive work in so few hours, Lord Justiciar. Was this roundup planned beforehand?"

"Somewhat," the prince interjected. "I saw to it that the cult was infiltrated by our own agents, naturally, as soon as the first threat to the Crown was manifested."

"Thank you, Prince Llewyn," Inhetep murmured, and before the royal scion could correct Setne as to how to address him, the Ægyptian urged the Behon on. "Who else on that list is notable?"

"There are a few more dweomercræfters and other strong practitioners, and an assassin as well, but most notable, dear Magister, are three members of this very household—that is, men in royal service."

"Their positions?" the wizard-priest snapped.

"Pantler, the second valet, and the chief clerk of the royal steward—all sufficiently high in position and trust so as to be able to wreak mischief had we not managed to connect them to the plot!"

Setne seemed impressed, but he also made it apparent he had a reservation. "Such a wide and complicated web. I am rather surprised that there are none of your nobles involved. . . ."

That made Prince Llewyn sit bolt upright. "Why do you say that?!"

"A simple matter of deduction, Highness," the green-eyed priest of Thoth supplied mildly. He sat back, relaxed, even as the royal scion of Lyonnesse remained tense. "You see, the Master of Jackals was after more than a few million in gold, great as such gain might be to most of us here. The demands for replacing the established pantheon of Avillonia with the pseudo-Ægyptian ones, and giving over your mighty Wheel of the Tuatha de Danann, point to no less than an attempt of rebellion."

"Rebellion?" The prince seemed shocked.

"Just so. Think you it unlikely that the folk of this kingdom would stand still for the imposition of foreign gods and a rabble of outlaws in government? Impossible! Murder if you don't comply and civil war at the hint of acceptance. And, my dear Crown Prince, whomever led the law-abiding folk of Lyonnesse against those who supported the Master of Jackals, or even bowed to that one's demands, would be a hero and more. I suggested some involvement of aristocratics and nobility, for what better opportunity to gain the throne of this land than with that?"

"Damn, Inhetep!" blurted Tallesian. "You might have something there!"

"Yes," the Behon said in a serious tone, "I believe he does. Have I your leave to—" He was looking at the crown prince as he spoke, and he left his sentence unfinished.

The prince had a somber expression as he nodded. "I understand, Lord Justiciar. You have my leave to depart. Tell the inquisitors that I would have knowledge of any noble name even hinted at by their prisoners. Tell them that I am most anxious for speedy news. Then return."

The man bowed and took leave immediately. While the Behon was absent, the remaining four sat and said little. After a few minutes thus, the prince signaled to Tallesian, and the druid stood up and hurried to Llewyn's chair at the table's head. "My liege?" The crown prince whispered something, then added in normal voice, "And have servants bring us a course of refreshment, too." Tallesian hurried off to do whatever the prince had ordered. Rachelle looked inquiringly at Setne, but he seemed distracted and did not respond in any fashion.

"Your Royal Highness."

"What is it, Magister?"

"Have you considered the possibility, however slight it might be, I will hasten to add, that one or both of the men now absent from us might be involved in the plotting and murder?"

Llewyn opened his mouth quickly as if to speak, then shut it with an audible click of teeth, and his ruddy complexion seemed slightly more flushed for a moment. He stared hard at the Ægyptian for several seconds, then dropped his gaze from the unwavering eyes of the shaven-headed priest. "Very well, I shall tell you, but it must never pass beyond the walls of this chamber. Do you both agree to that? Swear on honor and life?"

Both Rachelle and the ur-kheri-heb nodded, and the nobleman seemed satisfied by that small affirmation. "I am destined to sit on the throne one day, and as the future king of Lyonnesse, I am trained to trust no one entirely and to investigate any and every small suspicion. When the blackmail first began, I had my own secret agents delve into the activities of all three—the Behon, Tallesian the Archdruid of our Realm, and, yes, the Gwyddorr as well."

He paused and thumped a fist on the rosewood table to emphasize what he said. "The two former vassals were found absolutely upright and above reproach in all respects, but there was some slight question as to Aldriss—mainly a matter of his morals. I ignored the report. That is a hard lesson, Magister Inhetep. It is one I shall never forget!"

"By the Black Bull of Apis," the wizard-priest murmured as he shook his head in sympathy. "I don't envy your position now, Prince Llewyn, but the cares of crowned heads are ever thus, I suppose."

A very odd expression crossed the royal prince's face as he digested what Setne said. There seemed to be an irony in the Ægyptian's words, and a tone of voice which wasn't quite right. There was a sharp rap at the door. Prince Llewyn bade the one without to enter, and a line of servitors filed in with all manner of food and drink. These were placed on the table at the prince's order, and then the servers departed. "Help yourselves to whatever you like," Llewyn said, but he still eyed Inhetep oddly as he toyed idly with a plate of fruits and sweetmeats which had been set before him. As if on cue, both the Justiciar and Lord Tallesian returned before the three had had more than a mouthful to eat or drink. "Well?" demanded the prince, pushing aside the refreshments before him.

"I have a list of several nobles, Royal Highness," the Behon said, as if he were reciting some lesson in a classroom. "Two are mentioned here who are thegns." At this juncture the man swallowed and gave dramatic pause. "These nobles pretended to be friends and counsellors of your own Royal Father."

Prince Llewyn waved to silence the shocked gasps from Tallesian. "How many?" he demanded of the chief judge. "You have men ready, Archdruid?" he asked.

"Aye, Prince Llewyn, I do," the druid murmured.

"In addition to the two thegns, Highness," the Behon said as soon as his compatriot had ceased speaking, "there are a baron, two lairds, and an assortment of bannerets, vavasors, and landed knights."

"I'll stake my reputation on the fact they possess unusual riches and seemingly have utmost loyalty to the Crown," Inhetep said loudly, looking with fixed stare at the reader. That made the Behon uneasy.

"How did you know that?"

"Treachery is most often apparent and predictable," the ur-kheri-heb announced to the room, giving especial attention to the Kellts. "Treason even more so, it would appear," he added. Then looking only at the prince, Setne asked, "And you, Crown Prince, I think you have anticipated something of this nature too, haven't you? Lord Tallesian, your trusted cleric, has a force of agents now ready to hunt down these offenders, right?"

"Exactly, sagacious priest and magus. It seems you anticipate all I do here. Your Pharaoh is not well-served by your wanderings, Magister. You should be in your native Ægypt to assist and counsel your king!"

Inhetep smiled. "Thank you, but I wouldn't miss this sort of adventure for the vice-royalty of all imperial lands ever ruled by a Pharaoh," he responded. "So you have the whole affair wrapped up in a neat and tidy package after all. The dead Gwyddorr, Aldriss, was none other than the Master of Jackals, all of his minions are safely shut fast in dungeon cells, the treasonous nobles will be brought to justice—and the extortion money?"

"Unrecovered save for a drib and drab, but a cheap enough price, all in all," the royal prince commented.

"That's so, for those who are found guilty forfeit all—" Tallesian started to say, biting off his words when Prince Llewyn gave him a withering look of reprimand.

"Nothing left to do, then, but report the whole nasty affair to His Majesty, King Glydel," Setne said with finality.

"What? What did you say?!" The royal prince of Lyonnesse, first son of the king, was near purple with anger. "If you so much as breathe a word of any of this I'll have your *head!*"

"I see," Inhetep responded calmly, laying his hand on Rachelle's, for the girl was about to draw a weapon from her garments. No one could safely threaten Inhetep's life in her presence.

"My Royal Prince simply means that this sort of thing must be kept from our monarch. The king is no longer young, and Prince Llewyn fears for his health. If he found out this dark treachery, why it would break the good king's heart." The Behon was conciliatory.

"The Crown Prince will see to the scourging of the traitors," Tallesian added stoutly. "I am his instrument in that regard."

"You and the Behon there, and Prince Llewyn are instruments of perdition," Magister Setne Inhetep said harshly. "The king must be told, for his heir and trusted advisors are the ones who plot treason and murder—have committed those crimes, too. I am here to tell you that I know the whole truth, my lords, and to tell you that you will be brought to justice!"

"I had planned for this contingency, too," Llewyn snarled. Inhetep's chair suddenly dropped through the floor. Rachelle's fell with it. "You, Ægyptian dog, will now serve to be the greatest of the offenders, the Master of Jackals himself. Too bad that neither the magick of the Behon or prayers of our Archdruid will ever be able to discover your true motives." The two men laughed as their prince closed the yawning trapdoors. They had assisted in the preparations, so both knew neither magick nor physical prowess would enable the two victims to escape the certain death awaiting them below.

14

THE JACKAL'S PACK

"So much, Myffed, for the dupe you planned for."

The Behon bowed at his prince's scornful words. "Even the greatest magicks can not always accurately predict human irrationalities, my Royal Lord," he said humbly. "Yet now we have what we desired anyway."

Crown Prince Llewyn sneered at the gray-locked ovate. "Only because I had the foresight to prepare for this contingency, Behon. Let us hope for the sake of my coming rule, and your continued position, that your judgments will be better in the future."

The chief cleric of Lyonnesse was uneasy at the exchange, especially since he had supported and assisted in the development of Behon Myffed's plan to use the now-dead Ægyptian as their tool in the affair. "Wise Prince," he said in his most unctuous tone, "I congratulate you, as does the Behon, in having determined beforehand the likely reactions of Magister Inhetep. I know I speak for Lord Myffed, as well as myself, when I state that is the reason why the two of us are your willing and obedient vassals. Under your guidance, Lyonnesse will assume her rightful place in Avillonia's affairs and all of Æropa's, too."

"Don't flatter me," Prince Llewyn said, but there was no force in the command, and he smiled. Flattery or not, he thought to himself, what the druid said was no more than truth. Did that then obviate the intent and change the matter? He decided to forget about it as quite unimportant. "What about your men, Tallesian. Is all in readiness?"

"All of the nobles you would strike down, Royal Highness, are enprise," the druid assured him. "Forged documents and false evidence have been planted so as to be discovered when the time comes, and the agents who are there to make the 'discoveries' are fools who are totally unaware of what has been so carefully staged."

Llewyn stared a long moment, looking at Lord Tallesian as if he were a strange insect under glass. "Good," he finally said, but his tone was such that the two men who served the heir to the kingdom knew that any mistake would be unforgiven and fatal. "And you, Behon?"

"The roundup of the leaders of the cult of Set and all the faithful we could lay our hands on is complete, my Lord Prince," the sage related with assurance. "In this regard, the interfer-

ence of the meddling Ægyptian served us well.
Agents are now abroad with rumors of what occurred in Glaistig Pool—how Lord Aldriss was
slain by some foreigner, and that the bard was
probably leagued with the fellow somehow. A
case of thieves and traitorous ursurpers falling
out. . . ."

"Go on," the royal heir to the throne said
irritably.

"At the moment you command it, Your *Majesty,* there will be a new tale for all to hear. The
murderous priest and wizard, the shave-pate foreigner and none other, has struck again. Not
satisfied with slaying the Gwyddorr of Lyonnesse, the filthy Ægyptian jackal has assassinated Good King Glydel!"

A broad smile lit the fair face of the prince,
causing its ruddy patches to glow apple-red with
pleasure. "Fortunately, the Crown Prince was on
hand to lay low the vile regicide," he said with
conviction. "The killer and his whore died as
swiftly as his valiant father did under their murderous hands!"

"A murderous plot unveiled for all the kingdom to see, Highness—Majesty!" Tallesian corrected hastily. "The foreign killer could never
have managed his heinous crime save for the aid
of the vilest of traitors among the nobles of the
kingdom itself! They too will be brought to swift
justice—before they can utter a word in public."

"Then those who would suspect this matter,

THE ANUBIS MURDERS • 229

who have the means to find the truth of it, will be dead," Prince Llewyn said, "and all of their lands and wealth will become property of the Crown."

The Behon nodded and put on his most solemn and judicious face. "It is my ruling that all titles, properties, and possessions of these villainous rebels now and forever be forfeit to the Crown," he intoned. "The commoners will hear only vague rumors of the affair, just sufficient to prime them for what is to come. The gentry and nobility will be furnished with ample proof of the perfidity of the executed and those outside our realm."

"I will assuredly retain all of the estates as royal demesnes," he told the two men, "but when I rule as emperor, you will have whole counties to call your own!"

"Serving you is ample reward," the Behon said with a certain haste, as he looked at Lord Tallesian with a warning message carried in his glance. The prince had last told them that the lands and titles of the two thegns singled out for death—the two great nobles most loyal to King Glydel, of course, his closest friends and wisest advisors—would be granted to them, with Aldriss gaining the properties and wealth of a great baron and another lesser peer. Last promised, that is, until this moment. Trust not princes, Myffed thought. Yet he had no other course now. He would have to be most cautious in handling it, but the druid would possibly serve as a useful henchman should the time ever come to ... change one royal dynasty of Lyonnesse for another, one sprung from the power of heka, assuredly. "Lord Tallesian and I will be content with whatever is granted by you, Sire."

"Absolutely, absolutely!" The archdruid had caught the drift of things. "I am your man, Great Lord. To see you ruling this land is what my heart longs for."

"Well, we had better get on with things then," the prince said with firmness. "Are you two certain that all is in motion?"

"All know that it was your men who began the arrests of the offending cultists, my prince," the Behon responded. "Agitators now circulate among the lower class in all districts of the city to whip the folk into a frenzy against all concerned with the foreign gods. The lowest will be ready to tear them to shreds when they get word of the death of their king at the hands of the leader of the false cult."

"The rest is also as you command," Tallesian responded in turn. "Gentry and nobles alike will turn to you as savior of the realm, Majesty."

Llewyn preened under the title but admonished, "Be not so free with that title—yet! Soon enough I will bear it rightfully, but until the time comes, none must hear you speak to me thus, priest. You remember that as well, justiciar," he added, turning to the Behon. "Now go and fetch Sir Murdough, for he is captain of the guard this day, and he needs to be alerted."

The Ovate went off as if he were a page. In truth, Myffed trusted none other than himself in the matter. The knight was not far distant in the citadel, and the Behon soon located him sitting at ease in the office reserved for the commander of the King's Guards. Sir Murdough jumped to attention as soon as the justiciar entered the room. "Is it . . . ?" The Behon nodded. "Have your lieutenant assume command now, and come with me." The knight went to a side door and opened it. He spoke a few words with the soldier who was in the room there, then closed the door and bowed stiffly to the high justice of Lyonnesse. "Lieutenant Kerrier will be ready when it is time, lord. He will see that all unreliable men are out of the way, one way or another, so that only the loyal will be on duty."

"How long before he's done that?"

"I helped him with the plan, Lord Behon. At worst it will take but half an hour, at best no more than one-quarter of that time by the clock."

"Come on, then, Sir Murdough. His Royal Highness will have a few words with you personally."

"You are not aware of what is going to occur," the prince said flatly to the guardsman when Sir Murdough stood rigidly before him.

"No, Your Royal Highness. I know only that you will soon be king."

"That is because my father is unfit to rule,"

Llewyn said with a snarl. "He treats our neighbors as if they were equals, demands no conces-
sions or tribute, and has made the great kingdom
of Lyonnesse but a mewling kitten instead of the
roaring master of the Five Crowns. Know you
which is the eldest and greatest of the five kingdoms of Avillonia?"

"None but Lyonnesse, Royal Prince," the captain responded. "That is not but truth."

"You are correct, and when I wear the crown,
the other four kinglets will bow to us once again.
My doddering sire takes council with fools, but
one of those men, the Ægyptian called Magister
Setne Inhetep, will soon turn on King Glydel
and strike him down. When that occurs, you will
be there—understood?"

"Yes, Royal Highness."

"Godsdamn you, man, if you fail in any of
this! Listen carefully. The Ægyptian will flee the
council chamber, escape unscathed, but he will
take a wrong turn in his flight." Prince Llewyn
paused and looked at the knight.

"I will be in hot pursuit with a half-dozen of
my best men, Crown Prince," he said.

The heir to the throne smiled thinly. "That is
correct. The foreign assassin will find himself
trapped in a cul-de-sac, the Royal Library—you
know the chamber?"

"Well enough, although I am not given to book-
ishness, my Lord Prince."

"Never mind, fellow," Lord Tallesian told the

knight. "You must answer with a simple yes or no only, else we'll be at this all day!"

"Keep your own speeches brief, druid," the Behon said, for he had seen the expression on Prince Llewyn's face as Tallesian spoke.

"Enough! I am speaking," Llewyn snapped. "Sir Murdough, when you and your men enter the library of the king, you will find the bald-headed killer standing confused and uncertain. You will take that opportunity to cut him down, and you and your men will hack him to pieces! Is that clear?"

"Yes, Royal Highness."

"Not one or two thrusts, but pieces!' The guard officer nodded, not daring to speak to the prince, who was bright red with inner fury. Llewyn took a deep, gasping breath, calmed himself, and went on. "Then you will rush back to the chamber where the king lies dead. You will shout that the murderer has been found and exe-cuted. While our Archdruid, Lord Tallesian, at-tends to the corpse of the slain king, doing his best to restore the poor monarch to vitality, Lord Myffed will accompany you back to where the body of the Ægyptian dog who assassinated my father lies in pieces. I too will be with you on that return. We will bring the head of the of-fender back with us, and that will be the end of the matter."

Sir Murdough nodded again. "The king . . . ?"

"Beyond any help, even the best of my magickal restoratives, of course," the chief cleric supplied. "But with the Behon's assistance, we will discover the reason for the slaying of King Glydel. You see, Inhetep was actually the Master of Jackals, and when the king accused him of that, the Ægyptian coward panicked and struck him down. By that act he hoped to escape justice, but thanks to you, *Marshal* Murdough, that part of his vile plan failed."

Prince Llewyn smiled at the heavy-browed knight. "That is so, for the marshal you will be after this day's work. In fact, serve me well, and I will also award you the honor of a baronacy. Many noble peers of Our Realm will surely question you closely about all that occurred, and you must not betray the slightest portion of the truth of the matter. The office of chief soldier of the realm I will confer immediately upon you, a commission for your valiant slaying of the assassin. Thereafter, as you do your duty aright will come the elevation to the peerage as mine own baron, Murdough."

"I am ready now and will remain steadfast, Royal Prince," the man said, with that conviction a lust for position and power confers on those who live for such achievement.

"Back to your station, then, and attend the king when Lord Tallesian directs you to. Most of all, do not forget that the assassin, Magister Inhetep, is to receive no wound nor any real hindrance in his escape—until you bring him to bay in the library, and you must do your bloody work well then!"

The druid showed Sir Murdough out and saw that the knight went back as instructed; then the chief cleric of Lyonnesse returned to the place where prince and justiciar awaited. "All is now ready," he said with a hint of fear in his voice.

"Go on to your own part, then my stout Archdruid," the prince said, feigning kindness and trust. "At the striking of the sixth hour, go to the king in his council chamber and whisper your message. He will dismiss the others, of course. Then you will depart to send the 'magister' to his audience with my father."

Tallesian bowed low, his face pale but set in determined lines. When he was gone, the Behon looked at Prince Llewyn. "He is a reed."

"I have put some iron into the core of the reed, but even that metal will soon enough corrode."

"What of the girl?" Myffed asked, not wishing to pursue the subject of Lord Tallesian further at the moment. The druid was too ambitious for his own good. Had he not tried to displace him in the prince's favor, then Myffed might have done his utmost to see that Llewyn remained satisfied with Tallesian's service. As it was, the Behon worked to undermine the chief cleric, and in a few months or a year, there would be a new first priest of the realm where Tallesian had formerly stood—one who owed everything to the justiciar.

"Her? The Shamish doxy is to be kept drugged. In a few days she is to be sent north."

Myffed shuddered. "To Lo—" He cut himself off, as if his involuntary reaction would permit no further words. Then he managed, "I see . . ." with a weak and horrified voice.

Llewyn actually laughed when he saw the ovate's reaction. "She's nothing, a cheap enough price to pay for the aid we've been given and will receive!" The royal prince was telling only a part truth. Rachelle was meaningless to him, of course. Pretty women by the thousands would soon be available to him—not that he lacked for mistresses and conquests as crown prince. The price of his ascension to the throne was as high as could be imagined, only Llewyn had told no one of what it was. The great relic of Lyonnesse, the *Wheel of the Tuatha de Danann,* which was the source of kingly power, would also go north with the captive amazon companion of the dead Ægyptian when the time came—soon now, soon! There would be parity in Avillonia, though, and once he managed to gain suzerainty over the other kingdoms, he would use the combined might of the islands to regain the lost artifact— and more! In that the magus, Myffed, would be indispensable. After new power was available, perhaps lesser practitioners would suffice. Heka-benders were always a problem to the Crown, so necessary and yet so dangerous. That would sort itself out in due course. "Go now and prepare the Ægyptian for his part. Place him in the secret passage from the library to the cellars, so that when I come from my work he will be ready to confront the guards. When you have finished that task, attend me here, for it will be nigh onto time then."

The Behon murmured assent and departed hastily. Bah! Tallesian and the justiciar both were growing faint-hearted as the hour neared. Not he! Llewyn was firm, knowing that it was the only course possible. Long had he yearned for the throne, but his father was but fifty and still vigorous. The dotard would probably live to a hundred years of age, just to spite Llewyn. How old was Myffed? Well beyond the century mark, certainly. Leave it to Glydel and the ovate to use some magickal energy to live forever! Then, too, it was no secret that his father liked Llewyn but little, preferring his younger brother, Uthar, and even the snot-nosed child, Rhys. That forced him to walk a tightrope to avoid being disinherited and replaced as heir to the crown of Lyonnesse. Much had Llewyn foregone and borne because of his father—and his two brothers. There would be a terrible accident soon after King Glydel was buried and King Llewyn reigned. "King . . . King Llewyn!" The Atheling prince said it aloud, savoring its sound. He touched the ring he wore on his left hand's little finger. It was the token of his pact. On impulse he took hold of it, ready to pull it free and cast it from him. "No, not yet ..." Llewyn whispered.

An ancient waterclock on an ornate stand in the corner of the chamber dripped time away. The prince stared at it in fascination. Where was that doddering fool, Myffed? But a handful of minutes only had passed since the Behon had departed. Time seeped slowly, slowly. Llewyn willed the water to run as a mountain freshet, to pour out and thus speed the coming moment. The droplets seemed to hang suspended in space for eternity before completing their fall. He filled his heart with hatred and lust and envy and desire, the desire to own all, command all. Thus the crown prince stilled his own doubts and strengthened his resolve. He thought of the other kingdoms, too, of an imperial Lyonnesse.

On the surface it seemed a fair enough bargain. Lyonnesse to gain overlordship of Hybernia, the crown of Albion to be placed over that of Caledonia, and Cymru divided between the two greater kingdoms to be ruled as Camelough and Londun decreed. Fair on the surface, but the conniving monarch on the Albish throne would always seek an edge. His realm bordered on Cymru, and his army could easily invade the whole of that land. Then would the balance be gone, and King Dennis virtual ruler of all

Avillonia. Llewyn had pretended to be blind to that possibility, but ever since the conclusion of the pact, he had dwelled on the matter. Possibility had become certainty. Then he had realized how to forestall the matter and turn it to his advantage. The new-crowned monarch of Hybernia would be left co-equal to Llewyn, and the wild warrior bands of that island kingdom sent to ravage the lands of Caledonia. Lyonnesse would in the meantime have all of its forces to deploy in Cymru, so that kingdom would be totally his. When Albion and Hybernia were through fighting in the Caledonian lands, weak and exhausted, then would the Lion Banner move to take them. Albion first, then occupation of Caledonia in order to cause the Hybernian devastation to cease. Isolated, the green isle of Hybernia would then fall like a ripe and juicy pear. Five points and five jewels in the crown, his crown, and like none ever adorning any monarch of Lyonnesse before him.

What of the one who had been so useful in orchestrating this complex scheme? That made Llewyn pause a moment in his gloating thoughts of imperial splendor. The might of Avillonia was the answer. United, the greatest state of the West, much of the rest of Æropa would certainly hasten to make alliance with him—and the price of alliance would be high. Not too high, just enough to make his empire unassailable, and perhaps then would be the time to bring war to Skandia and beyond. Otherwise, assassins were worthy of consideration. How many hundreds could he send? Enough to do the job! Either way, the Behon would be useful, even Tallesian . . . perhaps.

"Prince Llewyn?"

He started, for he had not heard Myffed's entrance while in his reverie. Llewyn raised an eyebrow in inquiry. "Well?"

"I have done all you instructed, Highness, and it is now time for the final step."

"Get to it then, man! What are you waiting for?" The magus was beginning his ritual, a casting of change. Should Myffed choose, the prince would be at his mercy, much as any man might be beneath the razor of his personal valet. The Lord Behon was a good vassal, though, Prince Llewyn thought to reassure himself. The magick would be as he had commanded. Then he felt an odd tingling and pains in his body. "What have you done?" he demanded, half pleading, half angry.

"See for yourself, my Lord Prince," Myffed told him.

Prince Llewyn stared into the mirror which stood beside his chair. A hairless face, head bald, eyes green as spring leaves, confronted him there. He stood up in shock, and the perspective was wrong. He was looking down on the room from a place almost a foot higher than it should have been.

"Magister Setne Inhetep now stands ready to speak with King Glydel," the Behon said smoothly. "Here are your Ægyptian garments."

15

THE MASK OF DEATH

The two men went by hidden route to an out-of-the-way anteroom. Llewyn felt strange, dispossessed. He was sure it was due in part to the magickal alteration of his size and appearance, but he couldn't keep from wondering what part his own fear and anxiety played. He shook his head to clear it. "Are you feeling all right?" the Behon said with near-hysteria in his voice. "Of course I am!" the prince snarled in a strangely alien voice. "Get this charade moving," he muttered to the worried ovate.

The Behon went to an inner door and opened it wide. "This way, Magister Inhetep. His Majesty King Glydel will see you in his council chamber now," and with those words Myffed turned to a pair of guardsmen. "Escort Magister Inhetep to the king. Bring him back here when he is finished, then find me, for I am to personally take this man out of the citadel when his audience is completed." The senior of the two soldiers saluted, and both men fell into place awaiting their charge.

Llewyn stepped out into the broad corridor. He looked at the guards, but neither man seemed interested in him. To their eyes, Llewyn was nothing more than the bald foreigner. "Which way?" he asked one of the guards. His voice was that of the Ægyptian, with a trace of accent, too.

"You just foller' us, Worthy Magister," the man said, and he and his comrade marched off, just to either hand and a little ahead of Crown Prince Llewyn in his masquerade as Inhetep. They went for some distance, for the room was removed from the central part of the palace building. But the tall doors of polished walnut, thick valves carved with the armorial bearings of the king of Lyonnesse, came into view almost too soon. "In 'ere's where you'll be agoin', Sir Magistrate. Them fellas'll announce you, an' there'll be 'is Royal Majesty." He was a trifle condescending, treating the supposed foreigner as he would a stupid child of noble rank.

Llewyn swallowed hard. He was now quite nervous indeed, but that was fine, too. Inhetep might be that way, and as far as his father was concerned, the Ægyptian *would* be jittery. "Then announce me, lout!" The guards would be left with the worst possible impression of the wizard-priest. "Are all the soldiers of Lyonnesse garrulous old women? Or you an exception?" And he laughed softly as the man flushed and his face hardened. With absolute precision, the two guardsmen came to attention before the sentries on duty, stated their mission and charge, and stood rigid. One of the other pair cracked the door, and a subaltern's head appeared immediately. Hushed words were exchanged, and then the guards before the doors of the council room swung open the portal. The interior guard officer announced Llewyn thus:

"Magister Setne Inhetep of Ægypt comes before His Stellar Majesty of Lyonnesse, Glydel, craving audience!"

Llewyn bowed as he had seen Inhetep do, standing just inside the chamber by the double doors, as the guard officer peered intently toward the throne-like chair occupied by the king. Llewyn-in-Magister Inhetep form stood thus for what seemed hours, but it was merely a matter of minutes. King Glydel had been discussing something with emissaries from other governments.

The prince couldn't be certain, for he had never seen the three men closeted with his father, but they were certainly from Avillonia, and one was unquestionably a Hybernian. The others might be Cymric of Caledonian origin—not Albish. Odd, Llewyn thought, but not of any consequence now. The king was speaking too softly for him to overhear from this distance, but it was evident that his father was dismissing the three, for the men arose, bowed, and after backing the mandatory three steps away from the monarch, turned and strode toward Llewyn-Inhetep.

They passed without so much as a sidelong glance at him. Excellent. The dweomer was perfect in its transformative effect, and Llewyn was now fully confident that he could face his father without fear of recognition. "Please approach His Majesty now," the officer whispered. The prince went forward in his best imitation of the Ægyptian's long-legged stride. The sounds from behind indicated that the subaltern was again taking his attentive station just before the doors, too distant to overhear the words spoken at the table, near enough to spring into action. Not quite, Llewyn thought to himself with a broad inner smile of triumph. I can strike and be done easily before either fool can move! There was an arras to the right of the king's throne. Behind it were two doors. One led to the library, the other gave onto a hallway leading to the private apartments of the royal family. The prince knew this well, but the red-skinned assassin, a stranger from the land ruled by Pharaoh, could not, so it would be an even chance he would take the first door, the one leading to the library. Then he would be trapped in a cul-de-sac by that choice, and slain thereafter due to the error. Who would think of the secret passage? Certainly not the Ægyptian, for the vile killer had turned at bay and died—would die soon now. First he must do his work. . . .

A voice like his conscience spoke in Llewyn's mind. "Do you really wish to slay your father?" The prince stilled the thought. Yes! he shouted back to himself as he neared the seated figure. "Can you slay your own sire? He has been generous, understanding, good to you. . . ." Llewyn-Inhetep paused and bowed to King Glydel, and as he did so his thoughts raced. I am ready to kill him, I am able. He felt the cold hardness of the hidden knife at his side, a sharp-edged blade laden with the most potent of venoms. And I will not falter in this, for he is not fit to rule, he has loved me not, and I hate him!

"Please be seated, Magister Inhetep," his father said in even tones. The king was turned slightly away from his visitor, so that Llewyn clearly saw his profile. Straight nose, heavy eyebrows bushed out to match the long moustache and jutting beard. The king was just completing his reading of some document or another, for even as he spoke Glydel folded the parchment rectangle in half and thrust it into his robe, placing it just over his heart.

"Thank you, Your Majesty," the false Setne Inhetep responded. Llewyn thought that the document would soon be cut through and washed clean by the blood of his father. A victim? To all others, yes. To the prince, only a stupid brute about to be slaughtered as an unwanted dog.

"I have heard of your presence here in my Kingdom, and there are rumors of some dark business involving my son, Atheling Prince Llewyn. You will tell me all that you know," his father said, turning to stare directly into his eyes.

Llewyn fought for control of himself. He felt sweat beading on his forehead, and his limbs were shaken by tremblings. How fortunate he was here now, ready to strike, for the king was onto the game! "I had come to speak of other matters," Llewyn-Inhetep said slowly, fighting still to regain composure. "I . . ."

"You will obey the command of a king, sir," his father said sternly. "This is a command."

"Of course, Royal Majesty," the false Inhetep said, inclining his head so as to shield his eyes from King Glydel's all-too-penetrating stare. Impersonation or not, the eyes could give the game away. The prince thought fast, mind racing. He would begin to relate the whole business, voice low, and as the dark truths came out his father would draw closer in order to clearly hear all of this terrible conspiracy, and so as to be sure none other did likewise, the king would order his foreign informant to speak even more softly. "How much detail do you desire? For there is much, and the whole awful business will be lengthy in recounting fully, your Stellar Majesty."

"I am prepared to spend as long as needed, Sir Ægyptian, if what you say is accurate and meaningful," the king said as he straightened his spine.

That was no good at all. Llewyn thought

quickly—and acted cleverly. "King Glydel, there is treason in your realm," he said boldly, voice ringing. "The Crown Prince is implicated!"

"What? What is that you say?!" His father straightened even more, eyes blazing. Then he seemed to realize that the guards could hear the exchange, for he slumped a little, leaning toward the false Inhetep. "You had better have incontrovertible evidence of such charges," he snarled softly.

Llewyn knew that treason and royal misbehavior shamed the whole kingdom, but especially its ruler. "I would not speak were it otherwise," he assured the hard-faced monarch. This would be enjoyable work, for his father would suffer with the knowledge of the whole business before Llewyn put him out of his misery with one fell stroke of the poisoned blade he had ready. "Your eldest son heads up a network of nobles, court officials, soldiers, and others less important. He has stolen from your treasury, subverted your men, and plots your death."

King Glydel paled. Then he fell back in his chair, staring with disbelief at the man he thought an Ægyptian ur-kheri-heb, a wizard-priest of the ibis-headed god, Thoth. "Impossible . . ." he muttered, shaking his graying head of dark gold hair. "Yet . . ." he murmured on, "yet Llewyn has always been . . . weak, weak and selfish, and full of hubris, too! You might speak true."

"Weak?" Llewyn felt rage surging through his

veins once again. The old bastard dared to call him weak! Now his true feelings were surfacing, and the prince was filled with relish as he thought of the deed he was soon to perform. How joyful and fulfilling to plunge the steel into the hated breast! "He is not weak but strong!" Llewyn contradicted the king's words, not caring of consequences. A dead man's ire was nothing at all. "To devise and execute a successful murder demands strength far above the normal— heroic strength and resolve."

"Successful? I am still alive and ruling this kingdom," Glydel spat back.

"But for me here now speaking," Llewyn said with absolute veracity, "you would be dead. The royal prince is prepared to do the fell deed from selflessness, too, for he is determined to rule Lyonnesse and bring her to greater glory than ever known! Is that selfish? Nay! The sacrifice of personal pursuits, devotion of all energy to the glory of the kingdom bespeaks the greatest of spirits."

"Does it now, Ægyptian? . . ."

"Yes. And who could say that pride in the accomplishment of such a scheme, the years of dreaming, the months of planning in fear of discovery and execution, and the final fulfillment of the whole betokens overweening pride? Crown Prince Llewyn is filled with the grand and glorious sense of accomplishment, not hubris. It is the pride of nation, kingship, and what will be wrought by an imperial Lyonnesse."

"Then my son is a fool," King Glydel sneered. "He builds mist castles and dwells in the realm of the demented, for no such things as you speak of have or will come to pass."

"Were Crown Prince Llewyn here now before you, king, he would be prepared to say you were a fool and addlepated."

"But he is not!"

"Come near to me, so that I may tell you where the prince is even now," Llewyn whispered softly.

"Eh, what's that you say?" King Glydel asked, bending towards the impersonator.

Llewyn-Inhetep grasped the hilt of the envenomed knife inside his garment as he and his father leaned toward one another. "Your own son, your firstborn but least-loved, the one you have so often belittled, despised, and denigrated, Crown Prince Llewyn himself, is most near to you now," he hissed, staring into the king's blue-gray eyes. The blade came free, and he seized his father by the folds of his robe.

"Wha—" was all the man was able to get out before Llewyn drove the bright steel into his chest. The force of that blow sent the poison in the hilt jetting through the narrow tube in the weapon's spine and into the body of the Lyonnessian monarch. There were strangled sounds from the king's throat as the venom coursed through his body, and Llewyn relished those noises. Then King Glydel's head wobbled and

fell forward. The prince released his hold on the
royal robe, and his father's head thumped loudly
on the table. King Glydel was dead. Long live
the king, King Llewyn!

This final interplay had taken only seconds.
Llewyn hoped that his father had realized who
had slain him thus before he died. "May your
spirit wail in the deepest nether-realms!" he
shouted, springing up and upsetting the chair in
which he had been seated.

"GUARDS! MURDER! TO ... THE ... KII-
ING!" The shouting of the subaltern of guards
there in the chamber with Llewyn-Inhetep came
as if from a slow, basso voice, so stunned were
the prince's senses. The whole room seemed to
whirl as he turned his head sharply to see the
man calling for the armed soldiers just outside.
"Plenty of time," flashed across his mind, but to
be safe, Llewyn began edging towards the arras
as he watched. The guardsman tugged upon the
door nearest to him, so panicked that he forgot
that it opened outwards. Just the thing to make
the young fool seem as if he were assisting the
assassin, for he was suddenly jerked off his feet
and asprawl. Four of the men outside, two
guards on each door, had yanked the heavy wood
panel open. Sir Murdough was there as he
should be. Llewyn began moving more rapidly
now, even though his soon-to-be-slayers seemed
to be responding in ultra-slow motion; the prince
knew that it was only a few seconds' time since

he had murdered his own father in cold blood. In truth, the guards were seeming to speed up as the rush of adrenaline began to trickle away from Llewyn's body. The captain actually trod upon the prone subaltern in his feigned eagerness to come to the king's aid. Seeing that, Llewyn turned away from the scene and made for the arras with all speed.

Cries and shouts full of alarm and hatred filled the chamber behind him as the prince disappeared behind the arras. He heard the thunking sound of quarrels impacting on the thick cloth. Murdough had been wise in having the arbalesters ready and then blocking their arm for the time needed by Prince Llewyn to get safely behind the hanging. He jerked open the door to the private library, slammed it, and shot home the heavy brass bolt. It would keep the guardsmen out just long enough. Dodging the long reading table in his path, Llewyn made for one long section of inset bookshelves. For the past month he had studied the room so frequently that he could have run through it in the pitch dark, though soft, golden witchlight now illuminated it perfectly. The shelves masked the secret passage to the private subterranean cavern belonging solely to the king. Of course, most of the royal family and its trusted counselors knew about it. No matter.

"Open, damn you!" Llewyn hissed, as he triggered the catch with one hand and shoved with

the other. The heavy unit swung inwards soundlessly. He nearly leaped back at that moment, for
there stood Inhetep! It was as if he were looking
in a mirror, save that the Ægyptian's face was
blank, eyes staring vacantly into space. "Well
met, Magister," the prince said with mock sincerity and warmth. "I jape," he added, "though
my heart is truly glad at the sight of you, un-
gainly and copper-skinned as you—we are! You
see, my dear fellow," Llewyn continued as he
entered the little passageway at the top of the
stone stairs leading down, "you are now to play
the part of a prince—or is it playing the part of
a prince playing the part of a wizard-priest?
Now . . ."

There were heavy blows raining upon the
locked door. Swords and glaives would soon have
it a splintered ruin, and the guards would come
pouring through seeking vengeance upon the one
who had murdered their sovereign. "Now, Setne
Inhetep, go out and play your role in this
masque." The witticism made Llewyn laugh. It
would be a brief dance, while he escaped to regain his own form. He had been masked by magick to perfectly resemble the bald foreigner, and
soon no one would ever be able to unmask the
ruse. Inhetep was a mere automaton, standing
still until led, moving woodenly when so guided.
Llewyn hastened the Ægyptian along so that he
faced the assailed door. The tip of a sword
showed that it was about to be sundered. "Out

you go," he grunted, shoving the obedient form just far enough into the library so that Llewyn could close the secret panel behind the drugged man. It closed with a reassuring click. The prince stood in darkness.

It was easy for Llewyn to get to the stairway nonetheless. Three long strides, then a cautious probing with his left foot. "Ah," he breathed aloud. Once he felt the hard stone edge of the flight, he went swiftly down the steps. Ten stairs, turn left, eight more, turn left again, and the last ten stone steps to the hidden rooms below the palace. He groped along the right-hand wall and found the little leather bag he had placed there. Inside was a crystal bearing a spell of witchlight: a soft, pink radiance further reduced by the cylinder containing the stone, so that only a small ray of the reddish illumination went forth. The light enabled Prince Llewyn to pass through the several rooms and halls he needed to traverse so as to get to another secret stairway, the one leading to his own suite.

"Behon!" he cried as soon as he had dashed up the long flight and passed through the door concealed in the side wall of a storage closet.

"I am here my king," the mage responded. "Hurry, for I must remove the dweomers which give you the Ægyptian's form. They are crying alarm nearby even now!"

"Stop yammering and do it!"

Myffed began muttering hastily, making passes with his hands as he spoke, and then tapped the prince three times with his forefinger, once on the head, once again on the head, and then on the chest. "The dweomer is broken," he said.

"I feel no different," Llewyn said, but then he was struck by a wave of dizzying energy, and blackness closed his vision. It passed swiftly, perhaps four or five heartbeats, and Llewyn felt perfectly normal. "Is it now done?"

"You are your true self," the Behon said with conviction.

Just then there was a heavy hammering on the door to the outer hall. *Dum! Dum! DUMM!* Weapon metal being beaten on wood regardless of dents ruining the precious panels of exotic timbers. "Prince Llewyn! Are you there?! Come quickly—your father, the king! He has been attacked!"

"Open yon portal, dear Myffed, and let in those noisy guards so they can observe Atheling and Ovate in this far corner of the palace, see our shock at the news they bear, our worry and our grief. Hurry, man!" The regicide actually laughed with joy as he spoke, and he had to work very hard to compose himself as the justiciar jumped to the door and opened it.

"What's that you said? My father, my king, harmed? If this is so, heads will roll!"

The guardsmen blinked and pulled back, but their officer had to relate the news. "I fear it is very bad, Your Highness—Lord Justiciar. Lord

Tallesian has sent us here to bring you instantly to the council chamber, for he thinks that King Glydel has been struck dead!"

Faces set in grimmest looks, both prince and magus went off with all haste after the two soldiers and their leader. Now was the time of conclusions. They must complete the charade before celebrating their complete success!

16

ROYAL JUSTICE

Six guards came to attention outside the fatal chamber. The subaltern from the private audience chamber was there, commanding the security force. "Your Royal Highness!" he cried, snapping to a salute before Prince Llewyn.

The atheling merely waved the man aside, walking on with even strides. Two soldiers jerked open the doors with unseeming haste, for if they didn't their crown prince, soon king, would have walked into them. "What has happened?" Llewyn demanded with a shout. There were guards everywhere, and a knot of people were clustered by the table where he had sat as Setne Inhetep but a few minutes before. Not ten minutes before, he thought with secret malign pride. It was all going just as he had anticipated and planned.

The archdruid was kneeling by a still form. "It is your father, Prince," Lord Tallesian cried. "I am doing my best to—"

"See that you succeed!" Llewyn rejoined with

a hard voice, a voice filled with concern, anger, and regal tone. "You there, Captain! Who did this?"

Sir Murdough was standing with four other guardsmen atop a tangle that had been the arras. Behind the five men Llewyn could see the splintered door, but the library itself was obscured from sight. "A foreigner, Your Royal Highness," the captain said without blinking an eye. "The Ægyptian who was known as Magister Setne Inhetep." The prince came closer. "Was, you say?" Murdough nodded curtly. "Aye, Lord Prince. Was. We cut the assassin down. Here. See these blades still red with the foul blood of the man who dared to strike the king of Lyonnesse!"

Very good, almost as if he were not acting. Prince Llewyn turned to the chief cleric once again, forming his face into an agonized expression. "Tallesian—how bad is my father's wound?"

"It is ... I ... The stroke went to King Glydel's heart, Highness. Worse, the blade which pierced it was laden with poison."

"Magick, then! Use your powers to command heka, Archdruid, and mend the flesh, make harmless the toxin. He must live!"

"Of course, Prince Llewyn, of course. I do all in my power, but I fear that the Ægyptian used some foreign dweomer to make triply sure of his foul deed."

"What do you mean?"

"None of my healings, negations, purifyings,

or restorative castings have yet worked, though I have now laid nearly six upon my Sovereign's poor body.''

Hiding his inner joy, Llewyn hung his head and squeezed a pair of tears from his eyes. It was a trick he had used as a child, and that he could still produce such moisture by dint of will stood him in good stead now. Lifting his face so that all could see the streaks, Llewyn called to Myffed: "Come, Behon, follow me. I would see the corpse of the vile Ægyptian. I want you to ply your art to see if it cannot be forced to reveal the secret of the magick it used to lay low the king—my dear sire.'' The Ovate almost scuttled in his anxiety to comply and appear befuddled. Perhaps Myffed was near hysteria. Llewyn repressed an urge to slap the old man into sensibility, then turned and started toward the library. He was almost inside the room and could see the splatters of gore when a voice called.

"My Royal Prince!'' It was Lord Tallesian. He looked worried, and his eyes shifted slightly as they contacted those of the prince. "I beg you to come here with me and attend your royal sire a moment.''

What was the fool doing? This wasn't according to their careful plan at all. Something had gone wrong! Impossible. The stupid druid had forgotten something or blundered somehow. He would have to see what the idiot needed. "Come along with me, then, Behon.''

"No, dear Prince. This is a matter which only you can be privy to," Lord Tallesian cried, raising one hand as if to fend off the advancing high justice of the kingdom, and looking at Prince Llewyn with a warning message in his eyes.

The archdruid held up Llewyn's father's head with his other hand. The atheling stared. King Glydel's skin was pale and suffused with a bluish tinge bespeaking the poison which had doubly smitten him down to his well-deserved grave. This was impossible, this idiotic behavior from the bungling druid. How could he have ever placed so much trust in Tallesian? The dolt was about to do something absolutely incriminating. He'd have to intervene, do anything the fool asked now. "I understand, Venerable Archdruid," he responded as calmly as he could. The tremor in his voice would surely be taken for that of grief and dismay. He looked at Myffed. The magus was standing frozen and wild-eyed, for he too realized that Tallesian might unravel and somehow destroy their whole scheme. Llewyn couldn't leave him standing there in the middle of the room, alone and exposed. "Lord Justiciar, please go before me into the library and carry out what magickal inquisitions you can upon the murderer's dead body. I will join you in due time."

"Thank you, Prince Llewyn," the Behon breathed with an explosiveness indicating how much tension had built up within his chest waiting for the prince to show him some escape.

Llewyn watched the Ovate enter the library, then turned and took five paces so as to stand beside the kneeling cleric. "What is this, Lord Tallesian?" He spoke calmly enough, but there was a dangerous undertone directed squarely at the druid. Llewyn hoped the sound would put some mettle into the fool.

"Please, Prince, I must needs ask you kneel here beside me for a moment."

"Are you ...?" Llewyn allowed the rest to go unsaid. Kneeling as requested, he then spoke again. "Are you telling me the worst?" Those words should serve well. They would strengthen Tallesian and supply to the others that which they would assume was the remainder of the question he had swallowed.

It was as if he could see himself from a distance, as if he were an actor on a brightly illuminated stage. He had been perfect when following the scripted parts of this deadly drama. Here, now, with naught but extemporaneous speech and improvised roles, Llewyn was rising to even greater heights.

He took his father's still, ghastly head in his gentle hands. "Move aside, Lord Archdruid, so that I may cradle the poor cheeks with mine own hands as you tell me your rede." Tears now streamed down Prince Llewyn's cheeks, as he seated himself upon the floor and pressed his dead father's head against his thigh. He shuddered, but a sob made it seem as if the motion was but the wracking of his body from grief. Llewyn looked at Glydel's chest, the place where he had sunk deep the steely blade. Bright red blood oozed from the wound!

"The corpse doth bleed again!" Tallesian hissed in the prince's ear. "Your presence will unmask our crime, for all here know that should the murderer touch the corpse of his victim, the wounds will again gush gore!"

"Quiet, fool!" Llewyn hissed back. "It is you who will betray us—you alone! The corpse of Glydel bleeds only because I have lifted it and stuff from inside now drains out. What is the matter with you? Say those words which we have rehearsed—or make up what you must—but be calm. We have gotten cleanly away with the deed, save that you must now play out your last little part."

The greatest ecclesiastic of the realm gaped at Llewyn. There was a strange look about him, but the words from the prince seemed to steady Tallesian somewhat. "Then you are prepared for me to say the final bit?" Llewyn nodded. "So I must tell you that news which is the worst you might hear, Prince Royal?"

"Yes, fool, yes! What is the matter with you?" the prince hissed in a vehement whisper. Then aloud, so that those nearby could hear: "I ap-

THE ANUBIS MURDERS • 263

preciate your prayers and advice, Archdruid, but what of my father?"

"Look upon his face, Prince Llewyn," Lord Tallesian said in tone equally clear and ringing. "Look." He paused, forcing the prince to turn slowly so as to play out the scene fully. Then, as Llewyn turned to stare at the dead face, Tallesian went on: "King Glydel is . . . ALIVE AND WELL!"

Delusion. A nightmare from which he would awaken in a moment, finding himself in the king's bedchamber, and the time some hours after the day of the fell murder he had done. Alive? Well? Never could that be, nor could those words have come from the druid's lips. Llewyn turned to gaze at the dead face of his father. Glydel's eyes opened in an unbearable gaze of coldness and death. "NOOOOO!" He shrieked in hysteria, leaping to his feet, heedless of what happened to the blue-hued corpse and with no thought to those who stood watching. "You are DEAD!" the prince shouted accusingly, pointing at the corpse which now sat upright, eyes still fixed upon the one who had assassinated him. "I thrust the knife into your filthy breast with my own hand, thrust through that heart which never cared for me! Such poison went into that wound, Father-whom-I-Hate, that a dozen bulls and more would be slain thus. I killed you and you are *dead*!"

"I live," the blue lips said flatly, and King Glydel arose.

"Myffed! To me! You must use your magick to slay—slay all here who would undo us!" Llewyn screamed, then turned to face the druid. "Tallesian! You will suffer death for your part in this. Don't stand there like a post—strike with your own heka or you are lost as I will be!"

The chief druid of the realm stood unmoving, gazing with the same look in his eyes as had Prince Llewyn's father. It was a mixture of contempt, revulsion, and disgust. Tallesian had the hard and unpitying look of an executioner. "It is time you knew, Llewyn. Lord Tallesian lies bound in the dungeons beneath this fortress."

"You are gone over the edge! Crazed! You are Tallesian!"

"No more than you were Inhetep," the man rejoined. "You see, dear prince, I am Magister Setne Inhetep, the man you impersonated."

"BEHONNN!"

The young subaltern's head appeared from behind the ruined arras. "I must report to you, Prince Llewyn, that the Lord Behon, Myffed, has been slain resisting arrest but a minute ago. He is beyond your voice's command now, sir."

Llewyn stumbled back a step, collapsing weakly into one of the padded chairs in the chamber. "I am hallucinating," the prince muttered. "None of this is happening . . ."

"But it is," his father's voice came to him.

Cold, laden with impending doom, the words were like cold water to him.

"Your flesh—blue and dead . . ."

His father spoke again. "Woad and some creams used by ladies to beautify themselves. Magister Inhetep's own assistant, Lady Rachelle did the work. "You are testimony to her skill—murderer, traitor, and coward!"

Llewyn attempted to stand. Perhaps he could make a dash for it, escape in the warren of hidden passages. His legs were too weak to hold him. The prince looked at Tallesian, still doubtful. Where the archdruid had stood the tall Ægyptian was now standing. He had not lied. "How?" It was all the prince could stammer.

"Ere I came to you and your two cohorts, prince, I had sussed out your plottings and knew all. I went so far as to alert the rulers of Cymru, Hybernia, and even high Caledonia."

"Why do that?" Llewyn asked, for it seemed to have no bearing on matters.

"Those worthy kings understood. Their agents went immediately to your own father, alerting King Glydel of the treachery and villainy."

"I am ashamed to say that I called those good and noble emissaries foul names and believed them not. Not until Magister Inhetep showed me proof positive. Then we prepared this bit of play-acting to counter your own charade. Do you know that I went through all this because I thought you incapable of patricide? To the last

I expected you to flinch, confess, beg forgiveness. Had you done so, I would have spared your life and sent you into exile with all the comforts any man could want for the rest of your life."

"All I could want? Never! I want all Lyonnesse! I will rule all Avillonia!"

"No." That simple, flat denial from the wizard-priest was a blow across the face to the prince.

Llewyn stared at his accusers, his tormentors. "Proof, you say? What proof was there for Inhetep to display which would convince a *loving* father of his son's deceit?"

"Golden coins, Llewyn. Magister Inhetep brought me a pair of griananas which he had gained in one of the supposed temples of Set."

"That's no proof!"

"He asked me then to examine my treasury, to see if one thousand of the same golden coins weren't missing, the theft carefully hidden by false bookkeeping."

The king paused, wiped at his drawn face with a hand. "To prove him false I did as he asked, investigated, and proved him right instead. You were tried and condemned then for theft, treason, and worse. Yet I would have forgiven . . ."

Llewyn spat. "Be damned with your miserable forgiveness! I'd take none of it. All I've ever wanted from you was your life and crown."

Glydel turned away from the raving prince.

"You will soon enough have no head to wear the noble mark of kingship," Inhetep said. He was not gloating, nor was he baiting a fallen foe. The Ægyptian simply found this parent-slayer so hateful that he had to speak out.

"Damn you, too, dirt-skinned dog!" Llewyn shrieked. "How did you keep my blade from striking down the filthy tyrant?"

"It was simple enough," Setne told the man. "A talisman can take almost any form, and I prepared one especially for your father. You saw it, I'm sure. It was a sheet of parchment which made him proof from injury by blade, and even death from the most virulent toxin conveyed thereby."

"You could never have guessed I would strike with a poisoned knife as I did!" Llewyn denied.

"You think knife or dagger unusual tools for a regicide? They are old, Cæsar himself was struck down thus. I had no guesswork to do, however, prince. The servant sent by Lord Tallesian to fetch the venom was easy enough to get the truth from."

"The fool druid was to get the stuff himself!"

"Perhaps. He ignored your orders for once, though, Llewyn. I suspected some poison would be employed in slaying the king, so agents went round to all those dealing in such substances. One admitted selling a special venom to a man in the employ of Lord Tallesian. Magick can be used for many purposes, and I used much to garner the form of your deed. Sir Murdough recalls it not, for he was under a geas, but he revealed most of it."

The pale face of Prince Llewyn was a mask of hatred. "That fool soldier knew not half!"

"You forget I am a cleric as well as a mage," the Ægyptian told Llewyn. "I used the former to overpower the mind of your chief druid, and the latter to spin such dweomers as to find the whole web you had set out. Then and there we might have brought you to heel, but your father loved you too much, thought you would repent before striking, just as he said. Thus, we all had to act out our parts in this pretend murder. Thanks to the power of the talisman I wrought so carefully for him, you would not have succeeded had you plied a greatsword laden with the poisons from a score of death adders."

"But you were dropped into the prison pit! The fall, the paralyzing gas, the drugs which the druid used . . ."

Inhetep shook his head. "I expected the fall, and as Rachelle and I plummeted, a charm secreted on my person was invoked, and the lady and I fell to the hard stones with hardly a bump. As for the gas, your father's stout retainers had already cleared away the numbing stuff, replacing it with harmless vapors of similar color so had you looked you would have noted nothing amiss. When the druid applied his mind-blanking herbs to the two of us, he did so with-

out knowing that he saw but phantoms. As Tallesian suspected no dweomers, he sought for none
and understandably failed to notice the illusion
cast to make the whole seem real. We watched,
as did your own father, as the archdruid performed his vile duties."

"So there was never a chance?"

"That is so," Inhetep answered.

"No," King Glydel corrected the wizard-
priest, "there was a chance." He looked at his
son, and his eyes were misted. "You could have
done other than you did."

Llewyn hung his head, saying nothing more.
Inhetep had to tell the defeated man the final
portion. "I took Tallesian's place after he thought
he had administered his drugs to Rachelle and
me. The king gave me permission to do so only
then. The form that you thought was me was a
construct I fashioned with magickal energy,
mine own heka, using naught alive or ever living,
save blood from a slaughtered pig, so that when
the automaton was hacked by the guards it
would appear to die properly in a welter of
ruddy gore. There you have it all, Prince."

"All. Yes, I will have it all! Somehow I'll escape and get revenge on you all! I'll get aid—
yes, that's it! I can call for aid from the north!"

"Silence!" Inhetep shouted the command, and
the prince obeyed. He could not do otherwise,
for Setne had laden his word with magickal
power, which silenced the man. Turning to King

Glydel, Inhetep said, "You must not allow your son to speak as he was about to, for who can say what might occur if he did so."

"I understand, Ægyptian wizard-priest," the monarch replied coldly. His anguish was turning against all now. "Guards! Chain this criminal, for before you all I disown him as my son, deny his royal blood. He is a common criminal, and you will treat him as such."

"Majesty . . ." Setne prompted. "He must not speak!"

"Gag the criminal," the king said in a grating voice. "Put him in a special cell below, one reserved for confinement of those capable of using dweomers—just as is the case of our former chief druid, Tallesian."

The soldiers hastened to obey. Llewyn was dragged out, and then the bodies of the Behon and Sir Murdough followed. King Glydel stared at the procession a moment, then looked at Inhetep. "I should thank you, Magister, for your work, for saving my life, but I cannot find it in my heart at this time. Goodbye," he said, and without anything further, the ruler of Lyonnesse left the chamber.

17

1 REASONED THUS

The council room was now deserted save for Inhetep and the young subaltern of guards. The
Ægyptian was seated in a chair, staring sight-
lessly into space. Anyone who knew Magister
Inhetep would have realized he was both reviewing in his mind what had occurred and at
the same time feeling discontent. For almost half
an hour he sat thus, and the young guardsman
remained quiet, waiting. Inhetep seemed unaware that the officer was there, despite the fact
that he began to shift from foot to foot restlessly,
then actually paced here and there. Finally, the
guardsman came near to the wizard-priest where
he sat and cogitated.

"Setne?" the officer said with surprising
familiarity.

Inhetep started, glanced at the subaltern, then
shook himself, rising. "Ah, yes. Sorry to be so
dilatory, my dear. I had forgotten . . ."

"That's all right, Setne, I understand," the
guardsman said, laying his hand on the tall

Ægyptian's arm in a caressing gesture. "You have been through much these past weeks—but then, so have I," he added with a vigorous tone. "Can you manage to direct your attention to me now?"

"Your wish is my command," the man said, and without further discussion, Inhetep placed both of his long-fingered hands on the subaltern's shoulders and spoke four words. Rachelle's form replaced that of the guardsman. "Is that what you desired?"

"No," the amazon said with mock disappointment. "I had hoped you'd place a charm on the subaltern's person so that I'd be irresistible to the ladies-in-waiting here," she told Inhetep with a serious face. The wizard-priest seemed to be unaffected by her words, and Rachelle's expression changed from one of playfulness to concern. "Aren't you feeling well?"

"I'm in exceptionally fine health, and my body functions properly," he replied.

"No, silly old shave-pate. I mean, is your heart heavy? Your mind troubled?"

The green eyes turned to look into the almost black ones of his friend and confidante. Inhetep realized then, more than ever before, how much he truly cared about Rachelle, and she for him. Perhaps that was why he felt for her as he did. "I am troubled, dear little protectress, even though there is little or no cause for feeling thus. Something remains which is not right. There is a cloud of a malign sort which still prevails here in Camelough, perhaps pervading all Lyonnesse. I just don't know."

"Come along," Rachelle ordered, taking the tall Ægyptian by the arm and leading him from the chamber. "You need something to eat and drink, a rest—my care, too. In a bit you'll be feeling splendid elation. After all, you have done a magnificent job here!"

He pondered the case as they traveled the brief distance to their quarters. He had broken open the whole treasonous plot, and the worms involved had shriveled away in the bright light of discovery. Not only was this kingdom and its monarch saved, but three others, states and sovereigns alike, as well. The ruler of Albion was implicated. He would be dethroned soon, of course. His cousin, Richard, would in short order rule the kingdom of Albion, the fourth monarch of that name to wear its crown. Furthermore, his efforts had both allowed the Five Crowns of Avillon to retain their objects of power and prevented the most evil enemy on Yarth from gaining these artifacts. That was certainly worthwhile. But the Ægyptian still felt depressed, even after recounting all that in his mind.

After having herbal tea, biscuits, then some wine and fruit, Rachelle saw that Setne was still quite glum, so she resolved to brighten his spirits in a way no man could resist, let alone the cerebral wizard-priest. He was stretched out, half-reclining, on one of the several couches in the sitting room which divided their separate bedchambers. Without being asked, Rachelle brought a little tray of additional refreshments and placed it near the Ægyptian, then tossed a cushion on the floor beside his divan and sat down with crossed legs. "Setne, dear, can you please explain a few things about the Master of Jackals affair to me?"

"Explain? I'm quite uncertain what needs explanation," he responded slowly and without real interest.

"Oh, you know! I'm just not very good at solving problems—not like you are, anyway. I don't understand how you *knew* all you knew. Tell me how you caught on to Aldriss so quickly."

Although he strongly suspected she was manipulating him, Inhetep had to cease his brooding and give the warrior girl the information for which she asked. Pride of accomplishment and a desire to instruct his protégée demanded it. "More by chance than any inkling of the truth," he told her almost ruefully. "You know I have a penchant for learning new things—"

"More an unquenchable thirst after knowledge, you rogue." She smiled up at Setne. "You display an insatiable appetite for all things pertaining to heka, dweomers, and the arcane."

"Be that as it may—and I'll neither affirm that

assessment, girl, nor deny it—it was due to my curiosity that I caught on to the bard."

Rachelle knew he needed just a little more priming. "That's fine for you to say, and I know how your mind goes from one little curious bit to whole new realms of information, but I still don't know what you did, or what Aldriss did to reveal his duplicity to you."

Inhetep settled back in the soft cushion of the couch, fingers toying idly with the rim of the wine glass beside him. "You'll recall, dear Rachelle, that while you were busily accepting the compliments and unseemly attentions of the bard, I was attending to the magicks he employed."

"I recall your making notes and observing most closely," she agreed. Rachelle thought Setne's assessment of her reception of the bard's harmless flirting grossly overstated, but she was wise enough to allow that matter to pass.

"Exactly. That is what put me onto the right path, but later. Who could have guessed that three men traveling hundreds of miles to request my assistance in a matter of life and death could be the actual villains?"

"Never I," Rachelle said earnestly. "But you did—sooner than I, for you cautioned me about Aldriss in your note."

"The one you missed reading aright—but no matter. Outstanding was the initial choice of victims."

"How so? Svergie was the state, as I recall,"

Rachelle added as she puzzled over the matter. "It is a kingdom with sufficient wealth, rather cold and isolated, but . . ."

"But nothing! It is home to the Eldest Spaewife, the chief Wisewoman, and that is key."

"How so?"

"They are a counter to witchcræft, of course. Then the description of what had occurred in other places, Ys particularly, the inability to determine what sort of casting was employed to slay, the irretrievability of the victims, gave me concern. The first cause for that is evident."

She tugged at his sleeve. "No, it isn't."

He looked down at her dark ringlets, seeing that she was attentive and truly puzzled. "Yes, you do know, only you aren't thinking hard enough," Setne admonished. "Such circumstances point toward the involvement of great practitioners—ones at least *more* than human. In this case the *blame* was directed at Set, of course, and collaterally at Anubis. That was the first and grossest error in judgment the plotters showed. Had they determined to use someone else as their dupe, one not steeped in the pantheology of Ægypt, then the inclusion of Anubis would not have rung so false a note. After all, his association with death and the Duat tend to mislead the uninformed." Inhetep was warming to this recounting now, and he paused a moment to sip some of the light red wine and nibble a grape or two. "The second possibility with respect to the clueless murders lay in some unknown form of magick and a whole organization of criminals determined to use their abilities to evil ends. So, because a good detective never discounts the possibility of anyone with motive and opportunity being guilty, no matter where suspicion points, and regardless of seeming irrationalities, I kept the three Kellts as suspects in the back of my mind."

"It did seem a little odd that they knew where we were and came all that distance to find you," Rachelle noted.

"Hmmm, yes," Inhetep responded. He hadn't actually reasoned that way, because it was, to him, not all that strange that one of his talent would be sought out thus. There was a lesson in that, and the wizard-priest made a mental note not to be so smug in the future. "Anyway, my sharp-witted amazon, it began to come together after Crown Prince Llewyn displayed the statuette and told us all of the facts—what he desired us to believe as the whole truth, I should say. I had opportunity to study the dweomers used in the enspelling of the figurine, and I found strange similarities between them and the magick used by Aldriss when he hastened our voyage. Then I thought to compare what I knew about bardic powers with the practice of troubadours, skalds, and the rhyme-singers of Kalevala. There was the strand to follow! Still, it was a mere thread, so when I left you that warning it was vague."

Rachelle got up and brought the flagon to where they sat. "More wine, Setne?"

"Perhaps a few drops more, if you please," he replied without actually paying attention. "You see, the possibility of Set's involvement still remained. He too is 'of the North,' of course. When you were kidnapped, I took time to search out information in the underworld."

"You entered the Duat?!"

"Don't be shocked. It isn't so dangerous a thing as most would have you believe," Inhetep said with evident pride in his power in that regard. "What mattered wasn't the going but the reception which awaited me."

"Don't tell me that the terrible ass-headed one confronted you there!"

"I shall not, for quite the contrary occurred. The deities of the shadowy realms were incommunicado, as it were. Only wolf-headed Apuat was there to greet me and speak of what was occurring. In truth, even that one was of little assistance, though he would have had it otherwise. The lords of the Duat were constrained. Set could not accomplish such a feat, so some other involvement had to be considered. It was then clear that there was a vast and powerful organization of men, heka-binders, those in positions of rulership, and all manner of others involved in a fantastic and complex plot to disrupt the whole of Æropa."

Rachelle was now fascinated, for this was something she hadn't known about at all, something very evil and world-shaking in all probability. "Prince Llewyn was behind all that?"

Inhetep shook his bald head vigorously. "No. In fact, his inability to mastermind even the lesser web which was shown in the extortions and killings threw me off the scent for some days. No great entities were involved, for the lords who govern Avillonia, for instance, have no power to muzzle our own deities. Over and above the network of men—even powerful practitioners such as Behon Myffed and the druid, Tallesian, princes and kings—was some figure of supernatural power and force, one able to constrain gods."

"Who is so mighty as that?"

"None, at least in ability to force the matter. Yet there is one who with threat, trickery, and a certain reliance on the laws of Yarth could machinate things so as to arrive at the situation we faced. Wait! Don't ask about that one now, please." The wizard-priest had anticipated Rachelle's demand, and he wanted to complete the whole matter from start to finish and give the warrior girl a complete picture. "By thinking thus, I found that the skill of the bard was greater than others of his ilk because Aldriss had

woven another form of musical dweomercræfting into the bardic art.

"It became apparent that with that power, the
man was able to serve as the instrument of com-
bining magicks into a single casting form. Between the magus, the high druid Tallesian, and
the spellsinging of Aldriss, there was more than
sufficient power to bring about the strange and
unreadable magicks which struck down any who
dared to defy the demands of the so-called Master of Jackals. Yet the three hadn't been in Ys at
the time the cold-hearted master demonurge was
destroyed, let alone in all of those other, more
distant places. Those facts merely confirmed my
suspicion that someone of far greater ability was
serving to channel the power of those three to
work the mischief that one desired. The three
were dupes. Prince Llewyn was a puppet as
well, and so too the Albish king. The Master
Jackal is a long way from here and by no means
unmasked—save for me and you."

"But, Setne, I don't—"

Inhetep shushed her. "Have patience. In just
a bit, you'll be informed. You would have me tell
this whole thing in a jumble!"

Rachelle smiled wistfully. "Forgive me, my
lord ur-kheri-heb-tepi. I am but a simple girl unused to the intellectual exercise, just as you
seem quite unable to manage many of the pursuits I follow in the course of making sure I am

able to save your worthless, copper-hued hide
from—"

"I stand corrected, Rachelle," Inhetep interjected hastily as she warmed to her task. "The
jumble comes from me, for I have so many facets
to reveal, so many facts to set out for your exami-
nation." She snorted a little but allowed the
Ægyptian to continue. "Let's see, where was I?
Ah, I recall. Knowing that there was a puppet
master, I sought for the strings of the puppets.
The demon's words in Ys pointed the way. Then
I reasoned that money was used to buy many,
but the coin came from the extortions. The Master of Jackals had no interest at all in the wealth
gained by threat and murder, save to buy servants, to suborn and subvert. A thistlecrown
from Caledonia in the coffers of the false cult's
temple in Camelough led me to investigate all of
the nations of Avillonia. The coins were moved
from one kingdom to another so as to avoid suspicions—or throw them on another of the realms.
I was received well in Cymru, Hybernia, and
Caledonia. The plotters there were of high station and much power, but not so great as Crown
Prince Llewyn in Lyonnesse or the king of Albion. I already knew of that one's involvement
when I was nearly taken there. Had they found
me, they'd have killed me for sure!

"But why involve me, us, in the first place?
Some deity other than Set might have been used
as a god of straw, so to speak. It was evident that

there was never any intent that the foolish cult
do anything more than draw attention and bring
down blame and wrath upon the rabble serving
it when the true crimes were committed. This
affair became like an onion. Each time I pulled,
a layer came off, but another lay beneath. Magickal 'fumes' aplenty poured forth to dim my
eyesight, to carry the analogy a step further."

Inhetep fell silent, thought a moment, then
drew out several items of his magickal materia.
"We must now work with amulets, castings, and
hekau to make sure that we have no unwanted
eavesdroppers. Please assist me, Rachelle." The
girl was knowledgeable enough in the work, and
she complied quickly with the wizard-priest's
instructions.

"You have set a triple circle, Setne. You are
very serious about this matter, aren't you?"

"Most definitely, my dear child. The odious
heart of this whole vile plot is one who is so
wicked and powerful as to pose dire threat to us
even at a great distance."

"Will you tell me?!"

"Louhi, the Crone of Pohjola, is the so-called
Master of Jackals! Leave it to that evil Mistress
of Witchcræfters to use such a *pun,* for indeed
that is what it was. In her contempt for those
she used, she regarded them as slinking jackals—
and she the master of the whole pack she en-
listed. Louhi thus chose the appellation and devised the ploy of Set, a deity she has no little

admiration for, and Anubis, whom Louhi despises. It was thus gratifying to her to besmirch the jackal-headed one's name and repute in many ways. It was then no accident that the three noble lords of Lyonnesse sought me out. The crone had commanded it. I found that from my probing of Tallesian."

Rachelle came up on the sofa to sit beside him, for the girl was much concerned by what Inhetep had just revealed to her. "Why would the monstrous witch of the North want to harm you?"

"Harm? Eliminate in most foul fashion is more apt, Rachelle. I was to serve as the butt of all hatred, vengeance, and die horribly as the 'Master of Jackals' after all had occurred as the plotters wished. They would gain power, a throne in Llewyn's case, and subject kingdoms. Louhi would wrest the great objects of power from the five kingdoms of Avillonia, thus becoming even more formidable in her evil strength. But as to why I was singled out, I must say now, my dear, that I can only hazard a guess. I think that somehow I have interfered with the crone's schemes in the past. In addition, it just might be that I am becoming too strong an agent for right and justice to suit the vile witch. In any case, Louhi devised not a little of her whole scheme so as to bring me down and send me to the underworld."

"And by foiling her you have increased her enmity!"

"Most assuredly, Rachelle, most assuredly. Yet I would have it no other way."

Rachelle now had the whole of the picture, and she felt both happy and fearful. "You got onto the right track also because of the secrecy of the ones involved, I know. I was suspicious about the prince and his henchmen keeping facts from the king. That didn't ring true at all. When they let it slip out that no other monarch save King Dennis of Albion was aware of the matter of the demands of the Jackalmaster, I was confused, however, for that made me suspect that he was the one masterminding the whole business."

"Astute, amazon, very astute. The demands for the objects of power made it unlikely that one of the rulers of the Five Crowns would be found at the center of things, for such a one would never get the willing cooperation of the other sovereigns—or would-be monarchs. No, the relics would have to be passing beyond the grasp of each kingdom for such mutual skullduggery to occur.'

"I see. One small thing still troubles me, Setne. What about Aldriss? Why did the Behon so readily slay his fellow conspirator?"

Inhetep shrugged. "Only to save his own skin and that of Prince Llewyn. It was a snap decision, but a correct one. I was about to lay the bard by the heels, as it is said. Aldriss knew too much, and there would have been no stopping

me from prying it from his mind. Myffed wasn't
powerful enough to slay me, certainly not with
you there to assist in defense and attack. He had
only one choice, and that was to blast the bard
using the force granted to him by the crone. It
then became a patchwork which the conspirators
thought would cover their nakedness. To fob off
Aldriss as the sole mastermind of the matter was
sheer lunacy. That had a certain appeal. To use
that to lure me into their toils, to have both you
and I, Rachelle, at their disposal, would serve
perfectly. After all, I was to be sacrificed eventually, and with Aldriss' name to toss into the pot,
the stew might be more appetizing when I was
cooked in the mess."

"What do you suppose they intended for me?"

Setne shook his head slowly. "We'll have to
find that out, won't we, before the criminals are
brought to final justice."

That brought Rachelle's thoughts round to the
prince. "And Llewyn—was he planning all along
to have the Behon use a magickal guise to make
him appear as you and slay his father, King Glydel, with his own hand?"

"He *is* a foul villain, isn't he!" There was no
question in Inhetep's words. "Yes, the deranged
mind of the crown prince thought that fitting—
a form of retributive justice. Llewyn was weak,
selfish, and lusted for power. Somehow he blamed
his sire for that, thought that he would wipe the
stains of his own character away when he took

Glydel's life with his own hand. Perhaps the king failed to love his son as he might have, I don't know. Could you feel affection and heartfelt love for one such as Llewyn?

"He certainly had no love for anyone save himself in his heart. In truth, I think he hated himself more than those he used, even his father. By assassination and treachery he thought to rule Lyonnesse, conquer the other realms of Avillon, and perhaps even envisioned himself as master of all Æropa one day. Thankfully, he never got to his first objective."

"We speak as if the crown prince were already dead," Rachelle reminded the Ægyptian.

Setne shrugged again. "It is but a matter of a little time now.'

"I suppose you are right again, all-wise and hairless sage," she intoned solemnly. Then Rachelle laughed. Their mood was growing dark and heavy again, and Rachelle would have none of it. She and Setne should be rejoicing in their success. "Now how about you serving me for a change? I have an empty wine goblet and am quite famished. Bring me gallons to drink and mounds of viands, slave!"

"Famished as always, you mean, and I am not your slave—you are officially mine!"

"Only because I have never filed those papers," she responded. "Bring me my desired refreshments, please, or else I shan't speak another word to you today."

"Most unlikely," Inhetep muttered, but he arose and began pouring wine and selecting various morsels from the platters on the buffet. "Here, eat and drink until you burst. When you're finished, if ever, you may accompany me to the dungeons."

Rachelle had to wait a moment to clear her mouth of food before inquiring, "Such a lovely place you will show me. Why do we go to the dungeons?"

"Because we must find out what they planned to do with you. *That's* what has been bothering me since the prince was taken and this whole matter seemingly put to rest. In all of it, they seemed to have no use for you, so why not have you with me to be conveniently killed as a coassassin? To keep you sequestered in some cell would be to invite embarrassing inquiries. Never is Inhetep seen without his amazon guard and associate, Rachelle."

"Oh . . . you do make sense there, Setne. Do the men of Lyonnesse keep harems?"

"Don't be silly," he snapped. Then the wizard-priest saw her face and realized he was being goaded. He grumbled, then washed away those sounds with a big swallow of the wine. "Most amusing, I'm sure. No noble of this realm sought to prison you in his seraglio, but someone, somewhere, certainly had some purpose for you, Rachelle. Laugh at my concerns if you will, but it is a matter of some moment to me."

"Oh, Setne, I wasn't really laughing *at* you, how could I laugh at the man I—"

The rest of her words were interrupted by a rapping at the door. It was a messenger from King Glydel. Their presences were requested immediately.

18

THE CASE IS CLOSED

"You may feel some comfort, Royal Majesty, in the fact that the ancient crone who rules the northernmost realm was the instigator of it all," Magister Setne Inhetep concluded. King Glydel had asked both Rachelle and the Ægyptian magister for all they knew regarding the matter of the Master of Jackals. First the girl, and then the priest and wizard, found themselves doing exactly what they had done but a brief time before, discussing each detail of the case. Inhetep added those last words in closing as an offering to the monarch's peace of mind. No man, commoner or king, could pass off lightly a son's treachery, hatred, and will to murder.

"Only a weak and useless vessel would be so moved by the mother of witches as to act as Llewyn did. So whether from his own inner rottenness or from some pox caught from another, he is full of iniquity and deserving of execution."

"Aye, Majesty. I cannot but agree there," Setne murmured. "When . . . ?"

"In but hours. I will have him excised from Lyonnesse and all Yarth! It is customary to hold a trial before all peers of the realm in a matter such as this, but regicide and all the rest exempt me from the formality. It so happens that three of the chief thegns of the kingdom are here in the citadel, and there are a dozen lesser nobles come to Camelough for one purpose or another. I called them to judge upon the scant facts and evidence—scant save for what I, their king, experienced and testified to. There was a unanimous judgement. Death by beheading—too good for the man, but he is, when all is said and done, a member of this royal house."

"Your position is not enviable, Majesty, though you be king of the great realm of Lyonnesse," Rachelle said to him. "I am at a loss for any words of comfort."

"Say none, Lady Rachelle. I am king and need none, not even from one so lovely and talented as you. *I* have words for both of you, however. It is to my shame that I behaved so vulgarly when this whole nasty business was settled. I now ask pardon from both of you."

"But of course," Setne and Rachelle said almost in unison, and added individual assurances that they were neither offended nor was apology necessary.

"One million spurs, in gold, is awaiting you at whatever great banking house you name. That should suffice for your time, expense, and the discomfiture you both suffered in one form or another. To make doubly certain of the latter, however, I asked the peers assembled in judgment to agree to honors for you both. I could grant mine own, of course, but these are from the King and Peers Assemblage. You are both given honorary citizenship of Lyonnesse as nobles. Your Pharaoh might not wish to have his folk vassals to another monarch, so the honors are of a knightly sort and require no swearing. Lady Rachelle and Sir Inhetep, I give you these badges in recognition of service to Lyonnesse above and beyond the customary. Now both of you may be properly addressed as Knights of the Blue Moon—a rare occurrence, but one bringing brightness to the night. It is the order reserved for very special persons."

They thanked him sincerely, Inhetep adding, "Please, your Stellar Majesty, I have one small request. It pertains to the payment, for I need not the gold. I ask that you use a tithe to endow here in Camelough a small shrine to Thoth, he whose wisdom guided me in this matter. As for the rest, I ask that you distribute it in such fashion as you deem best so as to assist your own people—those deserving poor who want education and have not the means of gaining it."

"Granted," Glydel said, with a small nod acknowledging the Ægyptian's character. The king was about to depart when he recalled something.

"I almost forgot to mention two other things.

You may stay in this land, or not, as it suits you.
When you choose to depart, however, this writ
of mine will grant you passage to any port of call
for which a Lyonnesse vessel is bound, as honored guests of the king of Lyonnesse, naturally.
The other matter is one which you alone can
decide. Is there any boon I can grant to either of
you?

Rachelle shook her pretty curls, but the tall
ur-kheri-heb of Thoth did have a request. "Your
Majesty, may I have permission to question
Tallesian? Then may I speak—carefully, mind
you—with Prince Llewyn?"

"No!" Glydel nearly roared the refusal. Emo-
tion played across his worn countenance, but
then he said in softer tone, "Wait ... What matter do you wish to discuss with him?" The man
was torn between duty and desire.

Inhetep looked at King Glydel. "It is of no
import save to Rachelle and me. You see, there
is nothing to indicate what the conspirators planned
to do with her—neither any hint of murder or
durance, simply nothing."

"That's strange, Magister, for this very hour
my—the convicted felon mentioned that as I
questioned him."

"You questioned him? You mean that you allowed him to speak?"

"Certes!" Glydel was offended by the temer-
ity of the Ægyptian in questioning his royal personage thus. "It is the *right* of a king to do that,

and the right of a member of royalty, fallen or
not, to have last words of speech to his king and
the peers."

"What said he of me?" Rachelle queried
hesitantly.

"Something to the effect that he thought it a
pity he hadn't had you packed off to the north
somewhere, for you were payment or something.
It was confused, and I believe that his mind has
broken."

Setne gave his companion a meaningful look,
then said to the ruler of Lyonnesse, "He referred
to the *north,* as in the northernmost realm, the
dark land of Pohjola—Louhi's domain, Majesty."

"I see," Glydel said, not really in the least interested, obviously so distracted by his son's
treachery and impending fate that he made no
connection to the trouble and the hag-of-hags,
Louhi. "Now I must ask that you excuse me, for
I have affairs to attend."

"King Glydel, I fear to arouse your ire, but I
must request that I speak with Llewyn now."

"Are you mad? I go now to oversee his
execution!"

"That I know, but I must at least have the
opportunity to see him for but a minute, to speak
with the prince before justice is done."

With ill-grace, the king acceded to Inhetep's
request, so both the Ægyptian and Rachelle went
to the deep place where the offender was held,
escorted by men-at-arms, an entourage of nobles,

294 • GARY GYGAX

and the monarch himself. Upon finally coming
to the place, after passing countless barred doors
and guards, the dungeon's gaoler greeted all for-
mally, called for the turnkey to open for "King
and Retinue," and the whole procession crowded
into the narrow passage which fronted the four
special cells for prisoners of most powerful sort,
those with considerable powers of heka or likely
to have confederates with such powers.

King Glydel opened a small hatch in the thick
cell door and peered inside. "Here, Magister Inhetep. He sits now in a daze upon the bench. Is
the sight alone sufficient? Or would you speak
with him also?"

"I will hold brief converse with him, by your
leave, Majesty."

"Be brief," he said sternly, then called, "Llewyn,
this is your king. A man would have speech with
you. Do you consent?" No response was forthcoming, and after several moments of silence,
King Glydel turned away from the window and
toward the wizard-priest. "Sir Inhetep, the
prince makes no assent, so I must deny your
request."

Setne looked determined. "If I may not speak
with him, please allow me to view him closely."

"You may look through the grate on the window, but you may not enter the cell, for the
door is proofed against all dweomers and the
cell's integrity against interference and com-

merce from other planes and spheres is maintained by its closure."

"I am conversant with all such matter, Majesty. It shall be as you say." The tall Ægyptian went to the door and stooped a little to peer into the cubicle to see the captive therin. "Llewyn?" The prisoner made no response.

"I have come to give you priestly comfort," Inhetep said so that all could hear. "This ankh has much of divine nature in it—see its form?" and as he spoke, Setne held up the object he named. "It is yours," he then said, and before anyone could react, the wizard-priest had flipped the golden amulet through the iron grillwork and into the cell.

"What do you think you're doing!?" King Glydel demanded wrathfully.

"Serving as a bearer of ill tidings, I fear," Inhetep said with a grim-faced expression as he turned to the king and his nobles there assembled. "There is no prisoner in that cell!"

They all rushed to the door, looking in, calling for the turnkey to open it. After the dismay and disorder faded, the Ægyptian explained what had happened. "When the prince was freed of his gag, the encompassing magick was broken. He was left ungagged thereafter, so when whomever had done that left the cell, Prince Llewyn called upon his evil mistress, the Crone of Pohjola. Evidently, she isn't ready to discard her tool, nor finished with me."

"Eh? What do you mean by that, Ægyptian?"
King Glydel demanded.

"Look for yourself," Inhetep replied with an
equally sharp tone.

"At what? What do you mean, wizard?"

Setne held up the ankh he had recovered after
the cell was opened. The bright gold was slowly
darkening and becoming corroded. "Observe the
loop," he instructed. There, instead of the ovoid
of an ankh was the profile of a long-nosed, scrag-
gly haired female, a witch, the Crone herself.

A month passed before Rachelle mentioned
the matter again. They had left Lyonnesse almost immediately after the discovery of Prince
Llewyn's escape. The king was happy to see
them gone, for they reminded him of the sorry
affair. After crossing the channel and traveling
overland through Francia, including a visit to
Paris, of course, and thereafter crossing Arles,
the two again took ship, eventually landing in
Ægypt. Setne had to return home, ostensibly to
find a new ankh, but also for other reasons. Rachelle knew that the wizard-priest was worried
about the threat implied by Louhi's features
stamped out of the amulet's metal, and the cor-
ruption of the supposedly incorruptible gold.
Only after they had been home for several days,
and Inhetep had begun his work on a new ankh,
one to be imbued with more energy and might

than the formerly held device, did his companion dare to mention what had occurred.

"What would they have done to me in Pohola?" she inquired as they sat outside on a pleasant evening, with the first stars making little motes of silver upon the pond nearby.

"That's *Pohjola,*" he corrected, sounding the three syllables carefully for her, "Poe-*yoe*-lah."

"Never mind how you say it. I want to know what they wanted me there for!"

Inhetep looked at her and grinned. "They planned to turn you into sugarcake, just as the wicked witch of the wood did to all those children!"

"Setne!"

"I have no idea. Louhi is a devious bag, and the purposes she has to further her schemes are dark and vile. Whatever it was, she certainly planned nothing good for you."

"Does she have children?"

"I have heard tell she has a beautiful daughter."

"No sons?"

"You think that a possible son of hers was smitten by tales of your beauty and prowess so as to desire you for his own?"

"Well, it is possible, perhaps . . ."

"More likely that the daughter of the witch is a vampiress who must drink the blood of beautiful virgins in order to remain young and beautiful herself."

"Then she would not want me!"

"No, you are too ugly," Setne said firmly. Rachelle threw her chilled fruit juice at him, but he ducked. She pouted. "Oh, come on, girl! I can only speculate. Neither of us can know, not with Prince Llewyn escaped."

"What of him? He's of no use to the crone, is he?"

"Possibly. Don't underestimate that one, Rachelle. Louhi bent much energy to carry the prince away so. He might have been a pawn, but his planning and work were masterful in their criminal genius. I'd wager we'll hear of Prince Llewyn again in due course."

She nodded, for that sounded reasonable. "You don't think she'll send him after us?"

"No, although if he can Llewyn will seek revenge, for he is bitter and deranged. Louhi will have other uses for that one. Who can guess? She somehow taught Aldriss to meld the bardic enspellment techniques with those of the northern chanters, to use all manner of true names and to sing so as to blend the Law of Sympathy with those of Similarity and Contagion. What she can mold the prince into is unknowable to us now, but you can be assured he will be a willing pupil and a deft one, save for his instability."

"Now we have a truly formidable foe, Setne. You have always told me that in your detection of crime you sought the real challenge of a worthy and fell opponent. You've gained that antagonist, I think."

The Ægyptian made a cross face at her. "You make another of your little jokes, and I am properly amused. Now, let an old man sit and enjoy the evening in peace."

"Setne, come and sit by me. You're not an old man at all, and you shouldn't ignore a pretty girl."

"Bah! Go and fetch me some of that tonic you're always trying to pour into everything I drink. I am feeling logy and irritable."

She sat up, showing a long leg and a lot of thigh above it. "I feel positively full of energy. I'm so glad to be alive and here in our own home again that I think I'll stay up all night."

Setne grunted and looked bored, but he watched Rachelle out of the corner of his eye.

"I am ready for more adventure, though, my dear old ur-kheri-heb! Where will we go next do you suppose?"

"To bed, woman," Inhetep said with firmness, "definitely to bed!"

"Well, I suppose if we must, we must," Rachelle said with a giggle. "Let me show you the way."

The case of the Anubis Murders was thus closed at last.